WORDSMITH

Volume Two

The Thousand Eyes of Flame

WORDSMITH

A Science-Fantasy Novel

Volume Two

The Thousand Eyes of Flame

by

MICHAEL R. COLLINGS

The Borgo Press
An Imprint of Wildside Press LLC

MMIX

Printed in the United States of America

www.wildsidepress.com

SECOND EDITION

CONTENTS

WHAT HAS GONE BEFORE

On Omne, a world shrouded by a perpetual cloud cover, where science and technology are unknown and words have the power to create or destroy, young Davian Charl'an-born found himself at nightfall high in the mountain ranges, stranded just below the Veil of Heaven. Knowing that it would be foolhardy to attempt to return to his home in the absolute darkness of the Omnan night, he remained there, alone...and experienced a vision unique in the history of his world.

When he returned home the next day, he was met by an old man, Iam'Kendron, Master Maker of the Pillars of Beginnings and one of the most knowledgeable and powerful lore masters on Omne. Unaccountably, the old man seemed deeply intrigued by the boy's retelling of what he had seen, so much so that on the following morning, Iam'Kendron revealed that he had chosen the boy as his new acolyte. Almost immediately they set off for the Sanctuary of the Pillars of Beginnings, where Davian, now named La'am Iam'Kendron-word, underwent a five-Cycle tutelage in the lore of the Wordsmith. After the death of the old man, La'am journeyed alone to Los'ang, the largest city on Omne, to present himself as the old man's acolyte before the Makersraad, the council of Makers.

At the same time, the rest of the Makers had assembled to consider a growing threat to Omne—persistent rumors of the Return of the Wordsmith and the consequent upheavals in Omnan society—and to perform the ritual naming of a new High Magister. In the presence of Ranulf Mathom-son, they united their power to pronounce the official name that would symbolize his authority, but inexplicably the oldest Maker among them interrupted the ritual to speak a forbidden name and by doing so marked Ranulf not simply as Magister but as the last Magister of Omne and harbinger of the returning Wordsmith. With the Naming, the Council Chamber was suffused in an unprecedented display of Makers' light, the stone Magister's seat shattered, and the old Maker crumbled to the floor, dead. Even so, the name had been spoken, and the new Magister was confirmed as Zeta'Om.

On the following day, the Makersraad, with the new Magister present, assembled to appoint a Maker to fill the newly vacated Maker's seat. This time, the ritual progressed according to tradition, emphasizing the unsettling disruptions of the previous day. Afterward, the Makers again united their powers, this time to communicate with the single missing Maker, Iam'Kendron of the Pillars of Beginnings. Instead of establishing a mental connection with him, however, they encountered a barrier that forbid contact. While they were still in confusion, struggling to understand what had just happened, a young man entered the Council Palace and announced himself as La'am, Master Maker of the Pillars of Beginnings, throwing the council into even greater agitation: he was unknown to any of them, had never even been formally acknowledged as Iam'Kendron's acolyte, and had not been named as Maker—let alone Master Maker—by the Makersraad. Yet clearly he possessed all of the powers of a Master Maker.

Grudgingly accepted by most of his fellow Makers, ignored by several of them, and refused permission to return to the Sanctuary of the Pillars of Beginnings, La'am remained in Los'ang and immersed himself in the lore of the Wordsmith. Isolated and lonely, wandering through the city late one night, he met a boy who, like himself, was drawn to the beauty and mystery of the Veil of Heaven. Returning the next day, he discovered that, also like himself, the boy seemed to know things about the Wordsmith that no books of lore could teach. Without taking advise from any of the other Makers, La'am and the boy returned to the Council Palace, where La'am, acting by himself as Iam'Kendron had once done, named the boy Mord'am La'amword, acolyte to the Master Maker of the Pillars of Beginnings.

As disruptive as La'am had proven to the Makersraad, his naming was accepted and he and Mord'am continued studying the lore. Then, shortly before the celebration of First Day of Seed Time, two other Makers announced that, according to their reading of the lore, the long-prophesied return of the Wordsmith was imminent...that it would occur on First Day. And, indeed, during the ceremonial celebration itself, something strangely shaped and glistening descended, penetrated the Veil of Heaven, and arrived on Omne.

While those on Omne knew nothing of any worlds beyond the Veil of Heaven, considering themselves alone in time and space, the Exploration Service had long been searching to re-establish contact with colony worlds separated from the Comity generations before.

Then the chief archivist discovered documentation of one missing planet—Jamison's planet, reportedly a treasure house of unexploited mineral wealth desperately needed by the Comity. Under the command of Captain Haardt of the ExServ, a ship was dispatched to locate and assess the unknown planet.

This ship was, of course, the unfamiliar object that had penetrated the Veil of Heaven, revealing to the Omnans assembled in Los'ang that they were not, after all, alone in the universe. Since the ship's arrival had coincided precisely with the celebration of the prophesied return, the High Magister, the Makersraad, and all of Omne tacitly recognized Haardt as Wordsmith.

It didn't take long for Haardt to manipulate the Omnans' religious belief to his own advantage and in doing so alienate several key members of the Makersraad, including La'am, who realized that the Strangers were a threat. For his part, Haardt consolidated his authority by playing on the young High Magister's ambition and disdain for the Makersraad, alienating the Magistry further from the Makersraad and stepping into the resulting power void. Having done so, he turned his full attention to his prime objectives...to determine the extent of the planet's mineral wealth, to report his findings to the ExServ, and, should the occasion arise, to divert as much of that wealth as he safely could into his own pockets.

His methods were ruthless. Since the archivist's research into Omnan language and customs had revealed that the people had no sense of warfare or weaponry—that their language did not even include words to describe such things Haardt gave commands. The city was to be placed under martial law...his. The land was to be stripped of its vital resources, even if that included burning vast farmlands. The report to the ExServ was to be delayed until his own depredations were concluded and would therefore make no mention of any unique finds. The entire planet was to be tamed, controlled, and exploited within a month. Then he would send in an *almost* meticulously accurate record of what the planet offered.

Nothing could go wrong with his plans...but something did. Alerted by the Maker of one of the outlying Sanctuary that the strangers were burning unharvested crops, then devastating the landscape with their machines, the Master Maker of Omne confronted Haardt, who essentially admitted that all that the Master Maker accused him of was true, then, with a curt disinterest in any of the superstitions Omnans might have held about supposed powers held by the Makers, dismissed the Master Maker. Almost immediately he ordered a curfew.

Unaware of the new restriction, Mord'am had left the Council Palace late that afternoon and returned to the place where he and La'am had first met. Troubled by premonitions, he again broke with all tradition and initiated mental contact with La'am—the acolyte calling the Maker. At Mord'am's unspoken request, La'am allowed his acolyte access to the storehouse of memories that were La'am *and* Iam'Kendron; in return, the boy opened himself to La'am's mind and, finally, revealed both his promotion that La'am would soon die at the hands of the strangers and his decision not to allow that to happen. Startled and aghast, La'am tried to remonstrate with the boy, but suddenly the boy's mental patterns fragmented, distorted, and died. In a panic, La'am rushed from his chamber to find—and rescue—his acolyte.

Even before Mord'am had contacted La'am, an ExServ squad had begun patrolling the streets, announcing the curfew to all anyone they encountered. Everyone obeyed, until they came across one boy sitting alone near the shoreline. The squad leader called to the boy. The boy ignored him. The squad leader ordered the boy to stand and answer. The boy ignored him; and worse, his squad began to laugh at him. Furious, he struck the boy with a neural whip. When that brought no response, he struck again…and again….

When La'am came rushing to find Mord'am, he found the ExServ officer standing over the boy's body. Furious, La'am turned his Maker's power on the man, nearly killing him but in the end only blinding him.

Equally furious when he heard of the disaster, Haardt had the Master Maker of Omne brought before him to answer for La'am's crimes. The Master Maker refused to be intimidated, refused to surrender La'am to the ExServ, accused Haardt's men of murder, and demanded to leave Haardt's presence. When Haardt refused, the Master Maker began to summon not only his own powers against Haardt but also the combined power of the entire Makersraad. But before he could act, Haardt's men burst into the room and opened fire.

Finally understanding how completely he had underestimated the strangers, the Master Maker of Omne ceased to be.

PART THREE

CHAPTER TWENTY-FOUR

La'am stood, numb, unthinking.

Mord'am's body lay at his feet. Through the darkness, he saw flickers of the mechanical light the Strangers carried to pinpoint the path to the Council Palace and their vessel. He could identify the silhouettes of several forms, one supported by the others.

The man he had injured.

The man he had almost killed—would *have killed*—could *have killed as easily as thought.*

Seeing the consequences of this dangerous side of the Makerslight sobered La'am at once. His anger drained away, leaving behind only emptiness and fear.

The Makerslight could kill.

He had known that as an abstract fact, ever since the night he had confronted the wulf in the Highland marshes—if not before. But never had he considered it as a weapon against the Strangers.

Now he knew that the light could kill, perhaps without a Maker even being physically present. One burst of concentrated patterns directed toward Haardt.... La'am was certain that he could identify the patterns of Haardt's mind, even in the confusion of people in the Magistry, the Council Palace, and the Strangers' camp.

He glanced down at Mord'am's body. Tears welled up, and with them the anger. He clenched his fist and began focusing the power that would destroy the Strangers as completely and as viciously as they had destroyed Mord'am.

As they had almost destroyed La'am himself.

Then he stopped. He opened his fingers and dropped his hands to his side. He willed the surging Makerslight to withdraw back into himself. The Makers' powers had been given to preserve and defend, not to destroy. There had to be another way.

And, he realized with a suddenness that chilled him, his own position was threatened. He would soon be a fugitive. He knew enough about Haardt to know that. He must flee for his life. Now.

There was no time to waste.

But he couldn't leave Mord'am's body lying broken on the rough sand. Already the highest waves were beginning to finger damply through the boy's disordered hair, along the rough edges of the blood-stained gray robe. La'am stood back silently, then stretched his hand toward the boy. Blue fire slipped through the night, sparking against the gray robe, bursting into full flame and devouring all that was left of Mord'am—all, that is, except the immutable patterns firmly locked in La'am's consciousness.

There was a moment of dizziness as he felt himself splitting into several distinct beings—himself, Iam'Kendron, and now Mord'am. The different perceptions of each struggled inside him, gradually merging to create…someone new, capable of integrating the knowledge, experience, and wisdom of all three. The sum of their Makers' powers suffused him.

If only he knew how best to wield that power.

Then, as if a voice had pierced the stillness and cried in anguish to him, he felt the impulse to turn away from the pyre, to retreat into the darkness.

Mord'am's patterns were momentarily in control, La'am realized. He recognized the fact and chose not struggle against them. The boy had spent his life in Los'ang, including the areas near the harbor. He had known the streets and pathways intimately, and now his knowledge would guide La'am through the darkness. La'am set his conscious self aside, relinquishing control to the Mord'am-patterns. The Acolyte was now the Master.

This night seemed even darker than was usual at Seed Time. Haardt's edicts forbade any movement after dark, and even now the private homes of Los'ang were closely shuttered. (La'am wondered what edict he was thinking about; then through Mord'am's mentrans patterns, he remembered for the first time the curfew and considered briefly what might have brought it about—and with it Mord'am's death.) Only an occasional glimmer of candle or oil lantern mellowed the overwhelming blackness. And La'am feared to kindle the Makerfire, even faintly enough to guide his steps. The subtlest hint of blue would give him away when Haardt's men began searching for him—as he knew that they must.

For now, he had to trust Mord'am's memories of the pathways. Carefully, silently, he passed along the strand, a ghost in inky indigo, invisible against the backdrop of night, unheard in a silence broken only by ripples of waves breaking on unresisting sands. He saw nothing, heard nothing, felt nothing. His legs moved under a direction not quite his own, yet he was unafraid. The patterns were clear. He was as certain of his way as if he were walking along the docks in the brightest daylight.

He knew when he passed the last ship. He knew when he had to turn to the right in order to follow the Jamis River to the stone bridge he had crossed (*how long ago!*) when he had entered Los'ang for the first time. He realized with a shock that his perceptions of the structure were strangely distorted; he was seeing it simultaneously for the second time as La'am, perhaps the dozenth time as Iam'Kendron, and certainly at least the hundredth time as Mord'am. He stopped, shook his head and shuffled the various patterns into place until their blurring edges interlocked. Then he stepped into the night.

But when his foot touched the cold, smooth stonework of the bridge, the perceptions jarred out of focus again. Mord'am's patterns faded. The boy had only rarely been out of the city and had never walked on the western bank of the Jamis.

La'am faltered slightly, then searched his own memory for the details of his march along the foothills.

He moved unhesitatingly, unerringly among the rough, rock-strewn paths of the foothills until he came again to the cleft in which he had spent his first night in Los'ang.

More fatigued from his mental exertions than from the physical act of walking, he dropped into a protected niche. He wrapped his robe tightly around him, thankful that the late Seed Time night was warm and mild. He settled in against the rocks to plan and think. The fine texture of the granitic rocks scratched agreeably against his back. The confined heat of the day radiated out into the night, warming La'am, and soothing him.

He felt sure that Haardt would concentrate his search in Los'ang and the immediate vicinity of the Council Palace. Haardt would be confident that no Omnan would dare venture into the unrelieved darkness of night. And the Strangers, La'am knew, carried tubes that illuminated the darkness for yards, enabling them to search without having to wait for First Light. La'am did not know if they had instruments capable of finding him even without light; he hoped not. He raised his head above the level of the boulders and stared in the direction of the bridge, even though he could see nothing of the stonework in the darkness. He thought he could see the bobbing white light of one of the tubes circling the eastern limits of the harbor—perhaps they were already returning to find him.

He leaned back. He would have to leave soon. He did not know where to go or even how to find a path in the night. It would be the same as suicide to kindle the Makerslight this close to the city, however faintly; and his own trip down the Jamis River from the Sanctuary was well enough known to make it certain that Haardt would dispatch men to search along that route. Then, he asked himself, where *should* he go?

The Pillars of Beginnings, something whispered—not one of Iam'Kendron's patterns, not anything consciously La'am of the Pillars, but something deeper that for the moment frightened La'am. Then the whisper-pattern died and he was alone again. But he had his answer.

The Pillars of Beginnings, where everything began.

But how to get there?

He closed his eyes against the darkness (not that he could see anything, since darkness was long complete), concentrating on the patterns that still shifted uncontrollably, merging and joining to create infinitely more complex, more meaningful configurations—when he had the opportunity to study them. He—La'am—knew only one way back to the Pillars. Mord'am knew of none. Iam'Kendron had only made the trip a few times, either along the same route La'am had taken or along the even more heavily frequented trails through the Eastern Ranges—and neither of those two alternatives made any sense. The first was too well-known to Haardt as La'am's own path, and the second was the most direct—and hence the most suspect—for any travelers heading toward the Pillars. In addition, that way led directly past the Sanctuary of Joleckan of the Eastern Ranges, and Haardt would undoubtedly send out scouts to the surrounding Sanctuaries, particularly Joleckan's, since she seemed more aware of the Strangers' movements than were the other Makers.

No, neither path would suffice. He would have to find another route, one that would put the Strangers off his trail, at least temporarily.

He pressed himself harder against the stone. Eyes closed, he probed patterns, memories, words of ancient prophecies and lays. Hoping for an answer.

And received nothing.

Until another mind intruded.

The intrusion was immediate and abrupt. La'am was at first overwhelmed by an intense despair, then just as abruptly soared in triumph as he recognized and was recognized by Jorik. There was no opportunity for delicate, fragile initial probes. Jorik wrenched La'am's mind open and released into it the memories and powers of the Master Maker of Omne—patterns that had once been Iam'Kendron; Jorik's own patterns derived through nearly six Cycles as head of the Makersraad; and the patterns and powers Jorik had pulled from the other Makers during his impassioned confrontation with Haardt. La'am felt rather than heard the words that had preceded Haardt's attack on Jorik; felt rather than saw Haardt's apparently random fumbling at his belt; felt rather than understood Jorik's shocked pain as he was cut down. With a part of his mind, La'am knew that the frenzied mass of patterns contained in essence the entire knowledge of the Makers of Omne, concentrated by the Master Maker of the Council. The rest of La'am's mind, however, was numbed by the violence with which the patterns were forced into him.

Suddenly, they ceased. Then there was silence—and La'am knew what he had to do.

Jorik was dead. Mord'am was dead. All of Omne lay under threat of death. Jorik's patterns convinced La'am even more completely of his paramount need to reach the Pillars of Beginnings.

* * * * * * *

By First Light, La'am was far from Los'ang, well on his way along the coast southward to the Salton Marshes and finally—he hoped—to Jathanan's Sanctuary at Harborwatch. He had moved cautiously during the night, not from fear, but out of a desire to avoid tripping or stumbling—anything that would conceivably injure him and delay his flight. During the interminable hours, he had seen thin shafts of light piercing the air around Los'ang, generated by the Strangers' machines as they searched for him. He had walked steadily but slowly until he had reached the fringes of the long dunes that bordered the western shore of the Harbor. A remnant of a pattern transmitted from Jathanan through Jorik had momentarily surfaced at that point, illuminating La'am's mind and providing a flawless map of the complexities of the dunes; few traveled there but Jathanan had made the dunes an object of special interest and investigation. In her mind, as in no other mind in Omne, the area was familiar, even easy to traverse.

Gradually, as his body assumed the mechanical functions of walking and freed his mind for reflection, La'am tried to define precisely what had happened to him during the instant of contact with Jorik. He had always felt the presence of Iam'Kendron in his mind; those patterns had recurred often enough for La'am to feel comfortable with them. Now suddenly, to Iam'Kendron had been added Mord'am, who in death had imprinted La'am with patterns, anomalously mature and coherent for one of Mord'am's age and experience. Then came the unheard-of phenomenon of Jorik calling on the entire Makersraad and similarly flooding La'am with the cumulative experience of the seven remaining members of the Council and of the generations preceding them and embedded within them.

For the first time in Omnan history, La'am realized, one man had access to the secret thoughts, knowledge, and experience of a generation of Makers, including perhaps the greatest Maker of all, Iam'Kendron.

But knowing all that did not really help. He could not yet control the patterns, call one to his purposes and force the others to remain dormant. They seemed at war, with first one then another dominant momentarily before submerging as another rose. His desperate need to cross the endless dunes safely had apparently given Jathanan's patterns a kind of supremacy; even as he struggled to sort out the kaleidoscope he had suddenly discovered inside his head, La'am knew that he was walking in the right direction, along paths at best barely visible and more frequently impossible for him consciously to detect. His head ached from his concentration; his eyes ached from the strain of trying to sec an invisible path through impossible darkncss. His lungs and muscles ached from sheer nervous tension. But beneath everything, he could sense Iam'Kendron's patterns structuring the experiences stored in the multiple patterns, organizing them, separating them, in a sense acting as a water-gate for them, allowing those through that were most critically needed. The overwhelming sense of confusion slackened as La'am grew aware of the potentialities he now possessed.

He was oddly at ease, confident, considering his circumstances. Always, no matter which voice, which pattern was dominant, the Makerspower flowed through him. All of the discreet beings whose memories were trapped within him urged him to the same end—to understand the particulated fragments of ancient lore that each possessed, to defeat the Strangers and their machines, to call upon those reserves of power which the ancients had named the Wordsmith.

And La'am knew that he alone of all Omnans had any hope of succeeding. He was now doubly heir to Iam'Kendron, both as La'am Iam'Kendron-word of the Pillars of Beginnings, and also as heir-in-fact to Jorik, Master Maker of Omne and one-time acolyte to the old man. He could feel Mord'am's instinctive grasp of Makerspower and lore surging within him, growing in its conjunction with the superior training of the others.

The independent memories of Jorik, Joleckan, Jathanan, Jeriam, Kaleb, and the others blended, pieces of the puzzle settling together. Never before would such a blending have been possible. Their fears had been too strong; even when in confluence as a Council, the individual Makers had retained a portion of themselves, never quite sharing entirely their knowledge. La'am recognized the subtle hints of selfishness, ambition, acquisitiveness—none overtly strong but taken as a whole sufficient to thwart attempts at merging. Additionally, he now understood the fear each Maker felt at such a merging—the fear that the merging might never dissolve, that the individuals might remain forever within the dominating consciousness of the strongest Maker.

No, it had taken a crisis on a scale unknown in Omnan history to precipitate the kind of merging that had occurred during the night. And it had happened because of Jorik's inherent greatness. Before, La'am had occasionally wondered how Iam'Kendron, with his wisdom and understanding both of Omne's needs and of human character, could have selected Jorik as the Master Maker of Omne—and then quietly relinquished the position to the man years before death would have forced the honor upon Jorik. Now La'am began to see in Jorik the elements of mind that had undoubtedly appealed to Iam'Kendron—strength, stubbornness in the face of opposition, loyalty to the Lore of the Wordsmith, and above all, the courage to act upon a desperate decision forced on him by unprecedented circumstances. Jorik might not have known that he was going to his death as he crossed the bridge leading to the Magistry—and La'am noted in passing that even then, the Master Maker had remained true to his responsibilities, had whispered the Words of 'Waring as he had crossed—but when he had defined the threat that the Strangers represented, he had accomplished what no other Maker had ever attempted. La'am grieved for Jorik's passing…and felt pride in being one with the dead Master Maker of Omne.

La'am walked onward through the darkness, no longer alone.

* * * * * * *

With the first glimmerings of day, La'am's trek became easier and simultaneously more difficult. He could now see directly the landmarks that until then he had been following by intuition and by blind, borrowed memories. He could move more quickly, more surely than he had during the darkness. But by the same token, his enemies could now see him as well. La'am had no way of knowing what sophisticated tracking devices the Strangers might have—and even if he had known them by name, he would have been ignorant of how they worked. All he knew for certain was that Haardt had not yet spotted him or stumbled onto his trail, regardless of the frequent scouting flights that had crisscrossed the Veil during the night.

As he walked, he felt a prickling at the back of his neck. A scouter. He strained his eyes, scouring the Veil of Heaven.

There it was, a speck in the northern sky, half-hidden in wisps of the Veil itself. It was heading southward…directly toward him.

La'am scurried to a low, shrubby hillock of sand a few yards distant. In this light, the scouter would probably not have seen him, but when it came closer the chances of discovery would be much greater. La'am hunched down at the base of a gray-green bush, then crawled into the cramped open space beneath its dome of branches. Lying quietly in the deceptive shadows of First Light, he hoped to escape detection.

It worked. The scouter glided silently, just below the Veil. The machine's brilliant white light was no longer on. There must be enough light for the Strangers aboard to see without artificial aid.

Even though he knew that it was useless and foolish, he held his breath until his lungs burned. His eyes blurred with tears as he stared at the scouter.

Finally, it disappeared into the lingering gloom to the south. La'am waited for another few minutes, then he scrabbled out from under the protective shadows of the brush, stretching to remove cramps in his knotted muscles and flicking grains of sand from the skirts of his robe.

His hand froze.

It was now full day. The Veil of Heaven swirled with the fluid colors of Seed Time, as calm as if no Strangers had ever ravaged its isolation. In the light diffusing from the Veil, La'am stared at the sleeve of his Maker's robe.

The indigo was threaded with the yellow and grey of Makers and Acolytes—and with colors which no Maker had every worn. Suggestions of scarlet (La'am was reminded of the High Magister's robe), green, purple, russet, and ivory mingled gloriously with what La'am now recognized as the metallic gleam of gold and silver. The robe seemed alive. It billowed lightly across the sandy shallow where La'am stood.

During the night, he had felt himself becoming a different person from the La'am who had rushed from the Council Palace to answer Mord'am's desperate summons. Now the light of day revealed the extent to which he had in fact altered to something new, something unknown to Omne. But even as he watched, the play of color faded, first overlaid then replaced by the deep indigo of the Master Makers. La'am drew a cleansing breath, then resumed his journey to the south.

His progress was slow but steady. He saw no more scouters; apparently the one he spotted had returned to Los'ang along a different vector. In fact, he saw no life, not even the tiny lizards that lived in the dunes. Hour passed into hour to create a day without boundaries. The Veil of Heaven deepened to ashy gray soon after First Light and remained that way until the flow of colors returned again at twilight. And by then, La'am had entered the winding morass of the Salton Marshes.

On the entire circumference of Omne, the demarcation between sea and shore was clear, often (as at the Lesser Pillars) abrupt—except for at the Salton Marshes. The channels dividing the mainland from the stony islands five miles distant wandered and twisted among mazy shallows and sand bars. Waist- to head-high salt-sedges bordered shifting, narrow channels. Only the flat-bottomed skiffs of the few hermitic marsh-men could efficiently maneuver in the morass of mud and rotting vegetation. Other vessels, usually larger and with deeper draught, avoided the dangerous channels, choosing instead the longer but infinitely safer voyage south of the islands.

Nor was there a permanent trail through the marshes. Stone piers for roadways and bridges either sank noticeably into the sandy bottom or were washed away during high tides and frequent storms. La'am was forced to feel his way slowly through the sedges, relying on Jathanan's patterns to avoid particularly deadly pitfalls.

Night brought him to a halt. He was thirsty, hungry, and bruised from innumerable false steps; he did not care to compound his problems by stumbling into a quagmire so recently formed that not even Jathanan had discovered it. He dared a brief flare of Makerslight, enough to follow the trail for a few steps more to a hillock, reasonably dry and slightly elevated yet not prominent enough to attract the attention of any scouters. As the Makerslight died away his robe again flickered with strange colors, then faded into indigo.

He chose not to think about it. Instead, he curled up in the robe, settled as comfortably as possible in the persistent dampness, and slept.

He did not see the three scouters heading south, then shortly thereafter returning toward Los'ang, their green and amber lights fuzzy in the trailing fingers of the Veil. He did not hear the muffled report, or see the reddish glow on the horizon. He tossed restlessly and mumbled feverishly, but did not wake. The danger to him was not pressing enough, not yet. The inner controls Iam'Kendron had formed were creating a barrier against intrusion. La'am was exhausted and would be even more so before his journey ended.

For now, he slept.

With the arrival of day, La'am woke and again set off. He pushed his way through rasping sedges and hungrily sucking mud. He hitched his Maker's robe about his waist to protect it from the sludge of the marshes. The still air grew thick and warm...unusually warm, even oppressively warm, for so early in Seed Time. Well before midday, La'am stripped the robe off and rolled it into a bundle that he easily tied over his shoulder with the belt. Clad only in his rhiam clout, he continued.

By mid-day, he was parched, chafed, bruised, and caked with salt from having to swim several branching channels; but he was also—finally, blessedly—in sight of the first of the off-shore islands. The Salton Marshes were teeming with life, quite unlike the barrenness of the dunes the previous day. He had been enveloped a dozen times by swarms of tiny, biting midges hovering over particularly rancid-smelling pools. Eyes shut tightly against the tiny creatures, he had stumbled through the swarms. He shivered as the midges had crept along his flesh and stung him on the back, the chest, in his ears, everywhere, it seemed. Then, as suddenly as a swarm had appeared, it would disappear, leaving him hotter and more tired than he had been before.

Several times, he had nearly stepped on snakes and lizards basking in the heat. Fortunately, none had taken his intrusion as an affront or a danger; the reptiles had slithered or skittered into the protection of overhanging reeds or sedges, relinquishing their overlordship of the swamp temporarily to the human intruder. Yet even these signs of life had been depressive and had increased La'am's desire to walk again on firm earth.

As soon as he spotted the island jutting out of the marsh, he splashed noisily through the remaining pools and rushed through clumps of sedge that tore at his already raw flesh. Finally, he felt the rocks of the islands beneath his feet—sharp, hot, and bare, but dry and solid. La'am sat for a few moments on the first large boulder he came across, then set off again, following the eastward curve of the island toward the jutting peninsula that was Harborwatch.

He walked stiffly. One part of his mind directed his abused body while another part remained alert for any overt physical dangers, and yet another continued the struggle to gain control of the kaleidoscope of patterns. He had made some small progress. More and more, La'am could call up a pattern, a word, a color, a memory. More and more frequently several fragments could be integrated into something larger. More and more he felt himself becoming...more than himself.

Shortly after mid-day he came upon a fresh-water creek that tumbled down a narrow gorge to join the salty water of the Marshes. He washed his hands and face and neck, and drank deeply. He traced the stream for almost a mile to its source, a deep, cold spring inside a circle of boulders.

He rinsed his robe a few feet downstream from the spring, taking care not to muddy the water. As he washed it, he inspected it for any damage. Even after the wildness of the Marshes, the threads were unworn, the weave untorn. And the robe was again the solid, indisputable indigo of a Master Maker. He spread the robe out to dry, camouflaging it with branches in case one of the scouters should pass overhead.

Then he returned to the spring and bathed himself completely, washing the filth of the Marshes from his legs and feet and cleansing the tiny cuts across his chest and forearms where reeds had slashed at him. The water was cold and invigorating.

He could almost feel its cleansing powers seep throughout his body, removing his aches and the soreness from his bruises.

For the first time since his flight had begun, he allowed himself to relax. He emptied his mind…and abruptly confronted the undiminished depth of his pain and loss. Abruptly he stood, reached out for his robe and retraced his steps along the stream back toward the Marshes.

As he reached the mouth of the stream, he put his robe on and cinched it tightly about his waist. As the indigo fibers brushed against his flesh, he felt stirrings of hope. He felt taller, stronger, more powerful.

Powerful enough to confront Haardt if necessary.

He walked on, more openly this time since he now felt that the sky was safe, that Haardt's searchers were far away. He could not have explained how he knew, but he did. He marched swiftly and directly toward the peninsula on which Jathanan's sanctuary stood.

CHAPTER TWENTY-FIVE

As he drew near to the end of the island, however, La'am began to experience a definite sense of foreboding. Something was wrong. He began running. His robe fluttered behind him like the wings of some great bird of prey.

He topped a small rise overlooking the stony peninsula of Harborwatch...and saw only ruin.

The Sanctuary had been destroyed. Bits of blackened stone littered the landscape. There were no signs of life...or of death. No bodies, no charred remnants. Jathanan lived almost alone on the island with only her own Acolyte, Kar'an, and two or three attendants. Whatever had happened here had included not only the Maker but also her few associates.

La'am ran down the broken slope. Heedless now of any danger to himself, he leaped jagged, fractured chunks of rock that had formerly been walls. He reached the disrupted foundations and leaned breathlessly against a portion of the wall that was still standing, then forced himself to examine the destruction. Through Jathanan's memories, he saw the sanctuary as it had been—a large common room, much like the one at the Pillars of Beginnings, opening onto the private rooms of the Maker, her Acolyte, and the attendants. There were several small interior rooms for unexpected guests, but as far as he knew, no other Maker on the Council had ever visited Jathanan's island, not even Iam'Kendron. The harshness of the journey discouraged trivial visits, while Jathanan's intense sense of privacy made any prospective visitor uncomfortable about disturbing the Maker of Harborwatch.

At the rear of the main structure, La'am discovered the entrance to the caverns beneath the island where the records and artifacts of Harborwatch had been kept. He knew what had been here; the Council kept accounts of the locations of fragments of the Lore, although La'am admitted to himself that the records themselves frequently disappeared or became illegible with age. Of the Sanctuaries, Harborwatch had been the poorest, with few original holdings and primarily late copies of documents stored in other Sanctuaries. Perhaps part of Jathanan's strength derived from her knowledge of the intrinsic poverty of her Makerseat and from her desire to wrench from that poverty the last possible shred of knowledge.

Now La'am hurried through the rubble toward the cavern, scanning the blasted ruins for clues to the fate of the inhabitants.

Surely Haardt would not dare to kill a Maker. Surely he could not so hate the Omnans.... But Mord'am and Jorik *were* dead, La'am reminded himself coldly.

He arrived at the doorway to the inner caverns. The door was gone. Its wooden beams and leather hinges had burned away, leaving a gaping darkness. La'am paused, then entered. He raised one hand. A faint trail of blue light surrounded him, then preceded him through the darkness. The walls of the cavern were scored with ashes. La'am touched the stone, felt a lingering heat, and drew back a soot-encrusted fingertip.

He continued, searching for surviving fragments of the Lore, but everything had been consumed: documents, ancient scripts, a few artifacts of wood and—even more scarce—metal. All were gone, leaving only thick layers of black ash. Nothing had survived—no word, no letter, no indication that this had once been a vital storehouse of knowledge.

He gathered his glowing robe tightly about him. In the warm air of the dead cavern, he suddenly felt chilled. He stood silently, head bowed, near the scorched wall of the chamber.

As he stood, a gleam from the floor caught his eye. Stooping, he picked up a silvered lump, heavy and warm in his palm. It was a melted remnant of a metal fragment from the Ancient days. He held the metal in his hand and ran his thumb along the smooth, fused surface. The heat had to have been intense beyond all imagining to melt metal.

Tears of helplessness formed in La'am's eyes. Given this kind of power, what could he do. He was only one man, a young man at that, with fragmentary powers....

"*La'am.*"

There was no mistaking that pattern. Iam'Kendron's voice echoed through La'am's mind, simultaneously evoking subsidiary patterns...Mord'am's, Jorik's, each Maker's in turn, culminating with Jathanan's. Her pattern reminded La'am of the gray-green swells of the sea whipped up by the monster storms of Dark Time, the thunderous crash of breakers on the stones, and the whispering of the breezes as they played through the stones of Harborwatch during the calm nights of Growing Time. That was how Jathanan had impressed him. She was as changeable, enduring, unexpected, and rhythmic as the sea itself.

The pattern grew stronger, until it crowded the others back into the recesses of La'am's mind. Then the color-sounds began to form vocally.

"I am Jathanan, Maker of Harborwatch. I seek La'am, Master Maker of the Pillars of Beginnings." He started to respond with his own patterns, but Jathanan continued: "And Master of all Makers on Omne."

The phrase startled him. This wasn't merely a residual pattern; this was a flood of new mentrans patterns searching him out. Wherever she was, Jathanan was trying to speak to him.

"I am La'am of the Pillars of Beginnings," he sent, praying that he had enough control to focus on Jathanan and make himself understood. "Why do you seek me? Why do you call me by a title not my own?"

"La'am!" The relief in the old woman's patterns was nearly tangible. "Where are you? Are you safe? No, don't answer that. I don't want to know where you are. But are you well?"

"Yes. Where are you? What happened?"

"In Los'ang," the old woman answered, "in a chamber below the Magistry. We are all here—at least, I think we are—those of us who survive. When he could not find you, Haardt dispatched men to the Makerseats...to the Lesser Pillars, the Eastern Ranges, to Heartland. And to Harborwatch." Her patterns grew muddy and turgid with despair. La'am almost interrupted them when the color-flow began again.

"We had been warned," she sent. "Jorik called the Makers the night Mord'am was killed, the night Jorik died. He drew us into council, except for you."

"I know of the Council," La'am sent, "but I was not there. My mind was filled with Mord'am; I unconsciously blocked everything else out. I regret the exclusiveness of my grief. Had I known of Jorik's intentions I might have...."

"You could have done nothing. We had been warned. I intended to start for Los'ang at First Light, by secret ways if necessary, in order for the Council to meet. We all knew then what several had suspected or dreaded—that the Strangers were foreign to their fibers and their bones, unmentioned in our histories, opposed to our beliefs. We would have moved against them. But they moved first.

"Their ships arrived before First Light. I only knew about Harborwatch, but they attacked each Sanctuary on Omne. They seized every Maker and Acolyte.

"We did not expect them. We did not know what to do when machines settled down on the rocks outside the sanctuary, their white lights stabbing the night. I was studying in the caverns when Kar'an ran screaming in, followed by Strangers bearing weapons. They grabbed me and forced me outside, along with Kar'an.

"We were taken to the Magistry and held in a room, the same one, I think, where I am now. Later, the others were brought in, one at a time—Jabeth and Jothun, then Jerek, Joleckan, and Kaleb, and after a while, Jeriam, woebegone Jeriam, whose eternally dour face finally matched his circumstances. Our Acolytes were also present, except for Joleckan's Rhiama.

"When the Makers were all together, guards took us to the High Magister's chamber. Haardt was there. Zeta'Om was also present."

La'am sensed the heaviness in the pattern as the final words formed. Jathanan was disturbed by the High Magister's presence.

Jathanan continued, but her words faded and the color-sounds merged into figures and shapes, into tangible memories. La'am immediately recognized the room. The Makers and Acolytes stood in a line along one wall. The Stranger, Haardt himself, faced them from the other side of the room.

* * * * * * *

"Where is he? Tell me!" The order rang sharply through the room, breaking the silence that had prevailed since the entrance of Master Maker Jabeth of Los'ang, the senior member of the Council now that Jorik was dead.

The words faded. The deadly silence resumed. None of the Makers spoke. None moved. The gray-robed Acolytes remained as motionless as graven stones.

Haardt waited for a moment, uncomfortable in the silence. Finally, he burst out again.

"Where is he?"

The tension in his voice crackled like static. He felt as if control was slipping from his grasp—yet there was no reason for such a feeling. He held the strings, he commanded on this lump of dust. He ruled, he alone.

"No one will dispute my authority without suffering the consequences. I will have him, now, easily...or eventually, accompanied by death and pain. The choice is yours."

At that point, Panraak entered the room and edged over to stand beside the silent, withdrawn High Magister Zeta'Om. The archivist did not speak; he seemed speechless in the presence of the ExServ commander. Yet the expression on his face vividly communicated his horror at what was occurring on Omne and at his inability to argue against it. He edged back until the shadow of an overhanging cornice half hid him.

Haardt strode from behind the desk and began pacing back and forth in front of the Makers. Their impassivity frustrated him; normally, he would not have even reacted to primitives such as these.

"I give you one last opportunity," he said finally. He stared at the Makers as he spoke. "Where is he? Where is he hiding? How did he blind my man? Answer, damn you, answer!"

Nothing.

Panraak murmured something, then stopped. His voice seemed to vibrate through the room. Zeta'Om remained silent. His face was drawn and pinched, as if he were pressing himself to make a decision.

Haardt spoke again: "All right, then, since you so choose, I will answer for you."

He stepped back behind the desk and drew himself up. His face was immobile and harsh as he motioned to one of the guards. The man stepped forward. Haardt gestured again. Two others followed. Haardt jabbed his outstretched finger toward Jabeth, the only Master Maker present.

"Take that one out and execute him. Immediately."

Even as the man was saluting his obedience and moving toward Jabeth, Panraak uttered a stifled note of protest. The High Magister stumbled forward, into the center of the room.

"You can't do this!" Zeta'Om cried. "What has Jabeth done? By what authority do you condemn him to death?" He turned to face the stunned Council. "I will not allow it. I will not." His face was flushed.

Haardt turned to the High Magister, withering the boy with a glance.

"By *my* authority," he said. Contempt dripped heavily from his voice. He looked up, his glance sweeping across the room. "By the authority of the Wordsmith, I order this man's death. He refuses to speak when I command. He obstructs my investigations. He wears the blue robe of my enemies. La'am reviles me; Jorik threatened me. There will be no more wearers of the blue robe on Omne."

Haardt turned back to the guard.

"Take him. And take that one also." He pointed to one of the acolytes—Kyril Jeriam-word of Towerwatch.

One guard grabbed Jabeth by the arm; another tore Kyril from the line of acolytes and propelled her toward the door. Expressions of shock flickered across the faces of the Makers and their Acolytes. Yet in that instant, there was nothing anyone could do. Old Jothun moved as if to reach out for Jabeth; the nearest guard struck him brutally on the upper arm with the butt of one of the hollowed tubes the Strangers carried. The hollow *crack* of breaking bone echoed through the room. If anything, the sound deepened the Makers' confusion and growing despair. Jothun groaned once, a low, chilling sound, then pulled himself erect. His broken arm hung limply in the sleeve of his saffron robe, but he did not speak or move again.

The third guard closed the chamber door behind him as he left.

Haardt returned his attention to the Makers.

"Where is he?" This time his voice was soft and low, furred with a velvet threat. Somehow, this voice was infinitely more terrifying than his bluster had been.

Still, the Makers did not respond.

"So be it," Haardt said quietly. He stabbed at the command studs on his belt. The door flew open and another officer appeared.

"Now," Haardt said simply, his eyes never leaving the line of Makers.

The man saluted and left the room.

"I have ordered my scouters to return to each Sanctuary on Omne. They will arrest all persons at the Sanctuaries. And then they will destroy the Sanctuaries. Completely. Not a stone will be left standing, not a scrap of paper left unburned. Everything will be destroyed."

This statement shook the Makers more than anything yet...more even than the deaths of their members. Several figures in the line slumped and paled. The walls shimmered, wavered, faded.

* * * * * * *

The scene died. La'am became aware again of words forming out of color-patterns. Jathanan was speaking.

"One of my attendants spoke to me briefly when she was brought in. Those remaining at my Sanctuary were fearful and worried, both for me and for themselves. The Strangers had swooped down without warning once; what would keep them from doing so a second time? And their fears were well warranted. In the middle of the second night, the scouter came again to Harborwatch. The few women remaining on the island were herded into the ship and borne into the Veil of Heaven.

"The man in charge stopped the craft, made it hover motionlessly in the air. The women were forced to look on as a thin beam of red light speared out from the front of the scouter. It rested for a moment on the buildings of Harborwatch, and then the stones erupted as if a volcano had burst through the earth beneath them. They could see the flames—could almost feel the heat. Then the man turned the craft and the women were flown to Los'ang.

"I rejoice only that I was not present to see the end of my life-work."

The color-patterns rippled. La'am started to form thoughts, but the ripples smoothed and Jathanan continued.

"After First Light this morning, the guards returned again and again, each time taking a few of us from the room where we were being held. I don't know where the others are, but I think that they are in separate chambers here in the Magistry. I have been left alone in one of the lower rooms. The door is bolted and there are no windows. I am being well treated so far, but am isolated.

"There is the chance, of course, that Haardt may have others executed, but for the moment I think we are safe. I felt Jorik when he drew upon my powers; I knew that he was expending his full force as a Master Maker and that he was killed while doing so. Jorik's demonstration of that power has frightened the Strangers and they no longer allow us to roam at will on Omne.

"The guards have even taken our Makers' robes. They gave us new garments of alien make. I do not like them. They are dead, lifeless things, glittering and harsh against the skin. But no matter.

"I have seen none of the others, nor can I reach them alone. When I finally felt contact with a mentrans receiver, I knew that it could only be you, that you are now the Master of Makers."

With that final phrase, the long set of patterns dissipated. La'am was overwhelmed by the sorrow and pain in Jathanan's color-sounds. But he was even more concerned about the repetition of a title to which he had no claim.

"But I am *not* the Master," he sent. "What of Ky'lan? Why is she not the Master? She lives, I presume, or you would have mentioned her death."

He sensed a muting and distorting in the patterns as Jathanan responded.

"She is no more."

"Did Haardt...?"

"No," Jathanan broke in, "she is no more."

La'am caught the particular inflection in the old woman's patterns.

"She is no more."

To greater or lesser degrees, all Makers feared losing themselves in the patterns of another; only strong minds could retain separate identities when confronted by patterns stronger than their own. Yet Ky'lan had been promising and well prepared, groomed to succeed Jorik in the Makership.

Jathanan's patterns resumed. "She was caught up too closely with Jorik. She could have withstood the merging of patterns—hers with Jorik's, theirs combined with the Makers of the Council—had not Jorik been struck down at the height of his power. When his patterns shattered, hers were too close. They shattered also. We other Makers were only ancillary to Jorik and Ky'lan; we escaped unharmed. Ky'lan still lives, but her mind is forever closed. She sleeps now, until the sleep of death overtakes her."

La'am felt the crushing sorrow of Jathanan's patterns infusing his own. Ky'lan was young, beautiful, alive.

No more.

After a moment of silence, La'am 's thought formed new patterns. "What should we do now?"

"I cannot say," the old woman responded. "You alone are still free. You must not be captured or you will surely be executed, as was Jabeth. Haardt fears the indigo robes more than our saffron ones, although I think he refuses to acknowledge that fear, even to himself. We are probably safe...for the moment. You are doubly damned. Not only are you the only surviving Master Maker, but you laid your powers upon his man and blinded him. That was foolish, La'am, foolish and impetuous. It may have brought this devastation upon us before we were fully joined to counteract it. But I cannot find it within me to chastise you for your actions. Had it been my Acolyte....

"Perhaps everything happening now is beyond our control anyway. Perhaps all was foretold, and we merely act out pre-ordained parts."

La'am was disturbed by the fatalism in Jathanan's thoughts.

"No...," he began, but her patterns continued uninterrupted.

"We look to you. I can exchange patterns with you freely. Such an interchange is possible only between Master and Maker, or among the full Makersraad in Council assembled, through the mediation of the Master. I cannot call the others, nor should you. If only I know for certain that you live, you are that much safer. You have within you our combined knowledge. Now, you are the Master of Makers. You must seek the answer. And for your sake, for our sakes, for the sake of Omne herself, you must find it."

La'am was silent. He accepted her words instinctively. He had been chosen to carry on; he would do so.

Jathanan ignored the momentary barrier La'am had unconsciously erected as he contemplated his role. As soon as he lowered the defense barrier, however, she spoke again.

"Go north. Seek the Veil of Heaven. There you may find us all."

She fell silent. Her patterns subsided and blended once more with those of the others coiling in La'am's mind.

Her message disquieted him greatly. Events in Los'ang were moving at a pace far beyond his worst fears. The Sanctuaries themselves had been destroyed, their generations-long accumulations of knowledge now so much cold ash and black dust encrusted on blasted stone walls. And the Makersraad itself was essentially dead. The Masters had been destroyed—himself excepted—and he was effectively isolated by uncounted miles of wasteland and by the weapons of the Strangers from the surviving members of his brotherhood. And they were separated from each other. Some might be dead: all had been stripped of the rhiam-fiber Makers' robe, although the Makerspowers were only amplified by the rhiam fibers, not created by them. Ky'lan was not physically dead but was lost to the present world. That did indeed leave him alone to carry on, to find some way to use the power of the Makership against the Strangers—without unleashing it directly, and fatally, against Haardt. La'am's experiences with Streiter underscored his conviction that the Strangers must not be defeated by overt violence and death. No, Omne must shake them off without descending to their methods.

There was a way, There had to be!

But what was it?

La'am felt more alone than ever before. He must not call on the others, not even Jathanan. He missed Mord'am intensely, and for the first time felt no substantial relief when he searched and found his Acolyte's mentrans patterns.

He was alone. If any except Jathanan even knew for certain that he lived, Haardt might destroy them in the hopes of discovering the hiding place of the sole Master Maker. If the rest were ignorant of his fate, there was at least a chance that they might survive. La'am feared for Jathanan as well, until he felt her pattern surge once more, strong and as enduring as the sea.

She of all the Makers was capable of surviving.

La'am hurried out of the cavern, haunted by the ghosts of memories and lore now lost forever. Once outside the shattered Sanctuary, he ran south along the rocky shore of the island until he came to the small inlet which Jathanan's memories told him he would find. Already the daylight had diminished and lengthening shadows distorted La'am's vision. The shore line was rocky and rough but seemed unbroken. In fact, La'am almost passed by the low entrance to the hidden grotto. Only by chance, it seemed, had his eyes swept the face of the cliff to study the shadows at the base.

He reached down and pulled back the thick mat of branches and leaves clustered at the base of the towering wall. There, half obscured by the greenery, half by the fading light, he found the entrance. He had to bend nearly double to pass through. There was barely enough room on the narrow ledge for his feet. Below, and almost lapping the shallow stone, the water of the hidden inlet spread into the darkness.

The Maker could not see the opposite side of the cavern. As darkness fell, La'am released a brief flickering of the Makerslight. The grotto was small, barely a man's height and not more than double that in length and width. The boat took up most of the room, its wooden sides nearly scraping the stones.

In darkness, he pushed the craft from its berth in the stony prison and out into open air. He settled himself into the boat, feeling the water pick it up and carry it along to the open sea. He sensed that the waves and breezes were pushing him along to the east but he could see nothing. He had never before been on the sea, yet he felt no fear. Omne was with him, and Iam'Kendron, Mord'am, Jorik, Jathanan, and the others—assisting in the final struggle for Omne's survival.

The wind would bear him where he should go.

He slept—and did not dream.

CHAPTER TWENTY-SIX

When La'am awoke, it was day although he could see nothing except grayness. The Veil of Heaven had lowered during the night, obscuring the ocean with a thick coat of mist. Heavy fog was usual along the southern coast, particularly in Dark Time. But this fog was thicker than any La'am had ever seen before...and it was not Dark Time. La'am shrugged deeper into his robe, wrapping the folds tightly about him to keep out the morning chill. He lay quietly for several minutes before sitting up in the center of the small craft.

Glancing at the whiteness on all sides, he struggled to gain some sense of location or direction but could not. His thoughts were confused. He was barely beginning to return consciously to his world, a world in which everything was going wrong. People died, ancient landmarks and havens of learning were destroyed by machines that spit red flames from the air, and now he was floating alone on the ocean. La'am had never really even seen the ocean before his arrival at the Sanctuary of Harborwatch. During his youth as Davian Charl'an-born in the Northrill Vale, he had become used to the placid blue of mountain streams and lakes. As La'am Iam'Kendron-word of the Pillars of Beginnings, he had been only miles from the ocean, but those miles encompassed the impenetrable morass of jutting minarets and sheer faces that made up the Pillars. And as La'am of the Pillars, he had lived in Los'ang, on the marges of the Harbor. Yet in all of his Cycles, he had never once seen the vast, open sea.

Now he was alone with it, ignorant of how to survive although confident that the memory-patterns of Jathanan and Jeriam would surface should he call upon them in need.

He reached into the water and shook a few drops from his fingers onto his face. The salt burned his eyes and a small cut on his cheek. He must have received it during his flight through the Marshes. The smooth coolness of the water and the sharp stinging of the cut awakened him thoroughly. He sat upright and studied the mist.

He could see nothing, hear nothing.

It was as if he were the only being, the only physical object on an entire planet—and he was surprised to hear himself think that thought, that *word*, and thus tacitly accept the existence of other *planets*, other *beings*. Yet it was true; he was totally isolated. Even his senses were dimmed and shrouded in the mist. He could not see; the soft wash of the waves against the wooden planks of the boat was barely audible, muffled by the mist.

A dull scraping from the bottom of the boat startled him. There was a second scraping sound, and the boat jarred, as if it had caught on some projection on the seabed. After a moment, it surged forward again, unimpeded, only to stop again. This time the scraping sound lasted longer. La'am felt small vibrations where his feet rested against the bottom.

He looked around again. By squinting and straining his eyes, La'am could vaguely make out dim shapes ahead. He quickly searched the boat, finally locating an oval paddle strapped with rhiam cord beneath the single-plank seat. He undid the knot, careful to stow the rope safely beneath the seat, and dipped the paddle into the unresisting water, then pulled back. His shoulders knotted with the effort, but he forced the boat off the sandbar. When the boat was floating free again, he tested the depth of the water with the blade of the paddle. To his surprise, it was less than a yard and apparently getting shallower. He rowed the craft forward a few feet more, then looked again over the low bow. The ghostly outline of a small scrub brush blended with the background mist, yet remained clear enough for La'am to recognize as a form of ranya, dwarfed by the almost sterile sand of the southern shores. He pulled a few more strokes on the oar, then stood cautiously, not sure of his footing in the boat even though by now the bottom scraped incessantly on sand. He hitched the Maker's robe up about his waist and stepped out into the water.

It was pleasantly warm and soothing. The sand felt fine and firm beneath his feet. Running his hand along the edge of the boat, La'am followed the smooth curve of the gunwale around to the point of the bow. His fingers found a knotted length of rhiam line coiled against the small ration box. He pulled on the line and discovered that it was tied securely somewhere inside the boat. Hoisting the line over his shoulder, he waded toward the scrub bush, towing the bobbing craft behind him. It took only seconds for him to moor the boat to the ranya.

A few steps more, and La'am stood again on dry land. Here the sand, still fine, was loose and warm. The fog had grown perceptibly thinner. The sharp, pointed ranya leaves jutted distinctly on the nearest branch. A dozen steps beyond that, the fog ended. La'am noted the few visible landmarks carefully—a twisted wedge of ranya spreading like mountain alluvia from the mouth of a serrated gully; an undercut bank held together by webbing of roots until it finally collapsed in a pile of rubble not ten yards from where the boat was moored; a streak of crimson in the bluff above the narrow strand. The bluff was only about twenty feet high and would be easy to climb, yet it effectively cut off La'am's view of the interior. He did not know where he was, other than that he was along the southern coast of Omne. These low sod bluffs certainly did not belong to the massive cordillera that extended along the western coast, across the North, and partially down the East; nor did they fit the descriptions Iam'Kendron had given La'am of the vast, desolate dunes of World's End on the southern reaches of the eastern coast. Nor again were they part of the hillocky swampland of the Salton Marshes.

He did not hesitate to leave the scant security of the boat and the strand and scramble up the sloping face of the bluff. He had a purpose here, on this coast, of that he was certain. Yet, like so much that had happened to him in the past few days, this experience was completely hidden to him, foreign to his expectations. He urgently needed to reach the Pillars of Beginnings, yet Omne's seas had cast him here, upon this portion of the continent.

He would begin his search here.

By the time he crested the bluff, the fog, which had become the merest haze as he climbed, had dissipated entirely. The air was clear. Visibility seemed to extend forever, until a thin line of gray-blue marked the beginnings of the Eastern Ranges. In front, to the North, stretched an unbroken mass of blue-green ranya, the great forest of the South. To his right, to the east, he could discern a vague formation of granite, one of the two warders of the Harbormouth—Jathanan's Sanctuary on Harborwatch had been built on the second of the two formations.

Well, then, he was not far from where he had started the night before. During the short hours of darkness, he had apparently drifted slowly across the mouth of the Harbor, along the coast for several miles, and finally grounded here, between the Harbor and the Eastern Ranges.

He loosened the robe still cinched high around his thighs, allowing the dry folds to fall to the ground, where they nearly touched the rich brown of the Seed Time soil. He looked about for any signs of habitation and, finding none, set off across the open fields toward the ranya forest, angling toward the north and west as he did so. He could not have explained why he chose that direction, or why he had left the shoreline at all, yet he strode with confidence and strength.

Within minutes, he had crossed the open stretch of rhiam and was beneath the sheltering shadows of the ranyas. As always, the pungency of the trees with their sharply palmate and spiny leaves and deeply cleft red-orange bark, refreshed La'am. This morning, in the warming light of early day, the air was redolent with the ranya scent, almost overpoweringly so. He closed his eyes and drew in a deep breath. Instantly, La'am was temporarily transported to his home in the Vale, remembering the thick covert of ranya that surrounded the lakes of his native reaches. For the first time since leaving the house of Charl'an to follow Iam'Kendron, La'am almost felt homesick.

The emotion passed as a breeze from the sea fingered through the trees, diluting the scent. Opening his eyes, La'am turned sharply as he entered the forest, following a faint trail. The path was barely visible, as if once it had been a well-used but narrow road, but long since neglected. The hard-pack in the center of the trail was barren of any growth, although shrubs and even a number of rather large ranya had encroached along the edges. The path continued without bending, heading straight through the forest. As La'am walked, he felt an increasing sense of familiarity, as if he could almost—but not quite—remember having walked this path when it was new, when it was a road paved with crushed granite mixed with lime and sand.

Almost, but not quite.

Still, even with the lingering sense of partial memory, La'am was taken totally unaware when the road angled abruptly, heading back toward the sea. Thickets on each side of the trail proved impassible, obscuring any view to the sides. La'am followed the trail, more cautious now than he had been moments before, and turned when he came to the bend.

At first he did not see anything unusual. Then he began sorting out vague images. What seemed to be little more than light shadows among the trees resolved into solid walls of weathered stone, low walls huddled together as if for protection from the invading forest. The pathway widened, then became almost a street. Now, for the first time, La'am could trace the outlines of the original road. He could see the remnants of cobblestones outlined by thick tufts of vivid moss—greener, La'am thought, than anything he had ever seen growing on Omne.

He paced slowly along the deserted street. The few visible buildings crouched on either side were single-storied. The stonework was ancient, as was most stonework on Omne—the Cantorium at Los'ang excluded, of course—but here the buildings were in an appalling state of disrepair. Roof tiles had cracked and split; many had slid down the low pitch of the gables to lie in broken piles near the foundations of the buildings. The fine-grained cement used to join the stones had flaked away. La'am turned and walked toward the nearest building. He scratched at the wall with his fingers. The remnants of cement crumbled into dust.

There were no doors or windows, although empty openings bore mute evidence that such had once existed. Even the wooden lintels and frames had rotted away—along the stone threshold, La'am could see remains of long, narrow mounds of matted fibers. Occasionally a vine or creeper stretched through openings into a shadowy interior.

He returned to the road.

The place was dead. No one had lived here for Cycles. Probably no one had even visited in almost as long. Obviously, the Makers had deserted it. The ruined buildings could only be explained by the fact that no Words of 'Waring had been said over the buildings for Cycles. When the Makers had left....

La'am felt a stirring of excitement.

When the Makers had left! Of course!

This could only be the deserted Makerseat of the Two Isles. It was in the right place, inland and west of Harbormouth. La'am felt a rushing in his blood as he hurried along the overgrown street. To his left were the remains of cottages, probably for the crofters who had once cared for the extensive southern rhiam fields. On his right, he could recognize an occasional structure—a wayhouse, a warehouse. And finally, at the extreme end of the cluster, at the point farthest west and farthest south, La'am found the Sanctuary.

The place was unmistakable. Its dimensions were identical to those of nearly every other Sanctuary La'am had seen—at Heartland and the ruins at Harborwatch. It was larger than the Sanctuary at the Pillars of Beginnings, but then Iam'Kendron had long ago told him that the Pillars of Beginnings was not only the oldest structure, but also the smallest.

For a moment, La'am was surprised to find the Sanctuary untouched. Jathanan had said that Haardt intended to destroy every Sanctuary. Probably, La'am concluded, Haardt had decided not waste his time on the ruined, vacant Makerseats of the Two Islands, of the Highland Marshes, and of World's End.

And it was just as well, La'am discovered after entering the dark ruins, since there was nothing of value to destroy.

The interior was black and empty. The Makerslight La'am kindled threw no shadows but his own against the walls. There were no tables, no benches. He peered into the open doorways along each side wall. The inner chambers were as empty as the common room. The large chamber at the back of the Sanctuary was similarly empty. The artifacts and documents preserved at the Two Islands had been removed to Los'ang when the Makerseat lapsed. Not even a stray scrap of furniture remained to disturb the smooth layer of dust and dirt that hid the stone floor.

The darkness and emptiness depressed La'am. He had hoped unconsciously—and against all reason—to find something at the Sanctuary to further his search. He had assumed that he had stopped at this point on the coast for a purpose, and had connected that sense of purpose with the Makerseat, as soon as it became apparent what the cluster of ruins was. But there was nothing here that could help. Absolutely nothing.

La'am sent a pulse of mentrans.

Still nothing.

It was as if the Makers of Omne had never inhabited the place, as if the Words of 'Waring had never been spoken here. As if the deepest of the Makerspowers had never touched this place.

La'am felt isolated and cold.

He retraced his steps to the filtered light of the central street and returned the way he had come. Far sooner than he expected, he reached the limits of the Sanctuary-town. Now, approaching from within its original limits, he could make out the outlines of a low stone wall that had once marked the boundaries of the Makerseat. Now the wall was broken and crumbling, straddled by ranya roots, lifted and cracked by huge, muscular bulges in the earth. Again, La'am was overcome by depression and loneliness—and a cold sense of death. He had never seen Omne looking as dead as did this place. Yet if he should fail, the entire land might someday soon look like this.

He quickened his pace and re-entered the forest. Once, he reminded himself, there was no forest here, just limitless miles of rhiam fields, self-generating and self-sustaining. Only in the past two hundred Cycles had the forests encroached on the fields, and then only as the population in the southern reaches had declined. Finally, the Maker of the Two Islands had died and no Acolyte was chosen to replace him. The crofters left, most of them moving northward into the Eastern Ranges, or northwest to Heartland. With the land untended, the forests began their irresistible movement along the coast. And now even the stones of the Sanctuary itself were threatened by the destructive roots of the ranyas.

As he walked, La'am allowed his mind to reach inward, to search for a pattern that might show him what the Two Islands had once been, but there was none. He probed along the surfaces of inert patterns just below his consciousness, suddenly noting and appreciating the fact that he was alone, truly himself, for the first time in days. Even the patterns that were Mord'am and Iam'Kendron had retreated.

The air was still and warm as he walked. The sharp scent of the ranyas again assaulted him through in the shadows. La'am was tired and thirsty, but surprisingly content.

Gradually, however, the breezes rose again, this time from inland. He caught the faint fragrance of rhiam in Seed Time, the rich smell of fallow soil, untouched and untended for generations.

Then he smelled something else. He halted abruptly, almost stumbling on the smooth path.

Rhiam...burning!

Jorik's patterns burst upward, reminding La'am of the reports of field-burnings in the north and south, of Joleckan's reports of devastation in the fields of the Eastern Ranges.

La'am plunged into the underbrush, leaving the path behind. He rushed on, unmindful of potential danger. He could always find the ocean, he knew, and he was confident that he could return to the bluff where the boat was moored, if necessary. Right now, he had to find out about this acrid smell.

He did not have to travel far. Within minutes, the smell became stronger, bitter and frightening. A few moments more and La'am could see the edges of the forest, with the increasingly sparse stands of ranya...and through gaps in the growth, wild rhiam fields. Above them, in menacing patches, hung dark clouds.

No, not clouds—smoke!

As he approached the last scraggly trees, La'am slowed. His movements became more studied, more cautious.

Here and there across the fields, thin lines of flames crackled through new growth. And scattered through the open spaces already blackened and cleared by fires, the machines of the Strangers whirred.

Shining, clattering, ominous—they moved sullenly across the bare earth, gouging great chunks of soil with toothed scoops at their front ends, swallowing the soil, then evacuating it in dark clumps out the rear. Occasionally, silhouettes of men flitted from machine to machine. La'am counted three, perhaps four men. In the distance, through a haze of thick, black smoke and silvery dust, he thought he could distinguish the outlines of a scouter or a lander. He could not tell which.

For a long while, La'am waited, hidden among the ranyas. The clouds of smoke increased as the fires burned closer to the fringes of the forest. Finally, the air became so full of smoke that even the nearest trees faded to blue-gray. La'am crouched and began creeping out of the forest and onto open ground. His blue robe would provide a certain measure of cover among the blue-black shadows of the fields, but he knew that would have to move cautiously to avoid detection.

He knew the risk he was running. He also knew that it was imperative for him to find out precisely what the Strangers were doing.

He inched forward, stopping frequently, freezing at any slight sound. Fortunately, the haze was deepening, covering him more completely. Near the ground, the air was almost breathable; had he been standing, La'am would probably have long since been overcome by the smoke. He wondered how the strangers could continue monitoring the machinery as the air thickened.

When he was a dozen or more yards from the last of the trees, he crouched even lower and spread the edges of his robe. With any luck, he would seem only a shadow. He waited.

In the distance he heard the noise of the machines but for a long while none came near him. His eyes began to water from the smoke, and gradually his lungs began to burn as he drew in the acrid air. Once, twice he stifled back a cough, knowing that he would not be able to remain where he was for much longer. Even if the men did not notice him, he could begin coughing and the sound might give him away.

He forced himself even lower against the ground, until his nostrils picked up more of the heavy, damp smell of rich soil than the oily smoke.

Finally, however, his patience paid off. Just as he wiped his eyes for the dozenth time, he spotted the outline of one of the machines moving slowly but steadily in his direction. The noise from the machine was almost deafening. But a rapid glance assured him that there were no other figures near enough to see him. Rising in a single graceful movement, La'am ran over to the machine and pressed himself into a deep shadow underneath a projecting, wing-like slab of metal.

He waited for another few seconds, his feet moving silently to keep up with the stolid pace of the machine. From the shadow, his gaze darted from left to right, sweeping across the smoky fields. He still saw no one.

Only then did he turn his attention to the machine that sheltered him. Beneath the wing, the side of the thing was covered with panels that were subdivided into segments of dials and wheels and pulleys. At first, La'am felt at first awed by the obvious complexity of the thing. This was the first functioning machine he had ever seen up close, the first he could reach out and touch and feel the harnessed energy vibrating like something living from its depths. Not even the Strangers' flying ships—seen only from a distance or at rest—had impressed him so completely.

But this thing....

He circled it, looking carefully at the multiple, complex structures that composed it. Apparently it was not one unit but many, linked for a special purpose.

When he circled the side and saw the toothed scoop on the front, he drew back. The teeth on the scoop looked wickedly sharp. They were gouging at the burnt-off soil and devouring man-sized chunks of hard earth as easily as La'am might cut cheese with a well-made stone knife. But the cuts were shallower than he had expected, perhaps no more than eight or ten inches skimmed from the surface. Blackened fibers that had once been rhiam plants canted and tipped as the machine devoured the soil. Watching more closely, La'am was able to see a number of small nodules—charm stones—as they disappeared into the machine as well. They too were dulled and blackened by the flames, hardly recognizable as the smooth, bright stones he and so many others had carried for luck as children.

Other than that, he saw nothing except ash-blackened soil.

He skirted the scoop, keeping as far as possible away from the direct path of the thing. Fortunately, the smoke billowed past him more heavily than before, and cut the visibility even further. There was little chance that he had been seen.

The far side of the machine was much like the first, only from that side he was more exposed to view from the men who, some distance away, were flitting from machine to machine. He crouched again and half-crawled along the side.

Then he was at the rear.

Dirt was spilling out. He reached down and grasped a clump. He lifted it, smelled it, fingered it. Carefully he crushed it between his two hands. Fine grains sifted through his fingers, leaving a shadow of dust on his palms. He tried another, larger clump, then another. The results were always the same. The charm stones were missing, but he had anticipated that. According to the patterns Jorik had sent him, Haardt had acknowledged that the stones were what the Strangers wanted. Yet La'am now realized that more was involved than just some stones. Joleckan's message—relayed again through Jorik's mentrans patterns—had referred to the barrenness of the soil after it was processed through the Strangers' machines. Where the machines had been, nothing grew.

La'am had assumed, as apparently Jorik had also assumed, that Joleckan's words were figurative. Joleckan was an excessively motherly woman, as befitted her position as Maker of the Eastern Ranges. More than once, La'am had caught himself thinking of her in terms of the Earth Mother mythology hinted at in the ancient lore. She seemed to fit, with her bluff mannerisms and her earthy ways.

La'am raised his hands to his face and breathed in the odor of the processed earth. There were layers of new smells—hot, metallic smells that he had no way to define. But more critically, beneath those layers, something was missing.

The richness, the life was gone. All he held was dead dust.

Joleckan had been more precise than perhaps even she had known. She might have written figuratively, but La'am knew, without understanding how he knew it, that this soil was sterile. The machines had removed more than just the charm stones—or perhaps....

The charm stones!

They grew only where they could touch the rhiam roots. And they were always present, most prevalent in the most fertile fields. La'am could remember as a small boy trying to transplant seedlings into a small plot he had prepared behind Charl'an's house. Within days, the plants had died. La'am had been perhaps four or five Cycles old at the time, and like a child he had run crying into the house, brokenhearted at his failure. His mother had patiently explained that in order for the tiny plants to flourish, La'am would have to place a handful of the charm stones near the roots of each plant.

He had carefully replanted his small garden, laying four or five stones at the bottom of each shallow hole, then placed the plants on top of them and pressed damp soil around their stems. The plants had prospered.

La'am's mind was working quickly now, calling upon the stored knowledge of generations of Makers. Rhiam fields were rarely plowed. Usually, the plants took care of themselves, requiring only rudimentary weeding and then, near the end of the season, harvesting. The fields of Omne were ancient; few had been increased in size over the past five hundred Cycles, and only those in the southern plains had reverted to wild. No one had ever questioned these facts—until now.

La'am crumbled another clump of dust through his fingers. He felt it trickle down, he saw it fall in a small pile at his feet. This soil would never again bear fruit. Where the charm stones were present, the rhiam would grow; where they were absent....

The Strangers were destroying Omne.

Perhaps they did not realize that they were. La'am himself had only made the connection in the last few seconds, and then only because of the Makers' knowledge. But to remove the charm stones would render the soil barren. And where rhiam did not grow, Omnans could not survive.

"Hey! You, there! What're you doing?"

A strident voice cut harshly through the air.

La'am whirled to see one of the Strangers running toward him. The man's face was covered by a plate of clear material, probably a breathing device of some kind since the man did not seem bothered by the thick smoke.

La'am did not wait to investigate further, however. He spun on his heels and took off for the protective shadows of the forest. He ran for half a dozen paces, then crouched and began a zigzag race for the dark shadows that loomed not far away. Behind him, he could hear a cacophony of cries echoing among the three Strangers.

"There's one."

"He's got a blue robe, I think. Those are the ones Haardt wants."

"Don't kill him. We've got to take him alive."

"Come on. Leave the refiners. They'll be okay. Let's get him!"

Pursuit followed quickly. Haardt's orders had been brief and explicit: Any blue-robed Maker was to be taken—alive if possible, dead if necessary, but taken.

The three men monitoring the computerized refiners circled the bulky machines. Two of them spread out, trying to cut off La'am's dash for the trees. The third ran directly toward the fleeing Maker. One of them raised a shining tube and pointed it at La'am. There was a gout of red light, a sharp *craaack*, and one of the ranyas just ahead and to La'am's left burst into flame. La'am smelled hot air and, his lungs almost bursting from exertion and, laboring from the smoke-filled air he was pumping into his system, he forced his legs to speed up. He straightened and ran full out, sprinting for the trees becoming more solid as they emerged from the smoke only a few yards away.

"Stop," one of the other two yelled.

Another voice added, "Don't kill him. Not yet. We can get him!"

But La'am was too close to the protective shadows of the ranya forest, too close and too fast.

Almost before the third man cleared the machine and broke into a full run, the Maker was obscured by the smoky shadows filtering through the trees. He ran a hundred yards or so into the thicket, changing directions two or three times, then stopped. He was breathing heavily and painfully but he forced himself to calm enough to listen for sounds of pursuit. The Strangers were still far away. It sounded as if none had yet entered the forest. La'am scuttled through a clump of low-lying pyranth bushes and slipped behind the screen of dense foliage. He sank to the ground, then crawled on his hands and knees into the small hollow next to the pyranth trunk. The bush covered him like a roof. He could not see out—with any luck, no one would be able to see in. He was virtually invisible where his dark blue robe merged with the shadows and the lingering haze. He pulled his hood over his head, as much to mute the sound of his labored breathing as to hide his chalky face.

I am a rock, he thought. I am part of the earth. A shadow within a shadow within a shadow.

He closed his eyes and concentrated on the sounds around him.

A few moments later, heavy footsteps thumped by as the Strangers ran toward him, then beyond him and disappeared into the denseness of the ranyas. Then, shortly, he heard muffled voices.

"Which way?"

"Shit, I don't know."

"Over here, I see something."

The sounds faded until La'am heard nothing except the rustle of leaves and his own breathing, lighter now and less painful.

He waited a few moments longer.

The Strangers had lost the trail. More to the point, it sounded as if they had lost themselves as well. They would find their way out of the ranyas soon enough, but for the moment their eagerness to capture the blue-robed Maker had led them away from the machines they were supposed to monitor.

La'am crawled out of the shadows, stood, and after brushing himself off, retraced his steps toward the edge of the fields. The machines were still operating, independent of human control. They gouged at the surface, expelled their sterilized loads of topsoil. Beyond, now almost hidden in smoke, the form of the flying craft that apparently brought both men and machines loomed ghostly and fading. La'am cocked his head and listened intently. The men's voices were no longer even barely discernible. There was no sound of returning footsteps. For the moment, he was still safe.

He stepped cautiously into the clearing and approached the nearest machine. It kept gouging at the soil, like a huge creature oblivious to the nearness of a human and compelled by its hunger to eat and eat.

La'am glanced around. No figures barred his way, no voices challenged him. He studied the monsters. After a moment, he probed it with a small, careful mentrans burst.

It answered.

Startled, he almost broke for the cover of the forest. He was turned, his foot poised to begin running, when he caught hold of himself.

What he had felt was not possible. He must have been mistaken.

He came closer to the machine and laid his open palm against its smooth, warm side. He touched it lightly with his forehead.

And sent a second, small, careful burst.

It answered again.

Or, rather, it *seemed* to answer. Reciprocal patterns emanated from the machine, as if it were human. No, La'am corrected himself at once, not quite human. These patterns seemed almost like mentrans, but even as he sorted through them, he realized that they were cold and precise, clipped, simplified and repetitive. Not at all the brilliant warmth and vibrant color-sounds of true mentrans...but very like them.

Even so, somehow the Strangers had managed to infuse their human thoughts and fragments of their human personalities into the machines. He touched his forehead to the machine and sent a more complex pattern, one that asked for information, clarification, explanation.

When the machine responded, La'am found to his surprise that he could identify the patterns clearly and easily, something he had never been able to do with the Strangers. Their patterns tended to be confused and murky, compounded with emotional overtones apparently impossible for Omnans to penetrate. Had Jorik been able to search Haardt's patterns this clearly from the first, the whole tragedy of Omne might have been averted, La'am realized bitterly. Mord'am might still live.

The Makers could not communicate with the Strangers, could not even isolate identifiable mentrans patterns within the Strangers, but La'am could feel—and understand—the thought-patterns of the machines.

Dig. Analyze. Retrieve.

Dig. Analyze. Retrieve.

He backed away half a dozen steps, never taking his eyes from the machine, with its wicked-toothed scoop. He raised his hand and pointed.

A single short flash of blue Makerslight, and the machine chattered to a halt. The patterns that motivated it were now confused, incapable of directing the thing's mindless operation. The machine was not destroyed—indeed, it was not even materially damaged. Its brain was simply no longer communicating clear thoughts. A moment more sufficed to confound the remaining machines.

In the ensuing silence, broken only by the crackle of now-dying fires, La'am turned his attention to the flying ship itself.

Penetrating to its controlling patterns was more difficult, less precise. He dared not approach it any closer than he was, since it sat in the middle of the fire-scored fields, too far from the forests for safety. And even if he could have come closer, he was not certain that he would have wanted to. Even from a distance, the thing was huge, intimidating.

Instead, he reached out with his mind and imagined that he was stroking its unfamiliarly smooth metal surface, then descending into its depths.

And, weak from the effort, he found its center.

The patterns were more complex, more similar to those generated by the Strangers, and consequently more difficult to isolate.

La'am concentrated. A shimmering arc of Makerslight threaded itself through the smoky gloom, spinning out from La'am's pointing finger and resting finally on the indistinct outline of the ship. A small flash of flame, and the ship was like the machines—intact but inoperable.

From just that small contact, thought, La'am felt confident that he understood—rudimentarily and instinctively rather than experientially or intellectually—the basic functioning of the ship, although he had no words for the multiform components he intuited or for the harnessed forces his questing patterns had brushed against then carefully avoided. He now knew the ships; he could control them to some degree, if only by disrupting the memory patterns stored in what he could only define as immensely complex artificial brains.

If only the Strangers could be read equally well.

It did not occur to La'am that his ability to perceive and to transmit mentrans had increased immeasurably over his abilities of only two or three days before. Or that now those abilities perhaps exceeded the powers of any Maker in Omne's history. Yet even with his amplified powers, the Strangers remained unreadable to him. If only....

Suddenly realizing that he made a perfect target, standing in the open, La'am broke off his reverie, whirled, and ran for the safety of the ranyas. This time his eyes and lungs did not bother him as much—but, conversely, the air was clearer. The fires were burning themselves out and the breezes were carrying the smoke away from the fields. He could have easily been spotted and killed or captured. He sprinted to the edge of the forest, then angled sharply to his right, away from the last place he had heard any sounds of pursuit. He cut into the forest just enough to be invisible from watchers on the open fields, then began a jagged trek that took him south toward the shore.

With any luck, it would be moments more before the Strangers gave up the hunt and headed back toward the machines. By the time they discovered that their machines were not running, La'am was back on the faint trail he had discovered earlier that morning, walking quickly and purposefully toward the bluff on the shore.

He had learned much, about himself, about Omne, and about the Makers and their powers, and about the Strangers. Perhaps, he hoped, he had even found a key, a clue, a beginning glimmer of a weapon that could be used against them without compromising the position and principles of a Master Maker of Omne.

Perhaps.

But now, it was increasingly important that he resume the journey to the Pillars of Beginnings. He hurried on down the faint path, ignoring the seductive call he felt coming from the ruins of the Makerseat of the Two Isles. Sometime—another time—he hoped to return and study the ruins. But not now.

By late afternoon, La'am had returned to the low bluff. The heavy fog still stretched in an unbroken curtain across the ocean. From the top of the bluff, the water line was almost invisible. La'am could barely make out the tendril-like branches of the tree on the beach. He half-slid down the crumbly slope toward the sand. When he hit the bottom, he pinwheeled his arms to help regain his balance, and ran through the sand toward the tree.

Before he was close enough to touch its rough bark and search with his fingers for the rope he had used to tie up the boat, his eyes alerted him.

The rope was gone!

He leaped forward, ducking low hanging branches, and searched in the wet sand. He crawled along the edges of the waves that slapped rhythmically at the roots of the tree. Suddenly, something thin and black and supple, like a coiling snake, whipped into, then as rapidly out of his vision. It disappeared just as he reached for it, then reappeared a few feet further down the beach. It flickered back and forth in the misty edges of the fog bank.

He lunged, grasped it, and pulled on the sodden rope. There was a moment of resistance, then boat floated into sight.

It is time to leave this place, he though in the second that his fingers tightened on the rope.

Omne had almost taken his boat without him. A minute later—perhaps even a few seconds later, and the painter would have disappeared into the gray fog. And La'am would have been stranded in the southern wilderness.

With his free hand, he hitched his robe up around his waist, and then waded through the hip-deep surf out toward the boat. Balancing precariously on the side, he finally climbed aboard and fell onto the moist timbers. At that moment, the unseen hand of an undertow caught the beams of the craft and pulled it out to open water.

La'am lay without moving. He was exhausted. The emotional component of his exhaustion outweighed the physical, however; he had expended Makerspower to a degree unprecedented in his own experiences. He shifted his position until he could lean against the seat, and slept. He was unconcerned for the moment as to his destination.

CHAPTER TWENTY-SEVEN

When he awoke, it was already day. He had slept the entire night away, undisturbed by dreams. He sat up and glanced over the side of the boat. From the ripples widening out from the bow in two smooth curves, he could tell that he was still being propelled by the invisible current that had grabbed the craft just off the southern strands. The sky was still the dull gray of ocean mists rather than the pearly white of the Veil of Heaven, but in spite of having no landmarks to judge from, La'am felt strongly that during the night he had traveled far from the despoliation of Harborwatch and the lonely, ruined desolation of the Two Islands—far from the machines that were systematically mutilating the rhiam fields. He had known before he slept that currents were carrying him to the East; now the mild wind blowing from the east against his right cheek and ruffling his hair suggested that the currents had arched northward. He had rounded the southeast curve of Omne during the night, passing beyond the inhabited lands of the Eastern Ranges, beyond the ruggedness of the Range crests themselves, and was now somewhere off the wastelands and dunes of World's End.

Knowing this excited La'am more than anything he had yet encountered since his flight from Los'ang. Normally it would have taken far longer to travel the distance he had covered—weeks perhaps, if the winds were not favorable. Nor was there any lingering memories in the patterns within him of a current that could carry a craft all the way to World's End against the force of the usual east-to-west winds. In fact, the opposite was generally true. Most seagoers spent their time following the Lesser Pillars where they curved along the western edge of Omne; occasionally especially hardy crews might venture as far as the sheer bluffs that faced the Highland Marshes to the North. Only rarely did any vessels head along the inhospitable deserts of the eastern coast, especially since the destruction of the Sanctuary and city at World's End. Indeed, according to all reports, the rescue attempts at the time of the disaster that destroyed the city had been curtailed by adverse currents that had thrown three ships onto the shallows of World's End and ruptured their fragile hulls. Only one vessel had made it to within sight of the burning city, but even that one had been unable to approach land and find anchorage close enough to do any good.

Yet La'am knew that he was now just off that same barren, death-dealing coast, following an anomalous current northward.

Well, there was nothing he could do about it...or that he would do about it if he could. He was where Omne wanted him to be. That sufficed.

He lay back against the edge of the seat. He licked his lips and found them dry and beginning to chap. He looked around for a stock of supplies that Jathanan might have left with the boat but saw nothing. No food, no water.

And for the first time he realized that he was hungry. He mentally tallied the days, and was shocked to discover that he had not eaten for almost five days—not since the morning of the day on which Mord'am died. He was used to fasting, so the rumbles and grumbles he felt in his stomach did not disturb him greatly. He knew the differences between appetite and hunger, and also knew that he had not yet passed from the first stage into the second. More to the point, he was nowhere near actual starvation. If necessary, he could survive for many days more without food...and if he were forced ashore in the desolation of World's End, he might have to do so. He hoped to continue directly to the sea-side of the Pillars of Beginnings, however, where he had every chance of finding wild rhiam and other edibles.

He licked his lips again. He was not thirsty, which did rather surprise him. The coolness of the Veil had staved off the normal heat of the preceding day, and the mists of night had provided additional relief. Physically, La'am was well. Tired and hungry, but well.

He sat up again and toyed with the idea of using the oar to propel the boat even faster. But he quickly discovered that he could do nothing to alter the direction or speed of the boat; the oar had become unshipped sometime during the night and must have fallen overboard. At any rate, it was no longer in the boat. The loss should probably have worried him, since it left him the mercy of the ocean, the winds, and the currents, but curiously it did not. Jathanan's last warning had urged him to head North. Now he was doing precisely that. There was nothing he could do except relax.

For what seemed like several hours, La'am remained immobile in the bottom of the boat. He folded his robe into a pad to protect himself from the cool timbers, then spent the time lost in thought. He was largely unaware of his surroundings as he explored the new worlds of understanding and knowledge that had been thrust upon him. He wandered through the patterns he had so precipitously received, sorting them, interpreting some, setting others—more obscure than the rest—aside for later scrutiny. He began to feel a sense of control over the minds that now shared to a surprising degree his own mind. He felt that he could begin to summon knowledge and power when the need should arise. He began to understand the powers implicit in the Words he had been taught...and to sense the presence of Words beyond those known to the present generation of Makers. He began to know more fully what a *Maker* was—a *Maker*. One who could control reality by assigning names and words to ideas.

Gradually, he sank into a re-evaluation of his own youth. He was amazed at the clarity of his memories. He could hear and smell and taste and see as if he were once again Davian Charl'an-born of the Northrill Vale. He recalled the last years of his life in the Ranges, treasuring each moment. He followed himself again into the highest ledges and shoulders on that last climactic climb. He saw again the visions of the night sky and the obscure flowing of his dreams, culminating with the magnificent figure of the robed form silhouetted in the circle of light.

As that final vision crystallized in his mind's eye, he felt a small, scraping jerk, as if the boat had bottomed on some obstruction. He sat up, blinking suddenly at the brightness of the day as it filtered through the Veil. He was still closely enveloped in the mists, but now they seemed to flow with a hidden, white fire. The boat had stopped; La'am could hear a constant lapping as wavelets broke against the bow, but the boat was not moving. The current had apparently reversed itself and now was trying to pull the craft southward with it.

The Maker stood steadily in the boat, as steadily as if he were on land. Stretching his right hand, he spoke Words of Light—words he had never heard but which had formed themselves from the fragments of patterns supplied by Iam'Kendron, Jathanan, and Jorik. The Words trembled with power, yet La'am's voice was steady and confident. Even as he spoke, he wondered how many centuries had passed since these Words had been uttered. It must have many, for almost all memory of the Words had disappeared from the closely guarded Makers' Lore.

Unless....

He swallowed, choking off one of the Words. His hand trembled now, both with the exertion of power and with an abrupt awareness that startled him as much as the Words of Light themselves did.

Unless, for some reason unknown to generations of the Makersraad, the Words had been *hidden*.

La'am's mind made a sudden intuitive leap. The Words of Light existed and were potent; other Words must also exist, as potent and as unknown, purposefully concealed by...by earlier Makers?

As the final phrasing of the Words of Light passed his lips, a spear of Makerslight flared from his outstretched hand and burned into the Veil where it dipped down almost low enough to brush against the waves. The stabbing light touched the Veil, dissipating it and dissolving it. La'am stared unbelievingly. It was as if at that spot the Veil had never existed. He continued sweeping his outstretched arm across the bows of the boat until all around him he could feel the Veil of Heaven lifting.

Squinting against the brightness and turning his body in the boat until the westward wind blew at the back of his head, he could see a faint line of yellow stretching in either direction—north and south—until it disappeared beyond his vision. In a few moments more, the Veil had lifted so completely that he could distinguish unbroken lines of dunes, shimmering with a brilliance La'am had rarely experienced.

In that moment, he recognized the landscape. He was just off World's End, only a few dozen yards from shore. The ocean was impossibly quiet; there were no swells, no breakers spilling up onto the vivid sands, only rippling ruffles of foam rolling up and down on the shore.

La'am stooped down and picked up his robe, packing it tightly into a bundle, then wearing nothing but his clout and laced sandals, he slipped over the side of the boat. The water was not as deep as he had feared. It reached only to his chest. Its coolness pulsed rhythmically against his flesh.

He headed toward the shore, half floating, half walking. He could swim, but hesitated to allow the robe to get wet. He could not have defined the reasons for his hesitation, however, not even to himself.

Once or twice something nudged against his bare thighs, but whether living or dead, he could not tell. The water was shallow but murky with suspended sand. He could see nothing, and the nudges did not repeat, so he kept going. Every now and again, a small wave caught him and lifted him until only his toes remained in contact with the sand, and once he almost fell but recovered his balance at the last moment. The bundled robe was still high over his head and untouched by the water.

Finally, he reached the shore. He almost stumbled again in the shallows when he stepped on a smooth, slick, rounded surface that must have been a wave-worn rock, but once more he regained his footing and continued on to the dry beach. When he was well above the high water mark, he sat down on the golden sand.

Everything was hot there. The sand was hot, almost burning against his damp skin. And the air was hot as well. Above him, the Veil of Heaven had lifted further. The clouds here were different from those elsewhere on Omne. They contained little moisture; they were vaporous and thin rather than white and billowing.

He stood quickly, brushing at his legs. He was nearly dry already. The salt water had left a thin shell of deposits on his skin, which he rubbed off with his palms. As soon as he felt reasonably clean and dry, he replaced the robe loosely about his shoulders, more for protection from the heat than for any other reason. In only a few minutes, his shoulders had become unusually warm; he feared that his skin might burn in the harsh, unmediated glare of light at World's End.

The Veil of Heaven continued to lighten and lift. Offshore, the boat bobbed in the waves. Gradually it drifted southward, as if it had completed a mission and was now free to return home. For a fleeting second, La'am thought of trying to swim out and recover the craft; without it he was irrevocably marooned on the inhospitable wastes of the Eastern shore. He stepped forward, then stopped.

No, let it go.

Somehow, he knew that he would no longer have to rely on the ocean for guidance. Omne had brought him here; she would tell him how and where to proceed.

He turned his back on the water and faced the limitless stretches before him. To the south, he could see nothing except miles of unbroken sand, until finally the Veil and the desert shores merged and became as one. To the west there were more dunes, with the faintest suggestion of mountains far away—the slopes of the Eastern

Ranges, from all accounts as dry and as desolate as the dunes themselves.

Only to the north was there any discontinuity in the golden monotony of the landscape. A low cluster of shadows swelled against the sand, with an occasional glimmering of...something...to catch the eye.

La'am began walking north.

His sense of vision was distorted by the lack of any recognizable landmarks, any familiar shapes or forms to provide a matrix for his perceptions. The shadows had seemed close, but La'am walked for several hours before he could be sure that he had come any nearer to them than he had been. Finally, he could distinguish a thin line of darkness that stretched from the clustered shadows westward, eventually merging with the mountains. Closer and closer he came, until the shadows resolved into vague shapes—buildings perhaps, certainly man-made structures—and the black line into a solid wall of stone: the lava flow that had destroyed the Makerseat of World's End.

This was what remained of the twelfth Makerseat, a city overrun by a volcanic flow. Once a busy place, third in importance behind Los'ang and Heartland, it now lay empty, peopled only by ghosts and memories. As he approached the dead city, he could see for the first time that the landscape north of the ruins the terrain was more violently broken than the smoother deserts of the south. Great spurs from the southern fringes of the Pillars of Beginnings thrust into the wastes, carrying twisted, fractured roots of stone toward the boundaries of the dead city. Ahead, faint swaths of green appeared on the mountains, and—more importantly—a fragile glimmering resolved itself into a river cascading over the solidified lava flows.

Water!

La'am's thirst had mounted unbearably during the day.

He quickened his steps, hoping to arrive at the ruins before dark. He was hungry, thirsty, and tired after his steady march.

By the first moments of twilight, La'am stood outside the city. The river had been blocked by the volcanic flow. The old streambed was dry, veined with minor lava flows now hardened and cold. New branches cut through fractures in the sharp lava and spread in widening pools along the streets of the city. Clear water sparkled through doorways of stone buildings now congested with black rock. It gurgled across the low roofs of dwellings buried forever beneath cold remnants of fiery flows, dwellings now one with their destroyer. In the center of the city, he could identify the pyramidal form of an ancient Cantorium, still valiantly reaching upward, its lower half robed in black.

La'am had expected nothing different from what he found, but he nevertheless felt vaguely ill-at-ease at the sight. Buried beneath the lava were the bodies of hundreds of Omnans, including the last Maker of World's End—men and women who were asleep when the volcano to the northwest had suddenly belched smoke, ashes, and liquid fire, cutting off the only pass through the Veil, isolating the panic-stricken survivors, and finally consuming the city itself. La'am could almost touch the patterns of fear and terror still hanging in the air from that night. The Makerseat of the Two Isles had been cold and dead, as cold and dead in physical fact as was the ruin now before him; yet the Makerseat of World's End seemed still charged with the potential for life. The Two Isles had been willfully dead, voluntarily deserted by the Makersraad; World's End was equally dead, while still harboring vestiges of the violence that had wrenched the city from the Makers against their wills and desires.

He knelt at the far edge of a small stream and lifted a handful of water to his lips and drank. The water was warm but sweet. He drank again. And again. Finally, when he no longer thirsted he removed his robe and laid it carefully on the sand. He stripped off his rhiam clout and washed it in the stream, rinsing residual salt and dirt and body oils from the closely-woven material. When the length of fabric was clean, he used it as a sponge to rinse his irritated skin. Afterward, he cleaned the clout once more, wring it as dry as he could, and rewound it about his body. The cloth was damp and clinging, but its coolness was refreshing in the heat.

Then he put his robe on again, stood, and looked over the remains of World's End. A Master Maker of Omne, he stared at the ruined Sanctuary and the empty Makerseat.

After a long time, he decided not to enter the city. He turned inland instead and followed the winding path of the small stream.

There was no shelter immediately available, so as the Veil gathered and turned from white to gray, and from gray to dusky blue-black, he simply settled himself down on the warm sand and waited for night. There was no wind, no sound. He felt no thirst. His hunger was increasing, as was to be expected, but it was not yet severe enough to make appreciable inroads on his discipline. Now, clean, washed, and dry, he settled himself for the night, allowing only the faintest hint of blue fire to encircle him. He waited patiently, his mind reverting unconsciously to his boyhood visions of unnamed giants, sparkling orbits of light, and amorphous figures shimmering in circles of blue fire.

* * * * * * *

Several times during the past Cycles, La'am had awakened suddenly during the night to the sensation of danger. This time, however, when he suddenly woke—abruptly and immediately alert and waiting—he felt none of the threat that had stimulated him to action earlier. There was only a pervading aura of curiosity, of not quite fear spilling into his mind.

And the instant understanding that he had awakened—*been awakened*—for a purpose.

Although fully awake, he did not move. He could remember no mention in any of the records of dangerous beasts living in this desert. The land was too barren, too lifeless to support anything but the smallest of animals—lizards, small scavengers, an occasional serpent, fortunately benign and non-poisonous. The great wulfs of the highest ranges would never venture this far into the desolation.

His studies reassured him that there was nothing to fear here.

But there was *something*. It had awakened him. It was out there, waiting.

He straightened his head and looked around. The darkness was absolute. Even his own Makerslight had faded to nothing.

Perhaps some lesser beast from the Eastern Ranges had made its way to the dry slopes, however, and from there on to the ruins of World's End, drawn perhaps by the presence of water. If so, it would be best not to startle the beast.

La'am closed his eyes and strained to hear any sounds other than the deep silence of the night.

Nothing.

Not a grain of sand shifted. There were no sounds of paws or claws...or feet.

The only thing he could hear was the rush of blood through his own veins and the distant beating of his own heart.

After a long while, La'am's lips moved slowly and he again uttered the Words of Light, this time almost inaudibly. As he did so, he consciously held the Makerspower in check, allowing it to seep only slowly through him and spill into the world beyond.

A faint circle of light grew about him, at first nothing more than a glow at the fringes of his Maker's robe. Then it expanded, illuminating grain by grain the surrounding sand, spreading so slowly that its movement was nearly imperceptible. The circle grew. The light strengthened.

And he was not alone.

He saw a dim figure on the sand perhaps a dozen feet from him. He pulsed more force into the blue light. He could now discern a robe, a hood, a pair of eyes reflecting back at him.

Without disrupting the circle of light that now included two, he stood, then spoke aloud.

"Who are you?"

The form did not respond.

"I am La'am, Master Maker of the Pillars of Beginnings"—a slight pause—"and Master of Makers on Omne. Who are you?"

At his final words, the second figure leapt lightly, gracefully up and moved toward him as if it were floating on a thin cushion of light that showed beneath the edges of the robe. La'am noticed a faint glow embedded in the fabric of the robe.

A Maker? Here?

Impossible.

He allowed the Makerslight to brighten until a blue-white light as strong as daylight in the Northrill Vale stretched brilliantly upon the sand in every direction, spotlighting the Maker and the other form, casting no shadows but engulfing night wherever it touched. The deserted, lava-choked city across the water caught the light and threw it back almost laughingly, as if the lava still remembered its own crimson light and the valiant but futile efforts of the Maker of World's End to stem the fiery flow.

The figure drew nearer, until beneath the hood La'am could see a softly narrow chin and the angled shadows of high cheekbones that seemed familiar—but for the moment he could not place them.

Suddenly, the figure stopped and made a brief, hesitant bow, as if recalling at the last moment a forgotten protocol. At the same moment, a voice echoed from beneath the hood.

"I am Rhiama, Joleckan-word of the Eastern Ranges."

With that the figure threw back her gray hood and looked directly at La'am.

Rhiama! La'am had not seen her since their encounter on the steps of the Cantorium at Los'ang, on the day of the Arrival—if encounter could describe their momentary interlocking of glance and empathetic tendrils. She had returned with Joleckan to the Eastern Ranges shortly thereafter. La'am had seen her before, had spoken to her on occasion, but did not really know her. He had been too involved with the problems created by the arrival of the Strangers, and before that with his own involvement with Iam'Kendron, with the Makersraad, and with Mord'am to devote much time to the acolytes of the other Makers.

"But Joleckan...," he began, then halted. He motioned for the girl to sit. She did so. He lowered himself to the ground an arm's length away, then allowed the Makerslight to retreat until the two were enclosed in a tight shell of living blue.

"Why are you here?" he asked.

Rhiama's explanation was quiet, low.

"I was in the lower mountains two days ago. I wander through them frequently, and Joleckan does not discourage me, especially when I feel the need."

La'am nodded. He recognized the experience—Iam'Kendron had similarly allowed him to explore the Pillars during his first days at the Sanctuary.

"I remained out from First Light until almost midday," Rhiama continued. "But when I returned to the Sanctuary, I felt that a wrongness had entered the valley. I could not explain it or identify it, but I knew that something was contending with Joleckan for control. As I approached the final pass leading to the overlook above the Sanctuary, I slowed, keeping to shadows and avoiding open places. Fortunately so, for when I neared the Sanctuary, I heard cries. I crawled to the edge of the overhang and looked. I could barely recognize Joleckan from the distance, but she and three others—all apprentices to the Makersraad—were being forced into one of the vessels of the Strangers. When they were inside, it closed and rose silently, and disappeared into the Veil of Heaven."

She stopped. La'am knew what was coming but could think of no way to soften the pain Rhiama would feel in relating it. He waited for her to begin again. When she did, he could hear the tears trembling close to the surface.

"I started to enter the valley, thinking to find out what had happened, when I saw three Strangers standing just inside the shadows of the Sanctuary doorway. They held weapons. Somehow, I knew that they were waiting for me to return.

"I crouched back into the shadows and waited. All day I waited hidden, craning my neck just enough to watch the doorway. The three guards remained there, motionless, waiting as well. Finally, twilight came and I could no longer see.

"A few minutes after night fell, I was startled by a bright light in the Veil of Heaven. A second craft dropped toward the rhiam fields just beyond the Sanctuary. It was larger and slower than the first, but more frightening. The three guards emerged from the Sanctuary, bringing with them a handful of people. Apparently they took only those who actually worked within the Sanctuary—the steward, the cook, the servants. The crofters who had settled nearby were left undisturbed. Everyone seemed terrified; I could see white-clad figures edging out of doorways in the crofter's quarters, and the ones from the Sanctuary being herded into the ship were struggling and crying.

"The doors closed, and the ship rose silently, just as had the first one. But this time, before it disappeared into the Veil the ship stopped and turned. From one end came a great roaring and a gout of flame."

Again Rhiama's voice trailed to silence. La'am raised his hand to reach out to her, but stopped himself before he touched her shoulder. His hand dropped back to his lap. She did not seem to notice. Her eyes were closed against the tears.

"The Sanctuary exploded," she said softly, "exploded as if the fire-mountains of the Pillars of Beginnings and the Northern Ranges had suddenly vomited destruction.

"There were...people...standing near the buildings. Many were burned badly. Others were crushed by fragments of stone or cut by flying splinters.

"I went down to try to help, but there was little that I could do. I know only the minor Words of Healing, and many of the victims were too seriously hurt for my powers. I wept, wandering through the heat and flames, seeing men, women, and children I have known for Cycles dead, dying, or wishing to die."

She let out her breath in a long, painful sigh, then straightened. When she began speaking again, he voice was stronger, as if she had stepped outside of her experiences and could relate her story objectively.

"When I could do no more, I returned to the mountains and climbed. I had no purpose, no goal, only to be as far as possible from the Sanctuary. I could not go west, into the plains, for the Strangers are strongest there, and that I could not have borne.

"So I went farther and farther into the ranges. I followed the decaying roadway that once led to this place. No one saw me; I saw no one. I was completely alone. I spent the night in a wayplace near the road. It was a large cavern, once clean and well-stocked but now fearfully neglected. There was neither food nor drink, but at least I was inside during the darkness. The door still hung on its hinges, so I could bar any beasts that might have lurked nearby. There are many, you know, now that there is no longer a way"—she faltered—"*was* no longer a way through the Veil of Heaven to World's End.

"At First Light the next day, I rose and continued upward, toward the blocked passes and the Veil of Heaven. I had never been there before, but many of the hunters and young men at the Sanctuary had, and they had told me many stories. The lava there had poured like a waterfall into the high passes, freezing in places. The ripples and flow of the molten rock are still evident today. Then, according to the stories, the Veil of Heaven lowered unaccountably until it consumed the seething rock, cutting off all passage through the Ranges.

"When the passes were blocked, there was great weeping among the men of the Eastern Ranges, for many had friends and relatives in World's End—my own grandfather's brother had settled there—and suddenly there was no way to reach them. We could not even find out if any had survived the volcano's devastation."

Another long pause.

"I continued on. Finally, I reached the edge of the lava flow. It was as they had described to me...except that the Veil of Heaven did not quite touch the ground. It hovered just beyond a tall man's height from the surface. I climbed onto the rocks and began picking my way through the tortured curves and waves, my head sometimes coming so close to the Veil that I could easily have reached up and touched it.

"All the while, I felt something compelling me toward the dead city, along the roadway so long untraveled.

"Finally I crossed a narrow, level place. The rock here was smooth and unwrinkled. In front of me, the ripples and currents in the rock drooped slightly downward, away from me. I realized that I stood on the summit of the pass. In a few steps, I would have crossed the Ranges. I looked back and saw that the Veil had again dropped onto the lava. I had to go on, since I was now clearly cut off from any return. It was as if a huge curtain had been lowered behind me."

The girl stopped speaking. She shivered violently, although not from any chill—the desert air was cooling, but within the sphere of Makerslight La'am and Rhiama remained comfortable.

"I went forward. I spent the second night beneath a small overhang along the way. The wayplaces had mostly been destroyed by the lava, so I could find none. I was undisturbed by beasts or men, however, and ready to continue the next morning. By midday, I had arrived at the beginning of the ruins of the city. I wanted to cross the water and enter, but something held me back. So I climbed onto a finger of rock overlooking the city, the desert, and the sea, and waited.

"I must have slept because the next thing I knew, darkness was complete. I sat back against a smooth boulder, hoping that there were no beasts here. Then suddenly, I saw something—or thought I saw something. The faintest glow of blue far away, on the opposite side of the ruins. I was frightened but felt the urgency of going on, of discovering what had made the light.

"I crept out of my hollow and along the ridge of the outcropping, feeling my way blindly away from the main flow of the lava, down toward the sand, thinking that the sand would be safer to walk on at night.

"I made my way down slowly, searching with blind fingertips for handholds, feeling with my toes for cracks to support my weight. Finally I made it. I reached down with my foot and felt the grit of sand. I felt my way along the edge of the outcropping until I could see the blue light again. Then I walked toward it, shuffling through the sand to avoid any unseen obstacles.

"When I arrived near it, however, I could go no further. All I could see was a figure obscured completely in the blue fire of the Makers. Yet I knew of no reason why a Maker would be here, alone in the wastes; nor could I understand which of the Makers it could possibly be.

"So I waited, sitting upon the sand, just outside the fringes of the light. Then gradually, the light flared out, and I saw you standing there."

The girl fell silent. This time La'am understood that she was finished. She had reported to the Master Maker and had no more to say.

In the ensuing quiet, both La'am and Rhiama were startled by a long wailing cry echoing from the foothills to the west. The sound lingered mockingly, mournfully over the wastes of World's End, before fading away. Rhiama shivered once, twice, then moved to sit closer to La'am. He pulsed more force into the Makerslight, enlarging the circle about them. He felt her robe brush against his, then her shoulder resting lightly against his own. Protectively, he raised his arm and allowed himself to encircle her. They slept.

CHAPTER TWENTY-EIGHT

Later—perhaps an hour or two before First Light, but La'am could not be sure precisely when—he woke gently from a deep sleep. He was still sitting erect, circled in the blue Makerslight. Rhiama was next to him, huddled a bit closer maybe than she had been earlier, since the desert chill had now set in and the air was definitely brisk. La'am sat for a while, eyes closed, awake and aware but preferring not to move. He concentrated on the minutiae of sound and smell, isolating those that were exclusive to World's End from those that partook of Omne in general. They were all beautiful: a crisp hint of breeze from seaward, redolent with promises of mist and coolness; a scuttling, shifting of sand off to the right—either from a nocturnal scavenger or, more likely, simply from the wind.

Overpowering all else were the sounds and smells of Rhiama; no, *fragrances,* he corrected himself mentally. Her robe, like his own, was of rhiam and reminded him strongly of Iam'Kendron, of the Pillars of Beginnings, and of his own Acolyte's robe. Rhiama had evidently been walking strenuously for several days—her own story supported that conclusion. Yet her fragrance was more pleasing than offensive, and vaguely, disturbingly exciting as La'am inhaled deeply and sensed her presence. There were subtle hints of smoke clinging to her hair, and a softly feminine muskiness surrounded her that was unlike anything he had ever experienced. Not even Marina, lost to him for so many Cycles, had smelled so...so intriguing.

He ventured a quick glance at Rhiama's face. She was breathing evenly, as if she were deep asleep.

But she wasn't.

"Why are you here?" she asked softly without looking up at him, surprising him.

He started to answer, checked himself, then told as much of his story as he felt he could. He spoke briefly of the events of Los'ang—of the deaths of Mord'am and Jorik, of his own flight south, of what he had seen and experienced since then. He did not, however, tell her of his contact with Jorik or with Jathanan, or his rapidly—and frighteningly—increasing awareness of the complexities of the Makerspowers. He did not understand them fully himself. Until he did, he realized, he could never explain them to another, not even to a fully installed Maker. And Rhiama was only an Acolyte.

Occasionally, she would intrude a comment: "I would rather have seen the desolation of the Two Isles than witnessed the violent death of the Sanctuary at the Eastern Ranges." Or a perceptive and incisive question: "Could you tell if there were more machines operating elsewhere in the southern fields? Did you disable them or destroy them?" But in general, she allowed him to tell his story as he chose. He could see in her expressions that she sensed untold experiences and was stifling the impulse to ask even more questions. But she also intuited his reserve and respected it.

When he was finished, he asked a question.

"Rhiama is a beautiful name. But why? It is not generational with Joleckan. Do you mind talking about it?"

Rhiama had half-turned her face, disappearing noiselessly into the shadowed cowl of the robe.

Now she turned back to him.

"No, I don't mind. In fact, there is little to tell, and what there is I do not claim to understand."

She paused.

"I have only been an Acolyte for a Cycle. Since last Seed Time, in fact. Before that, I lived at the Eastern Ranges, training with other apprentices. I was chosen to replace Joleckan's first acolyte, who had fallen ill some weeks before and who had died in spite of the Words of Healing. When I was chosen, I could barely believe it. I, Petran of the Ranges, might actually become a Maker!

"I suppose that the Installation went smoothly. We did not travel to Los'ang because of the late rains last Cycle. Instead, Jorik came to the Ranges."

La'am nodded absently. That was why he had so rarely seen or heard of Rhiama. In his own isolation at the Pillars of Beginnings, such news filtered only slowly to him, if at all. Iam'Kendron did not always tell his Acolyte everything he knew. And Rhiama's isolation at the Eastern Ranges must have been almost as complete as his own, Cycles earlier, at the Pillars. No wonder they had not become known to each other.

"Jorik arrived with Ky'lan on the same day that Jerek of Heartland arrived with his retinue. The Makers retired first into the inner chamber of the Sanctuary, among the relics of the ancients—they are all gone now, aren't they?—and spoke in Council with the other Makers. Then they called me in.

"I don't remember the events very clearly. I guess I was too frightened to notice much at all, but then, toward the end of the ceremony, when Joleckan stood to Name me, she was silent. I remember that. The silence grew and grew until I thought that I could hear the stones of the Sanctuary itself in their motionlessness. I was at first curious, then embarrassed, and finally terrified. What if she could not Name me? What if no Name came to her? What then? I had never heard of such a thing happening before, and my ignorance was probably more devastating to me than any concrete fear could have been.

"But even though the silence lengthened unbearably, neither of the other two Makers spoke out. They seemed more than content to wait for Joleckan. Finally she spoke. It could have been only moments later; it could have been hours. I don't know. But finally she spoke.

"'I am Joleckan, Maker of the Eastern Ranges,' she said in a voice unlike any I had ever heard from her. 'I am to Name this Acolyte; yet I may not. Her true Name is blocked and is not mine to give. She belongs to another. I will name her still, however, and in doing so I make of her a part of Omne itself. I am Joleckan. I name you Rhiama, Joleckan-word of the Eastern Ranges.'

"Joleckan seemed frightened by her words. Jorik was startled, I'm sure of that. But the Name had been given. I was Rhiama. Joleckan could never explain what had happened, or why she could not pronounce a generational Name.

"So you see, I am as ignorant as you in this matter. Someday soon, though, I think I will know what obstructed her. For now, I am content as Rhiama. What better name for an Omnan?"

"What better, indeed?" La'am said. But his mind was busy making connections. Another enigmatic member of the Makersraad. His own naming had shattered orthodoxy and he had become a Maker through a disruption of traditions preserved for generations. Now here, in this wilderness, he had discovered another of his own kind, one of the Makersraad, even though only an Acolyte—and the only other member of the Council he had ever heard of whose selection and Naming had been out of the ordinary. His sense of purposefulness in the apparently chance occurrences of the past few days was steadily strengthening. And he felt that that purpose was rapidly drawing to a climax.

Even as he mulled over these thoughts, La'am saw the precursors of First Light and noted an alteration in the cool chill surrounding them. When he dimmed the Makerslight that had shielded them during the darkness, La'am and Rhiama could discern faintly the flush of rose on the eastern edges of the Veil of Heaven. Another day had arrived. La'am calculated quickly; this was the fifth day since the death of Mord'am, the third since his mentrans communion with Jathanan on the Island of Harborwatch. And, he was certain, Haardt and the other Strangers would not have been sitting quietly, doing nothing during those days. Especially not when he received word that a blue-robed Omnan had appeared on the Southern Marches and had disrupted—seriously, La'am fervently hoped—whatever secret operations were in progress there.

What would Los'ang be like today?

What would the First Light bring?

Without speaking, La'am and Rhiama rose and stretched cramped muscles. They breathed in deeply, enjoying the rapidly warming air. He held out his hand. She took it, and hand in hand they crossed the nearest stream. It was less than knee deep, icy cold and so transparent that La'am could clearly see the intricate patterns of stones on the bottom. The patterns were random, to be sure, but they ultimately blended to create a complex, at times almost meaningful, arrangement of shapes and textures and colors.

Like life, La'am thought, just like life.

On the other side of the stream bed they turned right and walked toward the outskirts of World's End. In a few minutes, they entered the dead city together, an exiled Maker and a fugitive Acolyte.

As a child, La'am had heard stories of the expeditions sent by ship to give relief to the survivors at World's End, shortly after the only mountain passes through the Ranges had disappeared within the Veil of Heaven. By then most of the tales were full of fantastic rumors of strange sounds and sights, amplified by each teller until they attained legendary, even mythic proportions. Yet as a Maker, La'am knew that no ship had touched the shore since the volcano had erupted. Several had been sent but all except one had wrecked, and the remaining one could only drop anchor long before actually entering the mouth of the harbor. Winds and currents and noxious fumes rising from the ruined city had combined to deny entrance.

From the distance, the captain and crew of the ship had searched through the smoke and dust of the holocaust with straining eyes, hoping for signs of life. They had seen none. To all appearances, the entire city had succumbed to the flames and ashes and fumes of the eruption.

La'am had heard the wild tales of hellfire and earthquakes and tidal waves and, as he had grown older, had disbelieved much of what he had heard. Yet a certain hesitancy remained, a lingering fear.

When the time came to cross into the city, both the Maker and the Acolyte halted momentarily before stepping onto the lave flow that shrouded one of the oldest cities on Omne.

Rhiama tightened her grip on La'am's hand, and in turn he grasped hers more firmly, sharing her need to confirm human life and unity in this place of fragmentation and death. Together they walked slowly through time-deserted streets, once busy and active, now carpeted—or more often, choked—with thick layers of ropy black rock. They saw no signs of life, either animal or human, only weather-worn remnants of the panic of that single night so long before. What had been shops were still tightly shuttered. In spite of the intervening Cycles, the few unburned ranya-wood doors and window frames seemed sound and undecayed in the dry desert air. It would take many Cycles more before they would begin to disintegrate. La'am was relieved to note that there were no bones lying exposed; the bodies must lay far below, preserved by the lava that destroyed them.

La'am and Rhiama wandered aimlessly through a maze of half-obliterated streets. They turned left or right at random, altering their direction of travel in order to look more closely at a particularly anomalous formation or to investigate the upper story of a structure less damaged than most. La'am was struck by the differences between World's End and the Two Isles. The latter had been just as dead as the former, but with important differences. Two Isles was not only dead but also empty—deserted, inviolate in its emptiness. La'am had walked its unused streets with interest and curiosity but little else. World's End, on the other hand, was dead but thickly peopled with memories, with ghosts. In the one room they had entered, La'am and Rhiama had seen remnants of simple furniture standing essentially undisturbed. Wooden chairs still sat stiffly around a table; remains of rhiam-fiber coverings still decorated the cold stone walls, their threads clinging to each other as if they had just emerged from the loom a Cycle or two before. And beyond what could be seen lay the sense of presences watching, neutrally, neither approving nor disapproving this intrusion into their privacy—and of memories locked irrevocably into the stones of the city. World's End was dead...but paradoxically still subtly alive in ways that disturbed La'am profoundly.

Gradually, their wanderings brought La'am and Rhiama to the center of the city. Without planning to do so, they found themselves standing at the base of the ruined Cantorium. Next to it, and just far enough behind it to hide partly within its massive shadow, lay the remains of the Sanctuary of World's End. Only the upper lintels of its windows and the final few feet of walls just below the roof jutted out of the lava flow.

La'am stepped toward the steep steps, only to feel a sleight weight against his shoulder.

"Should we?" Rhiama asked. Her voice was soft but it echoed like a shout against the silence of World's End. "It doesn't feel...right."

Her question made La'am pause. He closed his eyes and concentrated.

"I'm not sure. There's no danger. But there is...something else. I'm not sure," he said without opening his eyes.

He fell silent again. Rhiama did not lift her hand from his shoulder, but neither did she speak. He felt the warmth of her hand, even through his thick robe, even through the desert heat already beating at him.

"There's something here I can't figure out. It seems like...."

She waited for him to continue. Her hand trembled—oh so slightly, less a tremor than a momentary vibration that nonetheless startled him and almost broke his concentration.

He didn't ask her to remove her hand but was not surprised when he felt it sliding from his shoulder along the length of his arm to rest just above his wrist. There, the warmth was more noticeable. Beads of sweat broke on his lip, and for a moment the patterns in him wavered and fluttered.

Then something clicked into place and he became aware of a shift in the mentrans patterns. He could still identify the individual memories and knowledge patterns of each Maker that he carried within him, but now there were new patterns superimposing on the old.

At first he thought they were Rhiama's, and his heart beat faster.

Then he realized that while hers were indeed there, swirling almost subliminally at the edges of his consciousness, the patterns he felt most strongly were old ones, superimposing themselves forcibly onto the new. At first he could not define them precisely enough to be sure. He forced himself to concentrate, to focus on them until his head whirled and his temples throbbed. He felt suddenly faint, and Rhiama's hand ceased to be merely a pleasing warmth and instead became a support as his knees threatened to buckle.

His eyes rolled back beneath his still-closed eyelids, and a low, creaking moan escaped from between his compressed lips.

"La'am?" Rhiama whispered as she tightened her fingers around his forearm. "What is it?"

He moaned again and trembled.

"What is it?" she repeated. "Tell me? Are you all right?"

"I'm...," he began, then with a cry he dropped to the ground and pressed his hands over his ears.

The screams!

The pain!

The dreadful anguish!

And then they were gone—or, rather, not so much gone as swallowed up, muted, tamed by the kaleidoscope of patterns inside La'am.

He dropped his hands and opened his eyes.

Rhiama was kneeling before him, her eyes even with his own. He read fear and concern in their depths...and something else that frightened him more than the deluge of pain that was rapidly ebbing.

"La'am," she whispered again.

He shook his head, as if to rid himself of some final, difficult memory, then looked at her again.

"It was them. It was their anguish. Maker, Acolyte, attendants..., the whole city." He licked his dry lips, abruptly overwhelmed by a burning thirst that he knew no water would slake.

Rhiama's hand touched the back of his, flesh to flesh. Unaccountably, it steadied him. He straightened, then stood and stared over the ruins.

"The patterns are blurred and dulled now," he said after a moment, "softened, as if by the passage of time. They are only faintly intelligible. I cannot gain any distinct impressions except for the rawest of emotions, those strong enough to survive the Cycles since the destruction."

And there he lost the words to describe what he had felt and seen. The color patterns had been disquieting, not focused enough to be interpreted as warnings but too strong to ignore. He felt a wash of empathy for the long-dead sailors on the single rescue ship that had made it as far as the lava-choked harbor. The fresh patterns flooding World's End that soon after the tragedy would have been virtually unendurable to any Maker attuned to receiving mentrans, and profoundly disturbing to even the least receptive mind.

"What is that?" Rhiama asked.

Her question drew La'am to the present.

"What?"

"Those sounds," she said glancing around cautiously. "What are they?"

Now it was La'am's turn to worry.

She heard them also, even now when the patterns were little more than echoes. But she had not felt the blast of horror that had so shaken La'am—and, more to the point, she was not a Maker.

Was it to begin again?

Memories of Mord'am—alive and dead—flickered through La'am's mind, and he discovered that they were almost more than he could endure. Would he have the strength to begin training a new Acolyte again, only to have everything end in....

For a second, he thought he understood faintly how Iam'Kendron must have felt. The old man, too, had suddenly had to begin again, training a new Acolyte.

Learning to love a new Acolyte.

La'am shivered at the image.

Then another thought intruded. Rhiama was already attached to Joleckan of the Eastern Ranges.

But if Joleckan was dead....

The complexities multiplied as La'am tried to work out an explanation. And nothing worked.

"Those are mentrans patterns," he said finally. "They emanate from the stones themselves. They transmit the final thoughts and feelings of those who died here that night. What do you hear?"

"Very little," Rhiama admitted. "Only an occasional flash of... something, a buzz or a crackle that flits across my mind.... It's something like a color, but not a color; something like a sound but not a sound. I have never heard...or seen it before."

She swallowed hard. La'am heard the sound of muscles constricting along her throat, of moisture forced through dry tissues.

"It frightens me," she said.

La'am nodded at the understatement in her words. He could recall vividly his own first experience with mentrans...and Mord'am's.

He fell into a swirl of memories that lifted him from the present and carried him into the past.

He did not consciously notice when Rhiama gently withdrew her hand from his and left him, to walk slowly along the remains of the Cantorium. Its stones were now hidden by solidified rivers of lava that reached nearly to the platform atop the stairs. He did not see her climb the remaining stairs, or stand on the flat, worn stone surface of the main level. He did not see her enter the black cavern that was the Cantorium.

But he did hear her piercing shout.

He jerked out of his reverie and, startled, stared around. He was momentarily lost and unsure of present reality—even of where he stood.

Then he heard her voice again, spiraling into a high-pitched cry unlike anything he had ever heard before. He mentally pinpointed the source and direction of the sound and leaped up the crumbling stairs. He crossed the platform in two long strides and burst into the darkness of the chamber.

"Rhiama!"

He called her name once again, sharply.

Rhiama stood alone in the center of the Singer's dais. She was surrounded on all sides by bare stone benches. Originally, they would have been covered with fine fabrics. Long ago, the Singer's dais might have been circled by the Maker and his household—Acolyte, attendants, servants—and perhaps a retinue of Makers and attendants visiting from beyond the Eastern Ranges. The first rows beyond the Makers would have been reserved for the Singers. And there, on the single smooth block of hand-carved stone in the center of the Cantorium, where Rhiama was standing, the High Singer would have stood, shoulders bowed with age, mind overflowing with the accumulated words of centuries.

Now Rhiama stood on the raised stone. Her hands were clenched tightly at her side—even from across the hall, La'am could see the stark whiteness of her bloodless knuckles. Her arms and neck were stiff and tense as if she were struggling against some unseen power. Her eyes were open but unseeing as she stared fixedly at an invisible spot in the air above her. Her voice carried across the silence in a hoarse whisper.

"Come here." It sounded as if she were speaking through frozen lips, as if she were afraid to move even enough to speak. "The sounds are clearer here. Come quickly, before I lose them."

La'am rushed across the chamber and onto the central platform. The instant his foot touched the stone, he knew that she was right. The vague patterns were focusing at this one point, immediately beneath the pinnacle of stone towering above them. The sounds—so faint to her that she had to strain to hear them—battered at him like Dark Time thunder. They roiled and twisted and coiled in loops of smoky darkness. La'am could not distinguish individual patterns or meanings; it was as if a thousand voices were shouting at him simultaneously, each full of its own message and trying to out-shout the others. La'am despaired for a moment, then felt those he carried within—Iam'Kendron, Mord'am, Jorik, Jathanan, and to lesser extents the remaining Makers of Omne—surfacing. They systematically absorbed the multitudes, sorting and sifting, keeping everything safely locked in La'am's mind but holding back most of it for the moment. They identified an occasional pattern, but most of the color-sounds remained gibberish. Some few patterns seemed momentarily sharp and clear, others vague, ancient, almost too faint to register.

La'am could not understand what had happened here.

Unless the Maker of World's End had had enough time to confront the magnitude of the disaster sweeping down from the high Ranges—and had recognized the futility of attempting to escape the fire of the volcano and the boiling steam that must have billowed from the sea when the lava flows screamed into the water. He must have gathered his entire sanctuary staff at the Cantorium. If he had stood here, where La'am and Rhiama now stood, and linked with the other minds around him, resonating from them, focusing his attention, he might have been able to....

But the Maker of World's End was not a Master Maker, and his city had perished with him, in flames.

The sounds tapered off gradually, but to La'am, they seemed to whirl and spin and ring and crackle with greater and greater intensity. He did not notice when the color-sounds ceased altogether—or if not ceased, then began again in the same patterns he had already absorbed. He was struggling with what he had heard, desperate to integrate bits of information as they filtered through from other memories.

Only slowly did he become aware again of his surroundings...and then only to receive a fleeting, ghostly glimpse of the Cantorium of World's End awash and swirling with yellow and gray robes. Faces and fabrics were uniformly stained with red light that reflected the fury of the flames. He almost heard a shout of warning from behind, almost saw the beginnings of unthinking flight as the first fingers of lava washed the steps of the Cantorium....

Then all was silent, empty, dark, and quiet.

La'am and Rhiama stood alone on the Singer's dais in a ruined building, alone in a ruined city, alone and yet infused with the patterns of men and women long cycles dead.

La'am reached out to touch Rhiama. As their hands met, he received her perceptions of the kaleidoscope of patterns—roughly the same as his own, but altered by her different background. She was an Acolyte, but he also felt her accommodate much of what she had received.

He spoke to her gently, drawing her from inner visions back to reality.

"Rhiama. Rhiama, come with me."

He led her from the chamber. They crossed the hall and stepped back onto the platform, into the brightness of daylight that sliced across the silvered dunes of World's End. The sudden brightness reflecting from sand and stone and water dazzled them. La'am threw his hands across his eyes, squinting to cut down the light. For a moment, he felt as if a huge ball of flame were boring into his mind, blinding him, burning him.

The feeling faded as his eyes adjusted to the light. He glanced sideways at Rhiama, his vision blurred. She, too, had covered and averted her eyes. She stood, head bowed against the light. She did not move. For a moment, he was afraid that she had somehow been hurt. Then he saw the slow rise and fall of her breast beneath her robe and knew that she was all right. She was just sensitive to the light. Her eyes had to adjust, as his had done.

But then he blinked again, rapidly, and he saw that there was more than that.

Something was different. Not wrong exactly, but decidedly different.

Then it registered. Even as he noticed that her robe was no longer gray, La'am realized that part of the symphony of color-sounds he had overheard inside the Cantorium had been an Installation! Voice echoing unimpeded through the cold stone, the long-dead Maker of World's End had pronounced her former name—*Rhiama*—and had Named her anew and blessed her and poured authority into her, suffusing her with Makerslight and Makerspower.

Had created her *Laral,* Master Maker of World's End.

La'am was not sure *how* he knew what had happened. Iam'Kendron's patterns were mixed with those he now identified as belonging to Freyma, Maker of World's End before its destruction. Again and again, Iam'Kendron had mediated for La'am, allowing him to comprehend what had occurred—impossibly, improbably, yet undeniably happened.

Rhiama was no more. In her place, swathed in indigo so vivid that it almost burned, stood *Laral,* of the Makersraad of Omne.

Laral, now the only other surviving Master Maker in the Land.

He opened his mouth to speak, and stopped. He saw her eyes sparkling their own excitement and intensity. She stared into his face for a moment, then her eyes dropped.

He glanced down as well.

She was a Master Maker; she wore indigo, yet she was not yet his peer.

He spread the folds of his robe, raising them like pleated wings and exposing them to the vivid light of the Veil of Heaven. The indigo was still there—predominantly so, emphatically so. But the robe was unquestionably no longer just indigo. The subtle play of colors that had appeared before so mysteriously, then disappeared just as mysteriously, had returned.

This time, La'am knew, they would remain.

The robe now contained not only the indigo, saffron, and gray of the Makersraad, but also a range of colors never before associated with the Makersraad—scarlet, purple, green, russet, gold and silver (he recognized their metallic sheens and their names, one good legacy, however slight, from the intrusion of the Strangers). And others hovered just beneath his consciousness. He raised his hand, bringing one fold closer to his face, and studied the tightly woven fibers, seeming to see in them the freshness of a Seed Time field, the solid power of the soil, the violence and splendor of the fire-mountains of the Ranges, the tumultuous sea crashing upon the Lesser Pillars; and encompassing all, the shifting spectrum of the Veil of Heaven itself.

Laral brought her eyes up again to meet La'am's. Then she looked down at her own robe. She smoothed the flowing fabric with long, thin hands, and stared at the deep blue of the material. Then she looked equally long and hard at La'am's robe.

"I am now Laral," she said, her intonation formal and precise. "I am Master Maker of this place and a Master Maker of the Council of Omne. I now know why Joleckan of the Eastern Ranges could not Name me—I belong not to her, but to Freyma of World's End. And I now know that Rhiama Joleckan-word is dead, just as I know that Joleckan herself is dead and has released me from her authority."

La'am reacted sharply to the last phrase. He sent a darting probe. Rhiama—*no, Laral*—was right. Joleckan was dead. Outside of La'am's mind, her patterns were simply gone, as completely as were Jorik's or Mord'am's or Iam'Kendron's, or—how many others? Now, La'am realized, Joleckan existed exclusively in the recorded memories and experiences that she had given Jorik and that Jorik had infused into him. And Laral recognized this.

"And you," she continued, "are the Master of all Makers on Omne."

La'am hesitated, biting at his dry lips. Events were proceeding far too quickly. He reached toward Laral. She stood stiffly, then reciprocated. Their touch sparked a mental interchange, but this time La'am felt that the communion was dual. He entered into her, following her memories and thoughts, just as she entered that part that had first been Davian Charl'an-born and now was La'am, Master Maker of the Pillars of Beginnings and Master of Makers on Omne. She did not try to enter into the other patterns, nor did they reveal themselves to her. They remained silent, just below the level at which Laral and La'am exchanged identities.

Suddenly, dual peals of laughter echoed through the sun-bleached stones of the dead city. Long, loud, joyous laughter sailed sweetly over scenes of newly forgiven bitterness, bringing life to a land of death. Two Master Makers raised their hands in a silent salute to the East. They smiled when they saw faint tongues of blue fire shooting toward the Veil of Heaven above them.

Laral lowered her arms first, turning away from the black maw of the Cantorium. Back proudly straight, she began descending the steps toward the blackened streets of World's End. This was now *her* domain. It would live again. When Omne flourished in peace, World's End would experience a new beginning. Here, there would be no more ghosts or death—at least not for her, the Master Maker.

And as was appropriate in her own city, even for the Master of Makers on Omne, La'am followed the Master Maker of World's End down the stairs and through the streets—*her* streets—until they reached the outer boundaries of the city.

Then La'am stepped forward a pace and, side by side, the two Master Makers headed northward, toward the Pillars of Beginnings.

CHAPTER TWENTY-NINE

The first leg of their journey northward lasted only a few hours, however. Long before twilight dropped into night, La'am and Laral angled sharply to the west, crossing a single stretch of desert before coming to the first broken foothills of the Eastern Ranges. Behind them—and stretching from the sea to the north and to the south—lay the great, seemingly endless Dunes of World's End. To attempt a direct crossing of that desolation would have been fatal. It took Laral only a moment to search Freyma's patterns and confirm that no water was known to exist along the entire expanse of coast between the Pillars of Beginnings and the oasis-making river of the Makerseat itself. Even the cataclysmic upheavals that had destroyed the city would probably not have erased the fundamental aridity of the coast.

So to the west it was, and from there steadily northward and eastward along the curving spine of the eastern mountains. There at least an occasional spring, even a small stream encouraged the otherwise scant greenery that provided occasional small umbrellas of shade and offered hope of some respite from the heat. Neither La'am nor Laral was used to the terrain since only here, on this most unapproachable segment of Omne, were there any appreciable desert. As they marched stolidly across the sand, La'am realized how restricted the dunes near the Harbor in fact were. There one could cross the region lengthwise in an easy day's walk. Here, the sand seemed to stretch illimitably into the distant horizon.

Unfortunately, the foothills proved only marginally less inhospitable than the lowlands. There was water, but more because of the unusual wetness of the preceding Dark Time and the early Seed Time than because of any permanent flows. What vegetation the Makers encountered was vestigial—scrubby, pithy bushes that seemed averse to putting out any perceptible new growth...and then only where there would be sufficient water as the Cycle passed and dampness gave way to dryness. The land was cautious and eerily silent. Throughout the remainder of the first day's trek, the Master Maker of World's End and the Master of Makers on Omne saw nothing living except their own heat-distorted shadows floating in twin blurs beneath them. They saw no animals, no skittering rodents, no basking lizards or coiled snakes. Nothing.

Even so, they could sense a throbbing pulse of life as they passed along the backbone of the ranges. The heavy scent of water hung over small ravines and larger gorges that angled sharply toward the higher reaches. Occasionally, the two humans felt as if inscrutable eyes rested upon them, and almost heard half-imagined sounds of cautious trailing. But they never saw anything.

Finally, by twilight, both of them gave way to semi-fears and began searching overtly for shelter. There were no wayplaces here. No one traveled along this region, much less attempted to tame and settle it. In this desolation, Freyma's patterns were as silent as all of the others, for not even the long-dead Master of World's End could truly claim to know the lands to the north.

The shadows were deepening when, for the first time in hours, Laral spoke.

"Look, over there."

She pointed to a shadow marginally deeper, blacker than the others nearby. Only the tip of her finger showed beyond the edge of her robe.

Rather than speaking, La'am nodded, then picked up his own pace to match hers. The two Makers strode through the gloom toward the spot of shadow.

What they found wasn't much, little more than a narrow bluff overhanging a flat, rocky stretch. They crouched just enough for their heads to clear the rock, then settled back against a crumbling, damp natural wall.

For a moment, as he leaned his head against the packed earth, felt his travel-weary muscles unknot, and breathed the dark, rich smell of Omnan soil, La'am was forcibly reminded of his first night with Iam'Kendron. The rocky cleft Laral had found was practically identical to the other one; the same faint blue Makerslight illuminated the shallow recess and revealed a thick mat of detritus, mostly windblown from higher ranges.

And, like that first night with Iam'Kendron, this one passed in silence. Neither La'am nor Laral chose to speak—or even felt the need to speak. What they might have said was superfluous to their purpose, and besides, both were engrossed in sorting out the experiences of the preceding day. Both were growing and maturing in their new roles.

And more quickly than either would have believed, both were asleep.

At the earliest glimmer of First Light, La'am woke, stood, and stretched. He had slept in fits, disturbed by dreams now almost entirely forgotten—except, that is, for lingering, vague feelings of disquiet. He stepped out into the light, squinting at the brightness. Here, beyond the Ranges, the day was more direct, the light more glaring than at Los'ang. La'am felt that he would never get used to such light. There seemed to be a difference of quality as well as of quantity about it.

Laral moved quietly behind him.

"It's beautiful," she said, gesturing with one hand across the landscape below them. They stood on the lower slopes of the hills. Stretching out beneath them the desert shimmered golden in the early light—beautiful, glistening, barren.

La'am nodded. His eyes searched the land, but as far as he could tell, the desert was as lifeless and unmoving as the tapestries hanging on the walls of the Magistry—and infinitely older, of course. Nothing had ever flourished here. The coast of World's End was precisely that...World's End, the single portion of Omne that had been, was, and would remain barren.

Without speaking further, La'am and Laral left the overhang and resumed picking a trail through the boulder-strewn shoulders of the mountains, paralleling the wastes below them. The air was already heated and promised to become incinerating in its intensity before long. After the first few moments, the landscape changed again. The scrub brush disappeared for long stretches, leaving nothing in between but heat-cracked rocks and hard-packed dirt. In those long stretches, there was no shade, no shadows along the foothills.

After a few moments more, La'am appreciated even more than before the voluminous folds of his Make's robe. He was protected from the heat, from the brightness of the light reflecting murderously upward from the sand. He could tell that his hands and face—wherever his skin had been exposed during their travels of the past day—were unusually warm. He glanced at Laral. He could see almost nothing of her skin, but the little he could see was reddened and enflamed. La'am shrugged deeper into his cowl, welcoming the darkness of shadows on his face.

The morning passed slowly and uneventfully. Both Makers struggled wordlessly to find the strength and endurance to continue.

Fields of boulders the size of small children cropped up with irritating frequency to obstruct their march. Gullies and ravines opened precipitously beneath their feet, forcing long detours down to the desert floor. And, unlike the terrain of the previous day, these clefts rarely contained water. As the Makers proceeded further north, the land became drier and more barren—bone-bare rocks and coarse, eroded soil.

La'am and Laral stumbled on.

By mid-day, La'am could detect a slight alteration in the landscape. The line of foothills they had followed arced gradually toward the east, cutting off the desert sands and forming the southern perimeter of what would become the Pillars of Beginnings. Scraggly grasses and stunted scrub growth appeared in the shadows of the largest boulders, softening the harshness of the hills. Laral stopped occasionally, sniffing at the stifling air.

Finally she burst out excitedly: "La'am, water." Her tongue flickered out to taste the air. "I can feel the moisture in the air."

La'am paused and breathed deeply. He analyzed the stifling air, realizing with a leaping stab of joy that the air, although still furnace-hot, was no longer as dry as it had been. Somewhere close by, there was water—perhaps a small river, perhaps the sea ahead and to the east. But there was water!

He grinned at her—a surprisingly boyish grin to anyone who might have known him for longer than a single day. She grinned back, and they both picked up their pace.

Within hours of twilight, La'am and Laral reached the beginnings of the long curving ridge that cut toward the west. They halted, squatting uncomfortably in the scant shade of a head-high, dust-covered shrub—neither Maker recognized the species, but then neither observed it closely either. For long moments, they sat silently, drawing deep breaths, feeling the rush of oxygen stimulate bone-weary muscles.

"What now?" Laral asked quietly. She nodded toward the arc of the foothills, implying with the gesture her question—should they follow the ridge on toward the sea or angle northward, across the spine of the Eastern Ranges, and intersect the sea at the base of the Pillars. The former would be longer but easier; they had but to follow the increasingly smaller spurs until finally the foothills ended at the sea. The latter would be shorter, but less certain. Neither knew anything of the mountains, nor of the conditions they might find.

La'am remained silent, considering the alternatives, weighting safety against speed, certainty and caution against possibilities and unknowns. Finally, he decided.

"Through the mountains, I think. We must hurry. Haardt will not be waiting patiently for us to appear. Every day we spend here increases the strength of his hold on Los'ang, on the Makersraad and the Magistry. On Omne. If we cut through the mountains we should be able to reach the Pillars within a day or so." He shaded his eyes with one hand and stared along the curving ridge. "The longer route might add an additional day, perhaps two, to the march. Days we cannot afford to give the Strangers."

"Through the mountains, then," Laral said, nodding her assent. She stood, leaning back against the rough surface of a nearby outcropping of granite to survey the desert and the foothills they had just crossed.

There *was* beauty there, beauty and death. Did the one enhance the other? Did the existence of the barrenness at World's End help define the lushness and easiness of life everywhere else on Omne? Perhaps the Omnans were missing something important when they ceased striving to survive in the inhospitable desert and relaxed into the ease of the Heartlands. She looked down at La'am as he sat shadowed on the ground. He was of the Ranges; he had grown to manhood in a barrenness like this—not entirely, of course, since life in the Ranges, though difficult, was not too severe. But there was about him a sturdiness and strength that she had never seen in the men of the Eastern Ranges or those associated with the city. His hand was resting on a protruding root smoothed by Cycles of exposure to wind-spun sands and periodic waterfall. She could trace the lines of bone and muscle in the hand and the forearm, the implied strength of the half-clenched fingers.

Those hands could serve Omne well. She smiled. Reaching down abruptly, she touched his shoulder. The Master of Makers stirred from his own reveries, looked up, smiled in turn, and stood. He tossed the hood back from his eyes, releasing long, blond hair that was damp and matted from the heat.

"Ready?"

"When you are," Laral answered.

He slipped his hand into hers as they carefully picked their way up the slope toward the northwest, away from the foothills, away from the desert wastes and toward the Pillars of Beginnings.

* * * * * * *

By twilight, La'am and Laral knew that their decision had been correct. They had made far better time than they had hoped. La'am was now directing their movements according to sketchy maps he had seen as an Acolyte at the Sanctuary of the Pillars of Beginnings. Slowly, he began to recognize landmarks, faintly at first, and hesitantly, then with more confidence. One peak loomed above the others to bury its crest in the fluffy folds of the Veil of Heaven. Yet before it disappeared, the lofty pinnacle split into a triple crown, as if riven by a cosmic wedge.

"The Trinity," he explained. "It was named for one of the gods of the First World, I think. The name is very old, perhaps among the oldest on Omne."

Later, they passed a deep bay cutting into the sands of World's End. From their height, the Makers could not distinguish clearly the shape of the bay; the perspective was wrong, of course, and they could not see it completely. Their only glimpse was between two tilting slabs of granite wedged against each other by the forces of earthquake and erosion generations of Cycles before. Through the cleft, the water of the ocean sparkled vivid blue against the white sand. La'am caught his breath at the sight, then recognized the place.

"This is the Crescent. The water cuts into the desert here in an almost perfect half-circle. It is only a few miles below the point where the mountains meet the sea. We're almost there."

The sight encouraged them. The knowledge that they knew where they were strengthened them. La'am felt something akin to a homecoming as he walked on mountain slopes associated with the Makership of the Pillars of Beginnings, even though he had never physically been on this side of the range before. He hungered for a sight of the Sanctuary—then cut off that emotion as he remembered bitterly that the Sanctuary would have been destroyed by Haardt's ship. From what he could glean from Jathanan's mentrans patterns and Laral's story, probably only the Sanctuary at Los'ang, the Makers' Palace itself, remained intact. Yet he felt undeniable stirrings of memories as they trekked deeper into the mountains.

From the point where they had seen the Crescent, La'am and Laral angled sharply again, this time toward the north. They hoped to cut across the divide here, where the mountains were perhaps less lofty, and approach the Pillars of Beginnings from the west flank, from the face of the ranges on which the Sanctuary had been built. La'am both rejoiced and despaired at their decision, fearing yet desiring to see the rubble that had once been his home, and to stand beside the small mound of rocks that would still mark the grave of Iam'Kendron.

More than anything, he realized abruptly, he wanted Laral to stand there with him. He wanted her to imbibe the air of the Sanctuary and to breathe the breath of Iam'Kendron.

So they cut away from their trail and headed directly to the north, climbing higher and higher, until what had been foothills became mountains, and then the mountains finally evolved into the first ranks of the Northern Ranges. They had hoped to find a pass before twilight, but as they continued moving, encountering frustratingly unclimbable cliff upon unclimbable cliff, they realized the futility of that hope. The ranges would be closed to them until First Light. Already the Veil of Heaven was dropping, warning them of the coming night. The air was chilling rapidly—La'am found himself thinking half-wistfully of the withering heat of the desert, and wrapped his robe more tightly around himself. Finally, there was nothing left to do but find the best shelter for the night.

This time, not even Laral's sharp vision was of any help. Within a few moments, the Makers were huddled against a long, narrow boulder. It was poor shelter, both of them knew that, but it was the best they could find. The boulder itself canted nearly perpendicular to the ground; nearby, a second slab of granite had broken away from the cliffs and had fallen, striking the first head-high, and shattering. The rubble had settled around the base of the first. The result was a rudimentary shelter, vaguely pyramidal. A smaller cascade of rocks had closed the rear of the hole; when La'am kindled a small fire in the mouth of the pseudo-cave, the flames reflected both light and heat from the interior walls. La'am and Laral retreated to the back and rested against the rocks.

The fire blurred the night beyond, wounding it with red and orange and with slight hints of the blue Makerslight that had kindled flames in the twigs and branches Laral had gathered. At first, La'am and Laral sat stiffly. Their shoulders, arms, and thighs barely touched through the thick Makers' robes.

They had not spoken—La'am suddenly felt oddly uncomfortable around Laral...and aware of her not as a Maker but as a woman. Only twice in his life, since he had lost Brace as a birth-friend, had he opened his mind and heart fully to anyone.

Those two were now dead.

True, they existed residually within him as mentrans patterns, but the minds and souls that had formed those patterns were no more. Huddled against the rocks, La'am did not wish to speak, nor did he mind Laral's silence.

She, for her part, was equally aware of her loneliness. She had belonged to the retinue of Joleckan of the Eastern Ranges. She had been associated with the daily functioning of the Sanctuary and its surrounding circles of crofters' cottages. She had been constantly involved with people to an extent that La'am had not. And yet she, like he, knew that she was isolated even in her busy-ness. She did not speak lightly, nor would she purposefully interfere with her companion's obvious need for silence.

So they sat, side by side, their faces shadowed by a tiny point of light in an ocean of encircling darkness. Finally, the fire began to die down. As the twigs were reduced to ashes, the glow assumed a bluish cast; now the Makerspower itself became the primary source of light. Laral felt a languid relaxation stealing across her. Without thinking, she leaned against La'am. He did not move, and she did not notice how close they were. After a few moments, she fell asleep. Her head rested on his shoulder, her breath ruffled faintly the fabric of his sleeve.

Still awake and alert to her presence, La'am could hear her breathing, could smell the fragrance of her hair as she slept.

The fire faded to a cold blue glow. La'am noted that fact but was too near to sleep himself to do more than consider extending more Makerspower. The fire died to little more than coals. Laral shuddered in the coolness. La'am hitched himself more nearly upright and felt her settle against his chest. His arm drew up and around her, encircling her in his warmth. The loose folds of his cloak fell across her arm and side, providing additional protection. In her reciprocal warmth, La'am fell asleep.

He woke suddenly. First Light had just touched the Veil. He could see gray nothingness through the steep, triangular entrance to their shelter—but he could distinguish little else. A thick morning fog obscured his vision.

He started to move, then realized with something like a shock that Laral was still asleep, was still pressed tightly against his side. The comforting warmth of her body radiated against his own. She had reached out during the night, and her right arm now lay across his chest in a diminutive version of his own protective gesture. He smoothed a wisp of hair from her face.

She awakened at the touch,

"Wha... where...?" Her eyes wide and frightened-looking, she started back, throwing herself from him with an exaggerated surge of strength.

La'am cheeks and ears burned with a heat far beyond that of any desert-burn. He turned away from her. He had never been this intimate with a woman. As Davian of the Northrill Vale, he had been too young, too immature to do more than fantasize, although he had had hopes and longings that left him heated and shaking. Then suddenly and without warning, he had become La'am Iam'Kendronword, Acolyte to a Maker—and simultaneously subject to the rigid code that the Makers-lore imposed.

He had never known a woman—he would *never* know one, since the Makers were, by choice and by tradition, entirely celibate.

Yet he felt drawn to this woman, inextricably drawn to her—to another Maker, in fact! His embarrassment was obvious and immediate. Laral apparently shared it. She sprang to her feet and clattered across the loose stones toward the opening of the shelter. By the time she turned around, however, she had regained outward control, at least.

"Thank you for the gift of warmth during the night" she said, her words modulated into ritualistic inflections. "Maker to Maker I thank you."

That is that, La'am thought, disturbed by the heaviness he felt in his chest, a sudden ache in his gut. She had set him aside. She had repudiated the possibility of any reciprocal attachment. She viewed him only as a Maker...as she should. Any hopes to the contrary were dissipated by the formality of her tones.

He could, of course, brush lightly against her mind and read for himself the rejection—no, *rejection* was too strong a word. There could be no rejection where acceptance was impossible. But he refused to do so. Her attitude was clear; he was in error, not she.

He scrabbled to his feet and bowed slightly in answer to her, averting his face.

"Your thanks is well taken. The gift was freely given."

Thus was satisfied the protocol of the Makersraad. Now, to the task at hand.

La'am emerged from the shelter to stand in a world of gray. The fog seemed all-penetrating. Within seconds, heavy pearls of dew hung on the sleeves and shoulders of his robe. Raising his hand, he could even see the fog condensing on the sparse hairs on the back, bejeweling his flesh with moisture. Looking around, La'am could see virtually nothing. The ridge on the opposite side was completely robed in fog. Even the cliff face to the right—one part of which had fallen to form their shelter—was invisible. Laral moved silently up behind La'am and rested her hand on his arm.

He lowered his hand. She moved away a step or two and stared down the fog-shrouded cliff.

"Should we try to keep going?"

"We have no choice," La'am said fiercely—more fiercely than her question merited, he knew. He swallowed two or three times, then forced himself to speak more calmly, more carefully. "We must arrive at the Pillars as soon as possible, or all of our struggles will be in vain. Every second we delay puts Haardt more firmly in control. We may ultimately defeat him, but the damage he might do in the meantime increases with each minute. We must go on."

"In this fog?"

"We will have to climb carefully. The Makerslight will help."

La'am extended his hand toward the gray mist. He released a short burst of blue fire. A fragile cone of light stabbed through the mist, dissipating it locally but producing little or no increase in visibility.

"You must help me," he said softly.

Laral started to speak, then clenched her jaw. She had been about to plead her inability as an Acolyte—but she was a Maker now.

Perhaps.

She concentrated on the swirls of power within her. She raised her hand and pointed to an invisible spot next to the point where La'am's Makerslight disappeared into nothingness. A second flare of blue stretched toward La'am's and, at that invisible spot, merged with it. As it did so, Laral heard La'am speaking, almost mumbling. Half-consciously, she joined him, marveling as she did so that she knew the Words of Light. She had never heard of them, *yet she knew them.*

Somewhere deep within her, the patterns that were Freyma of World's End radiated warmly in satisfaction and achievement. Laral felt the words form, and flushed as her mind registered them: "*This one is indeed a true heir to the Powers of the Mastership. She will do.*"

The two Makers stood arm to arm and recited the words that filtered through their minds from generations past. As they did so, their eyes closed in utter concentration, the fog lifted gradually. First it paled to lacteal white, then it rose a few feet, until it touched—and merged with—the Veil of Heaven.

There was a faint, familiar crackling sound.

La'am opened his eyes.

The path was clear ahead of them for a dozen yards, until it angled upward and became again enshrouded in the Veil of Heaven. He started to climb. Laral followed.

Northward they went, ever northward, toward the Pillars.

At first, they made substantial progress. Small passes opened, allowing them to cross the outer ranges, each time drawing them nearer to the Sanctuary itself. La'am became convinced that they could cross the final range by late day. From there, they would be able to cover the remaining miles to the site of the Sanctuary quickly. They would be crossing terrain that La'am knew intimately. They would be walking by knowledge rather than by faith in old maps and older memories. If only their good fortune would hold.

It did not.

CHAPTER THIRTY

As the day wore on, the fog lifted more and more, until only the peaks of the far northern ranges were obscured—as usual—by the Veil of Heaven. The air was clear and fresh and crisp; as far as La'am was concerned, it was ideal for climbing. But far too soon to suit him, the passes disappeared. Again and again, La'am and Laral would follow a likely looking gorge for five minutes, or ten, only to arrive at an impenetrable barrier of smooth stone, unscalable and sheer, reaching upward toward the Veil. They would be forced to retrace their steps and begin again their scrutiny of the cliff faces, edging ever eastward in their searching. Time and again they found a promising cut and followed it, only to discover another dead-end.

By midday, La'am halted.

"We can't keep going like this. We're wasting more time than we can spare." He shaded his eyes and studied the surrounding peaks as much as the Veil would allow. He shrugged. "I think we are beyond the western shoulders of the Pillars. Even if we could find a pass now, I doubt that we could get to the Sanctuary without having to scale the Pillars themselves—and that's an impossibility. We can't turn back, and we can't keep trying each gully for a way over that may not even exist."

He fell silent, but kept his glance moving across the featureless stone.

"What then? To the sea?"

"I think so," he said after a moment. "Perhaps we should have chosen that route in the first place. I don't know. Right now, all I can hope for is to get out of these ranges in time."

"In time? For what?"

"I don't know," La'am said, flashing an embarrassed and quite boyish smile. "I really don't. But we have to hurry."

Laral didn't wait for him to say any more. She turned and followed the narrow crevice downward, toward the ocean glittering faintly in the distance.

The decision proved wise. Within the hour, the path they were picking out cut steeply down through a cleft overgrown with mountain ranya. The Makers descended rapidly, losing far too easily the elevation they had struggled so hard all day to gain. The northern walls of the canyon remained impassible. La'am had never seen cliffs so smoothly sheer, as if hand-polished. Yet their path continued in a straight line toward the sea, descending so quickly that the Makers frequently slipped on the loose rock and plummeted several feet—often as many as twenty or thirty—before they could grasp at a protruding root or worn knob of stone and break their fall. In spite of more than one tumble that threatened broken bones or worse, neither was seriously injured, although both tallied a fair number of bruises and scratches.

The miles melted away. La'am was a steady and sturdy climber; Laral was not far behind him in ability. Neither was encumbered by a pack or other luggage. Their hands were free to grip and grasp. And they were propelled by an increasing sense of urgency.

We must reach the Pillars—and soon.

By late day, the canyon had widened and leveled off. The Makers no longer slipped or lost footing. Instead, they strode forward confidently and strongly, their sandals scuffing against great shale slabs, nearly level and rippled slightly, just enough to provide secure footing. The enclosing cliffs slanted further and further back, opening wider to the Veil of Heaven above. Vegetation blossomed on the slopes.

Finally, Laral let out a small cry and surged ahead. The valley seemed cut off by an immense spur that jutted up from the southern wall and blocked the way. She ran impatiently, barely watching her step as she searched out a way over the northern flank of the spur. The slope was gentle and required little climbing ability; within moments, she was clambering atop a boulder perched on the crest.

"La'am!"

There was no hiding the exultation and excitement. Her voice was a clarion of triumph. "There it is! The sea. I knew I could sense it on the air."

La'am ran up the trail behind her and hoisted himself up onto the platform-top of the boulder. He stifled the impulse to laugh out loud, but inside he was as excited as Laral.

The sea.

Stretching virtually at their feet, unruffled and smooth, transcendent blue, until it blended with the Veil of Heaven at the horizon. The sea.

La'am turned and—without a second thought—caught Laral up in his arms.

"We made it," he yelled again and again. "We made it!"

An inner voice warned that there was still no justification for delay, but La'am was overjoyed at their achievement. From this point, the Pillars of Beginnings could be no more than an hour's quick-march up the coast. Squinting against the brightness of Veil and Sea, La'am felt certain that he could make out misty outlines to the north, above the low wall of the valley.

He gave Laral a quick, final hug.

"Let's go," he cried as he half climbed, half slid down the seaward face of the spur. His enthusiasm was contagious. Laral scampered down behind him and began running toward the water as well. The ground was softer than they had felt for days. For a narrow stretch between mountain and sea, it was true earth rather than sand or coarse gravel or rock. And it was festooned with hillocks of brilliant green—wild rhiam sprouting in the balminess of Seed Time and protected from the southern heat and northern chill by the ocean currents and prevailing winds.

Before either of them was aware of it, they were at the sea. Here the beach was less than a dozen feet wide. On one side rose the slopes of the Ranges; on the other broke fragile waves. And northward, clear and unmistakable and perhaps only ten miles away, rose the buttresses of the Pillars!

* * * * * * *

La'am and Laral looked up toward the Veil of Heaven where it clung whitely above the Pillars of Beginnings. The Pillars were unreachable from the sea—they could see nothing but rigid walls of stone, unscalable, smoothed by centuries of wind. The sand at the base of the Pillars was smooth also, scoured until not a single boulder or stone jutted above the surface. It was as if the sand had been consciously prepared for their arrival, had been neatened and swept and trimmed.

It was perfect.

As far as La'am and Laral could tell, it was also a dead end.

The two Makers stared in frustrated, anxious silence toward the Pillars and the Veil. They rifled through their own memories and those borrowed from other Makers to seek any references to invisible pathways up the sheer precipice looming over them. Laral looked into the patterns of Freyma of World's End—and of those allied through mentrans with him—while La'am peered into the deeper knowledge of Iam'Kendron. Somewhere, there had to be a way up the cliffs. Both of the Makers had experienced the same powers urging them to this point; both knew that this was their goal, that it would be disastrous, worse than useless to travel any further—that in some incomprehensible way their own understanding and the salvation of Omne depended upon their scaling the Pillars. And this was the only point at which that would be possible.

But their eyes told another story. After almost an hour of studying the cliffs, both La'am and Laral were forced to accept the simple fact that there was no way up, not even a promising initial foothold. They stared at the stony buttresses, following one shallow hollow with their eyes until it blended into nothingness. The light faded, twilight was upon them, and still they had no answers.

They moved closer together, slowly, not for protection or for warmth—the night was in fact quite warm, even without the added protection of their Makers' robes—but rather for a sense of sharing, of close contact that would allow them to resonate patterns throughout the darkness, hoping to find a solution.

Night came. And with it blackness. They saw nothing. They heard the low breakers whisper on the sand. They heard the wind curling along the Pillars. They felt the dampness of fog on their cheeks.

Neither slept, although both were lost to the physical realities of Omne during much of the darkness. They continued to explore their inner worlds, each separate from the other yet each intricately tied to the other by the common powers and hopes of the Makership. Occasionally one would reach out and touch the other, feeling the firmness of the other's patterns, smiling inwardly at the strength and warmth they drew from each other—La'am blending his headstrong faith in the Makerspowers with Laral's more temperate concern for Omne and her mild surprise at her own suddenly pivotal position in history. Their mental touchings never became probings. They never completely exchanged patterns. It was enough to know that the other was there, invisible in the absolute darkness, not even outlined by the faintest hint of blue Makerslight.

Only once during the night of searching did La'am break the silence.

"Laral?"

"Yes." Even though he knew she was not even an arm's length from him, her voice sounded distant and hollow.

"I..., did you..., I...." He stuttered to a stop. There was a long silence. "I am sorry again for last night."

"Last night?"

"For thinking...feeling...."

Again he fell silent. He did not have the words to express his emotions. Even had he had them, he could not have uttered them, especially not to her, a Maker of Omne. He had almost been able to ignore his feelings during the trials of the day. As night had fallen, his physical exhaustion and mental agony over their failure to find a way up the Pillars had distracted him completely. But now, with the night slowly edging away, he felt a flood of uncontrolled emotions.

He loved her; he even wished again for the warmth of her against him—yet he could not utter that love, that desire. He was first a Maker, then a man; and he was restricted by the lore of the Ancients.

"I'm sorry," he said lamely. "Never mind."

She did not answer. Again, La'am felt the momentary temptation to probe her patterns to discover her true reactions to him. Again, he hesitated too long. Reason took charge, and La'am retreated into himself. He was, after all, a Maker.

The night continued. The Makers searched relentlessly for patterns which might make sense of their failure. But nothing came.

Finally, however, La'am felt the first approaches of day. He could not as yet perceive any diminution in the blackness that surrounded them, but he could sense a subtle shift in the air, a hint of rising currents from the East with their warmer air bearing the fragrance of light and day. Only moments remained before the Eastern margins of the Veil of Heaven would take on the transparent shimmer of day. He stood and faced the East. As La'am looked across the invisible sea, he remembered his journey in the boat, scudding along on an unseen current, a river of water hidden beneath the placid surface of the sea that bore him as if by magic to unknown places.

Unseen, hidden....

Something crackled. Two fragmented patterns slid into one another and snapped together. The new pattern merged into another, then that one into yet another. Iam'Kendron's strong patterns mellowed with those of Jathanan to form a pattern known and unknown to either—or to La'am. It was not yet complete, but La'am could read its outlines. It resembled the Words of 'Waring that the Makers of Omne had spoken for generations to preserve the stonework of the Ancients. He had himself spoken them on the bridges and within buildings that had once been so easily constructed but that were now almost beyond the capacity of Omnans to restore or re-create.

Ancient things had been preserved from decay and change through the power of those Words.

And now there were other Words, startlingly like the Words of 'Waring but different, altered.

La'am swiveled on his heels. The Makerslight billowed from the folds of his robe, burning away the doomed darkness. Laral was also standing. She jerked her head up to stare at La'am as he stood there, arms stretched out toward the cliff. She had felt his disturbance, had intimated that action was about to take place, although she did not know what kind. She felt him calling her, urging her to join with him. She did.

As she merged her power with his, she too became aware of the new patterns—and of something infinitely more personal and, for her, more disturbing. In this moment of complete openness, she saw and understood finally the depth of La'am's love...for her. And she discovered that it was more than matched by her own for him.

Then the new pattern sharpened, clarified, and focused into the sound-pattern of Freyma, crystallized into a new pattern of Words flowing between La'am and Laral. The air between them was thick with Makerslight, congealed and palpable.

Together they spoke the new Words. "These are the Words of Discovery," Laral said. La'am nodded.

His voice trembled as the syllables passed over his dry lips. Here was a new power, one that had remained a secret through the generations, fragmented and hidden piecemeal among the patterns of a hundred individual Makers, living and dead, but not revealed until now. Not until the unique merging of La'am and Laral brought together Iam'Kendron's incomparable knowledge, Jorik's impetuous pride, Jathanan's courage, the incorruptible memories of Freyma of World's End, and the remnant patterns of every Maker before them—then mingled them in what once had been two separate individuals but were now one mind. Only then could the pattern be restored.

Even as La'am spoke, the two Makers braced themselves against the abrupt upheaval in the air. The ground shook beneath their feet, as if Omne herself were rising to the summons, as if the dead rocks of her foundations were quivering in their haste to answer the call of the Words, unheard for a thousand Cycles. The silence was first broken by La'am's voice and Laral's whispering, then shattered into nothingness by a massive roar, as if the Pillars of Beginnings had subsided into the sea, as had the Tower of Jeriam half a Cycle previously.

As at the Beginning, so at the End, La'am thought, not sure himself what he meant.

The sound ceased. The air was no longer fresh and moist. It was dry, caked, acrid and bitter. The darkness seemed to stifle rather than to enfold. Next to him, Laral breathed heavily through her mouth, as if her lungs were incapable of drawing in enough air to sustain her. La'am's head ached, and his wrists were as sore as if he had just carried a hundred-weight of dried rhiam.

"Laral?"

"I'm all right. You."

"I'm...tired. But all right."

"What happened?" There was just a hint of something tremulous in her voice, but it quickly passed.

Instead of answering, La'am extended the power of the Makerslight. For the first time, it hurt, a small tingling pain that ran along his wrist and forearm and skittered down to his fingertips. He concentrated, and the pain went away. The Makerslight grew until the blue circle lapped about the roots of the Pillars. The beach was no longer blanket smooth; in fact, there was no longer any beach worthy of the name. Instead, the narrow area between the mountain and the sea was studded with granite boulders—most of them large enough to fill a small room. Smaller fragments of stone and detritus filled in the rest of the nightmare landscape. The nearest of the rocks had fallen or rolled to within a few feet of where La'am and Laral stood.

That was how close they had come to being crushed to death.

La'am shifted his position and raised his hands higher. The circle of light, now twisted and broken into interlocking shadows where it struck the boulders, eventually flowed up toward the front of the Pillars themselves. As soon as the light struck the Pillars proper, it faltered, almost failed, then surged even stronger than before—a physical manifestation of surprise that, in spite of La'am's faith in the Makerspowers, now bordered on shock.

At that instant, La'am felt Laral's hand pressing against his arm. Her fingers were strong, their pressure against him equally strong. Looking at her, he saw that she was smiling at him—a tremendous, relieved, joyful smile that was almost painful in its intensity. But she was not looking at him. He followed the direction of her eyes, and of her pointing arm. There, at the eastern horizon, La'am could see the first play of color heralding daylight.

But in the center of the usual hints of color, directly to the east of where they stood, La'am thought that he could see—*something*. The sensation was momentary and brief, but distinct nonetheless. There was a flicker of redness, a flame like a great eye of opal gleaming through the Veil of Heaven.

The Eye of the Wordsmith, La'am thought, his mind numb with what he had just seen and what he was now seeing. *The Eye of the Wordsmith,* just as Iam'Kendron had described it, just as La'am himself had seen it in his dream-vision at death of Iam'Kendron. But this time the phenomenon was infinitely more real. The glow burned palpably in the dying darkness. It was larger, grander, more meaningful than before. It filled him with the same excess of happiness—the same ecstasy—that Laral obviously felt where she stood next to him. And yet neither of them understood what they were seeing.

Yet.

As instantaneously as it had appeared, the Eye vanished, leaving only the normal flow of First Light.

Yet even First Light was now sufficient to allow the two Master Makers to see the full extent of what had occurred during the night at the Pillars of Beginnings.

They turned away from the eastern horizon and raised their eyes to the mountains.

From foundation to Veil of Heaven, a rift had opened in the Pillars—or more precisely, immense quantities of rock had been removed from a hidden rift and now lay scattered on the sand. And, at the base of the rift, what looked almost like a twisting staircase was now open to full view. The chimney looked perilous, but it was clearly climbable. It was the route the Makers had searched for through the night.

La'am turned to Laral. His mouth was open and about to suggest that she wait for him, that the ascent into the unknown might be too hazardous for her. She forestalled him with a word and a sharp cutting gesture with her hand.

"No!"

La'am grinned broadly as she continued.

"I am a Master Maker of Omne." She glanced at his robe. It was dusty from their journal, but the flow of colors beyond indigo was still obvious. Her eyes grew deep with shadowed thought. "Right now, I am probably the only *true* Master Maker still alive. I am young and untrained"—La'am hesitated to admit that he too was young and essentially untrained, and so did not speak—"but I *am* a Master Maker nonetheless. I do not know how or why.

"Whatever waits up there waits for both of us, however. That I do know. You could not have arrived here without the knowledge that is now mine. I could not have done so without you and your knowledge. So now," she said as she straightened up, dusting moist grains of sand from her robe, "let's begin and find out together what *is* up there."

There did not seem to be anything left to say, so La'am said nothing.

They negotiated a tortuous path to the rift, avoiding the larger boulders and taking care not to stumble on any of the knife-edged, shattered stones at their feet. They stopped at the base of the rift. Looking up from the sharply angled perspective of the beach, the Makers could follow the undeviating passageway until it disappeared into the Veil. It looked formidable. Drawing a deep breath, La'am reached for the first handhold.

Whatever its purpose or its destination, and in defiance of their first visual impression of it, the cleft was not a stairway. It had not been designed for effortless ascent. Even though both had hoped for a quick climb, La'am and Laral were neither entirely surprised when they found themselves struggling for long hours in the tight chimney. The Veil of Heaven seemed unusually high here, the day unusually hot for climbing. Long before midday, they were both bathed in sweat. Their tired, cramped fingers slipped wetly on smooth stone. Here and there, they could see fragments of rock, different in texture and consistency from the surrounding material, that apparently had adhered to the Pillars even after the bulk of it had crashed down at the Words of Discovery. The remnants now served primarily for handholds and footholds. Without them, the Makers would not have even been able to begin the ascent.

They worked cautiously and carefully, trusting to nothing but their skills as range-born and range-bred climbers...and to each other as Master Makers. Several times, La'am felt a surge of Makerspower as Laral abruptly grasped his slipping wrist, or as he stretched his hand to aid her toward the tenuous security of a toehold that was little more than a faint indentation in the granite. More often, he felt heart-twisting lurches as the fragile rubble crumbled under the weight of a hand or a foot.

After a few hours of climbing, they reached a narrow ledge. It was barely long enough for the two of them to stand on and just wide enough for them to crouch against the Pillars. The two Makers squatted there, suspended to all appearances without any support, against the face of the precipice. Both were breathing deeply, both were nearer exhaustion than either cared to admit. The opportunity to snatch a brief moment of rest was as welcome as it was unexpected.

La'am leaned forward slightly, but even so most of his body overhung the ledge. He tried to estimate the distance between then and the beach below, now visible only as a hair-thin white strip twining north and south along the base of the Pillars. Then he leaned back and craned his neck upward, and tried to guess at the distances yet remaining until the Pillars disappeared into the Veil.

"We've come...about two-thirds of the way...I think," he said. Between pants, he continued. "A few minutes...then we've got to go. Okay?"

Laral nodded.

They sat for a few moments more.

"The rest of the climb looks harder than what we have done so far," La'am said. "We need a rope, to link us together in case...."

"Our belts?"

La'am nodded. "They'll do."

In fact, the rhiam cords that held the Makers' robes closed would do perfectly. The cords were long; tied together, they would provide a measure of security against accidents. And the rhiam fiber would never fray or pull apart, of that La'am was convinced.

They managed to remove the cords without mishap, even though there was little room for maneuvering. More than once, La'am felt Laral's shoulder, or elbow, or thigh touching his. He tried to ignore it.

Finally, though, he held both cords in his hand. He knotted them securely together. As he did so, Laral straightened as much as the narrow ledge would allow and carefully removed the robe itself. She was wearing a short chemise-like garment of undyed rhiam. She rolled the Makersrobe into a tight bundle, twisted the open sleeves through each other in a rough knot, and, thrusting her hand between knot and bundle, slid the robe up her arm until it rested on her shoulder.

As La'am watched her, she grinned self-consciously.

"It is far too hot for this robe today. Besides," she said, shrugging, "I can climb better with my arms and legs free."

La'am returned the smile.

"I know. I would have suggested it, but...."

He finished preparing the cords, then stripped his own robe off and folded it as carefully as Laral had folded hers. He unraveled the final foot or so of the rhiam cord and broke a single filament off. Even that took great effort. He tied his bundle with the filament, then stood, ready to begin climbing again. He was dressed only in a narrow clout, almost identical to the one he had worn on his last day as Davian of the Northrill Vale. He felt younger as he remembered that climb.

The two Makers passed the heavy cord once about their waists; enough remained linking them to allow for free climbing, although not as much as La'am would have wished. As he knotted the cord about Laral's waist, his hands brushed against her, involuntarily but necessarily. He flushed, aware of her nearness as well as of his own near-nakedness. Quickly, he turned and began pulling himself up the face of the cliff.

The last third of the ascent was more arduous than had been the first two-thirds. One climber would not have made it alone. For two, working in tandem and sharing strength, the cleft was difficult and taxing in the extreme and occasionally dangerous, but possible.

It was late in the day before they finally reached the lower edges of the Veil of Heaven. Their bodies were bathed in sweat from the climb. They were bruised and abraded from using knees, elbows, shoulders, and thighs as supports in the narrow chimney. The final few feet had proven virtually impossible. At one point, La'am had been convinced that the only thing that held him to the solid face of the Pillars had been the Makerspower flooding him and creating a mystical affinity between his flesh and the bones of Omne. It had almost seemed for that instant as if Omne herself had held onto him, pinioning him momentarily when his damp palms had slipped. Laral had closed her eyes in terror, concentrating her own Makerspower into La'am, willing him to hold steady, to adhere to the featureless cliff. And he had held. When the first moment of panic died, he had reached up, urging tendons and muscles beyond their capacity. His forehead, arms, and back were taut with effort. His body was drenched in sweat as much from concentration as from the heat.

For a time that seemed hours, he had been suspended on the cliff face by his toes and the fingertips of one hand. He had felt Laral's hand on his left ankle, less to support him than for the physical contact that provided a conduit for her Makerspower. His right hand scrabbled blindly along the featureless rock above his head. His fingers probed for any possible break in the smoothness. He glanced up and saw the lip of a ledge not a yard above him...but unreachable without one more handhold. He closed his eyes and focused all of his will power into his fingers.

They had come too far to be stopped now.

There was a thin *crack*, and the knot of rock that supported his right foot broke away. For an instant, his sandal-clad foot hung over nothingness, and he felt his body slipping to the right and away from the cliff. He lunged upward with his right hand.

And suddenly, it was over.

He felt a slight indentation, no more than a hairline crack in the rock. He pressed against it, feeling the thin sharp edge beneath his fingertips. It was not much, but it was enough. He pulled himself another six inches up the face. The muscles in his arm trembled from the strain, and in an instant of awareness, if seemed as if he knew intimately every contact between his body and the rock face, every fragment of light and heat beating on his back. He felt Laral's pulse where her fingers still touched his ankle, could almost count the beats of her heart as they were transmitted through her blood to her fingers.

He swung his left hang upward and found another crack, no deeper than the one that supported his right hand. He dug his fingertips into the stone facing. He dared a glance upward. The lip was within reach. He hooked the fingers of his right hand over the edge, careful that they were resting on solid rock rather than treacherously slippery fragments that might give way. Then he pulled himself up by sheer muscular power, until his shoulder was just above the level of the ledge and he could swing his other arm up to brace his weight. Then a knee, a foot, and he was crouching on the ledge.

The joined cord was stretched taut. He grabbed it with both hands and helped Laral climb up as far as she could along that final, impossible face. Then she too had one hand on the ledge. He reached over and helped her, pulling her up slowly, tiredly.

As soon as she was safely on the ledge, they both fell to their knees, breathing in great rasping gasps and numbly hoping almost without hope that this was the end of their ascent.

And it was.

CHAPTER THIRTY-ONE

La'am was exhausted.

Blood thudded in his veins, blurring his vision and spreading a russet haze between himself and his surroundings. He could hear nothing but the beating of his heart and the stentorian heaving of his own breath. His lungs ached. His fingers and palms burned as if he had thrust them into living flames. The muscles along his spine and in his thighs quivered painfully. It was all he could do to hold onto consciousness for the first few moments, until his heartbeat and his breathing dropped to something approximating normal. Only then did he move to raise himself to his knees and look around.

Beyond them stretched a narrow, level clearing. It was empty of anything living—not even a tuft of hardy grass or a stunted ranya. For the length of the clearing, there was just stone, brown and gray and black—but nothing else. The rock floor was unbroken and level from the edge back to where the cliff continued upward. In fact, the rock was so level, that as La'am focused on it, he wondered how the mindless force of wind and rain could have polished it so smoothly. He touched the surface with his fingertips. The skin tingled where it came into contact with the rock.

Laral spoke.

"The Veil ends there." Her voice was tinged with fatigue and strain but beyond that sounded normal.

She pointed beyond them a few paces.

As she had said, the Veil ended. Elsewhere on Omne, the Veil seemed amorphous and misty. When one approached it, there were no definite boundaries to warn that the impassable point had been reached. One was merely stopped—occasionally with a vivid flickering of blue light.

Here, however, the Veil *ended.*

La'am could see the sharp line of the Veil arching down from the grayness above to the rock floor on which he stood. He could not see it curve, but he knew that it had to be doing so. There was no perspective, though, nothing to give La'am and Laral a sense of size or distance. Somewhere beyond them—a few feet perhaps, or a few yards—the Veil simply stopped.

La'am took a step forward. Laral reached out and touched his shoulder.

"Not yet," she said. She rested her hand on the bundle still strapped across La'am's back. "The robes."

He stopped, half ashamed. In the excitement of the moment, in the final fatiguing triumph of the ascent, he had actually forgotten.

"Not yet," he repeated, echoing her words but altering their referent. He turned to face her, then moved back two steps and studied her. When he moved close to her again, he extended his hand toward a shallow, ragged cut on her right elbow. The skin had been ripped on some jagged outcropping and now bled slowly, oozing blood and clear fluid. He laid his finger on the torn skin. She winced at his touch; he had been as gentle as the feather touch of a spring breeze but a residue of salt on his fingertips—themselves cracked and bleeding—stung in the open wound.

He pulled his hand back at the sight of her pain, then reached out again. This time he moved more resolutely and recited the Words of Healing as he did so. His fingertips glowed lightly blue. Where he touched, the skin healed over; as they watched, it became again smooth and unmarked. Laral's eyes expressed relief and gratitude far beyond anything spoken words could have.

"Lay down," La'am said softly, motioning to the warm stone of the ledge. She did. Her face tightened in pain as tortured, cramped muscles—already tightened by the few moments of rest—were forced to stretch. She closed her eyes. She could feel warmth on her, then the coolness of his shadow as he knelt by her side. He passed his hands over her. He touched briefly the bruises and cuts scattered along her arms and legs. He lingered over one long, wicked scratch that extended along her calf from her knee almost to her ankle. As his hands moved, his lips incessantly repeated the Words of Healing, Laral relaxed. The lines of pain and fatigue disappeared from around her eyes and mouth. When he finished, she was on the verge of a deep, relaxed sleep. Her lips had curved into a faint smile and her breath had become normal.

La'am remained kneeling beside her for a moment. His hands hung motionless over her head, but he did not see her. He was lost in thought, remembering the flash of mentrans he had received at First Light, when Laral had joined her powers to his in searching for a way into the Pillars. He had seen...hoped he had seen?...his love for her and her reciprocal love reflected in the patterns they had shared. He opened his eyes and looked down at her. She seemed asleep. Her face glowed with a thin sheen and her hair curled damply around her face. Several wisps clung to the angle of her cheek.

Watching her, he felt a quickening of his own emotions. He dropped his hands to his sides but remained kneeling by her.

After a few moments, she stirred, then sat up. As he had done for her, she reached out to him and touched a spreading bruise on his naked shoulder. She echoed his own procedure with the Words of Healing. She did not ask him to lay down, but her hands trailed over his shoulders and down the length of his arms, then passed across his chest and along the top of his thighs, healing where they touched.

She dropped her hands and he stood up. Quickly he loosened the knot in the twisted sleeves of her robe, shook the worst wrinkles out of the fabric, and held the robe for her.

Moments later, both were again garbed as Makers of Omne. Only then did they walk slowly, solemnly toward the thin edge of the Veil. Hand in hand they approached the most secret place of the Pillars of Beginnings.

They approached cautiously. This experience was so far beyond the expected, the normal, that neither of them had any inkling as to what might lay beyond, nor did the accumulated memories within them. As they approached the edge of the Veil, La'am moved slightly ahead of Laral, conscious of the added dignity which he wore—literally, in the form of his multi-hued robe—as Master of Makers on Omne. He knew that he was certainly the first, and perhaps the last Omnan to bear that title. His robe momentarily deepened to the Master's indigo in the lowering air, then shimmered again into the multiplicity of colors that never had quite disappeared. The shimmering intensified as he neared the Veil; it was as if the colors were conscious of approaching the source of their strength.

Close behind La'am came Laral, Paran'born, Rhiama-Named, Joleckan-word, Freyma-word, Master Maker of World's End...and the only Maker La'am had ever heard of who had been Named by two Makers.

Together, the two anomalies approached the Veil of Heaven.

When they stood within reach of the gray barrier, they halted. The Veil had remained a perpetual mystery throughout their history. The few who had ever drawn near it and later spoken of the experience were impressed by its understated suggestion of power, by its absolute impermeability. La'am remembered vividly his nighttime introduction to it with Iam'Kendron. Now, no longer an untrained Acolyte but a Maker and Master of Makers, he nonetheless hesitated before he stretched out his hand. At the same instant, Laral likewise reached toward the Veil.

Their hands touched it simultaneously.

This time there were none of the sparks of blue fire that La'am associated with touching the Veil. Instead, there was...*nothing*. Not even a barrier. Their hands passed unhampered through what suddenly became no more than a thick mist. The lack of substantiality, of any manifestations of the Makerspower, of any sense of trial or victory, was fully as unnerving as...as whatever they had expected to happen.

There was simply nothing.

They could, if they so elected, walk through the mist and enter the Veil of Heaven.

They did. As the senior Maker, La'am moved first. This time the Veil was finally to be pierced, but not as occasionally happened when the Veil lowered until it became a fog on the land or the sea, as on the night when La'am had left Harborwatch. No, this time it would happen here, upon the stronghold of the Pillars themselves; and the Master of Makers must be the one to penetrate it. But Laral followed barely a breath behind him.

There was no opposition of any kind, no sensation of anything except a sudden coolness and dampness on their hands and arms. A diffuse light glowed from somewhere throughout the Veil, but whether from above, below, or beyond, they could not tell. They could see weather-worn stones beneath their feet. They could see a dimly bordered pathway leading across the level place and ascending unimpeded toward the highest reaches of the Pillars. Beyond that they could see nothing. There were no trees, no boulders jutting from the mists. There was nothing except the unending smoothness of living rock that formed a hollowed-out path their feet almost instinctively sought out and followed.

Neither spoke. There was no longer any need for speech. La'am and Laral could feel their patterns penetrating each other wordlessly, silently, but fully. Their earlier reticence disappeared, had already disappeared as each had reviewed the patterns they had exchanged that morning and discovered in them a mutuality of love. Without their consciously willing it, the Makerspower was merging the two, blending their patterns, heightening their perceptions and understanding of previous patterns, clarifying much and defining much more. The two Makers walked in silence, but as they walked, their robes glowed brighter and brighter, until the indigo of Laral's robe passed beyond the normal limits of indigo, and La'am's robe became a whirling blur of all colors and no color. No color? Or something beyond color for which there were no words? A blurring whirlpool of patterns that hovered on the verge of becoming sounds: laughter, weeping, singing, whispering—all sounds, all words, and none.

La'am and Laral knew that they were altering, although they did not know what form that change would ultimately take. They were discovering hidden depths within themselves, within each other, depths that had always existed but that no previous Maker or Makers had even primitively apprehended. La'am could feel the flow of his own blood in every portion of his body. He could see his own breathing. He could penetrate synesthetically into his own brain and watch the mentrans patterns swirling and kaleidoscoping in the pangs of merging and of birth.

The Makers stopped.

La'am and Laral jerked into awareness simultaneously, not understanding at first what had ripped them from their introspection. They had not stumbled. There were no obstructions in the pathway; and even when most remotely involved with internal searchings, they had released a portion of their consciousnesses to guide their steps. Yet both had stopped, muting the symphonies of patterns within.

La'am drew Laral's hand closer toward him. Her returning grasp grew stronger as well. Their fingers interlocked and tightened. Together, unified in fact and essence, they watched and waited.

The Veil of Heaven was thinning. Below them, farther back down the trail they had just climbed, it was as dense and as obscuring as ever. But beyond and above them burned some source of light and warmth beyond anything they had ever felt before. They could see nothing as yet, but the Veil shimmered with increasing intensity. The normal pearly white gave way to yellows, oranges, and reds.

They walked on, hand in hand, mind in mind.

The Veil lightened even more, dissipated, and faded until only a gauzy film remained in front of them. La'am and Laral reached out again, speaking simultaneously the Words of Light.

And the Veil was gone!

In the blink of an eye, the sharp intake of shocked breath, the Veil disappeared.

Towering above them were the hidden heights of the Pillars of Heaven, soaring higher yet than either gazer could comprehend. Below the small outcropping on which they stood, the Veil of Heaven curled like an ocean of smoky mist, pierced occasionally by lesser peaks of the Northern Ranges. Otherwise, as far as they could see, it continued unmarked, unroiled, untouched until it merged with... something.

A word came unbidden and, for a moment, unintelligible.

Sky.

Sky?

After the first dramatic moment, Laral and La'am did not see the mountains around them, nor did they see the Veil beneath them. They had eyes for nothing except a vast expanse of deep blue, indigo blue almost, especially in the east, in the direction they were facing. It was vast, like the ocean, yet infinitely deeper, bluer. It was without feature at all. La'am could determine no dimensions or degrees—the thing was far too vast.

The *sky.*

That word re-formed itself in concurrent patterns in both minds, then deepened until it became an image of the Master Maker's robe, of the rhiam fiber draping Laral, of the indigo underlying the prismatic hues of La'am's robe.

They felt heat suffusing itself on their backs. They noticed for the first time the crisp outlines of black shadows stretching in front of them, eastward, undistorted and unmoving on the smooth rocks.

As one body, one mind, the Makers turned.

Nestled in billowing swaths of crimson, scarlet, vivid violets and riots of pink, the saffron sphere hung, enormous and blinding, over the edge of the mist that was the Veil of Heaven. The sphere was eye-searing, yet neither La'am nor Laral blinked nor looked away; nor did either notice when the physical structures of their eyes altered, making it possible—for this moment, at least—to look directly upon that...that globe of fire without being blinded.

Or being consumed.

They fell speechlessly to their knees. Nothing in the legends, or the histories, or the lays and the myths could have prepared them for this. Everyone knew that the light of day and the heat of day filtered through the Veil of Heaven—but no one ventured to question where they came from or what their source might be. The Veil of Heaven was sacrosanct, to be penetrated neither physically nor intellectually.

But to find this...this brilliance...this light....

This...*SUN*—the pattern formed spontaneously.

To find this *SUN* was beyond belief!

Only gradually did La'am recover his senses. The two Makers had knelt motionless for long minutes while the Sun hung suspended between heaven and earth, while it grew larger and rounder, then touched the gauzy edge of the Veil and suffused the entire western horizon with liquid flame. The shifting saffron glow spread along the edge of the visible world, fading and deepening until the fingers of light circled the horizon and met again in the distant east, now darkened to a living indigo.

La'am was enthralled—enraptured—by the vision. He was delighted by the cooling breezes that signaled to his body the imminence of night. He reached out to Laral, and together they stood.

"The Sun," he said.

"I know. I don't know *how* I know, but I do."

"Gloriously bright. I hadn't imagined...."

"No one could," Laral said, speaking into the void created when La'am allowed his voice to recede into silence. "No one could have imagined something for which there is no word, no image. This is the great secret of the ancients. This is Life. This is...the Wordsmith."

But even as she spoke, La'am shook his head. An instant later she echoed his action and negated her own words.

"No," she said softly, "this is not the Wordsmith."

"It is something vast and grand beyond words, but it is not the final power. We must wait."

They waited. They sat upon the shoulder of the Pillars of Beginnings and waited and watched the play of brilliance across the Veil as day dissipated, died, and night drew on.

With the night, came the Eyes.

First one, then ten, then hundreds, and finally what seemed thousands of Eyes—glowing points of fire glittering through the blackness.

La'am immediately recognized the flames of his dreams. He recalled vividly that night spent upon the Northern Range; he now recalled the dream that even then he had not been able to recount coherently to Iam'Kendron. But in this instant the vision was so clear and its meaning so obvious that he laughed at his youthful ignorance. This was what he had seen, what Iam'Kendron had seen, what Mord'am—he felt a brief but fading stab of grief at the name—had probably seen on his own vigils along the Harbor strand.

Not actually *seen*, of course, but apprehended with powers beyond those of other Makers.

La'am turned to Laral. Her eyes reflected the shimmering lights of the night, but they also reflected more than the physical light. He was struck by a sudden understanding: She had seen them also, perhaps Cycles before. She had known them once as familiar friends, as....

Words failed.

In the presence of the impossible, the unbelievable, the incredible, La'am's thoughts ceased forming words. He shifted into mentrans. His patterns spread through the night and intercepting Laral's, understanding them but not becoming one with them. The two joined and spread outward as if to cover the entire world. They could feel the land, could hear the ceaseless ebb and flow of the sea. They became one with Omne, became in fact Omne, feeling her every movement, every fluttering through the rhiam fields. They wept for the flames and destruction even now arcing out from the wilderness toward Los'ang.

And then they were back, feet pressing into the cold stone of the Pillars of Beginnings. La'am retreated into himself and into the patterns that had once been other Makers and now were integral portions of La'am, Master of Makers of Omne and Master Maker of the Pillars of Beginnings.

With infinite care, he integrated perceptions, combined and joined patterns, as he did so becoming aware of ideas, knowledge, truths long obscured by the very Makersraad that had been created to protect and preserve them. The Makers had proven startlingly faithful to their responsibilities; so faithful, in fact, that they had submerged their individual particles of truths within themselves, surmising only rarely and briefly—as with Iam'Kendron—that the greater whole nonetheless existed and might be retrieved. Now La'am felt the retrieval beginning in himself and simultaneously in Laral. Patterns formed at a blinding speed; he could not comprehend their blurring outlines. In despair, he withdrew to the surface levels of his consciousness.

And found Laral waiting for him.

The night was half over. Below them on the surface of the planet, darkness would long have become absolute. On the exposed flanks of the Pillars of Beginnings, above the obscuring opacity of the Veil, thousands of stars lit the mountainside with a sterling light. Laral was silhouetted in the darkness of her robe. Her indigo robe deepened to black in the starlight. Her face, however, was exposed to the brightness and shone with a silvery sheen. She shivered slightly as if cold, but the night was warm, and the air was still and silent.

Without thinking, without speaking, La'am leaned toward her, pulled her closer to him, and kissed her slowly on her upturned lips. His eyes closed, as did hers, yet each could still see the other—could in fact see themselves as lingering shadows in the night. They drew still closer until they felt their radiating warmth even through the thick folds of their Makersrobes. Closer and closer, until Laral lay tightly enfolded by the curve of La'am's arm, and he felt an equal tightness across his back. Again they kissed, long and sweetly—and the patterns within them that had once been Makers of Omne applauded in joy, fell silent, and retreated.

Only Iam'Kendron remained. He was there for an instant, formed the Words of Joining in La'am's mind and in Laral's, waited for their wordless responses...then, silently, also withdrew.

* * * * * * *

It was not quite dawn when La'am rolled onto his back. His eyes sought out the mysteries of the stars, and noted that their patterns had rolled slowly across the sky.

Something touched his cheek.

Laral's fingertips.

"I had seen you before, you know," she whispered. These were the first words either had spoken for hours, yet they seemed as inevitable as if they were part of an ongoing conversation. La'am knew immediately what she was saying.

"I know."

She continued as if he had not responded.

"Years ago, while I was still a child, I dreamed you. I saw your face, your eyes. I heard the music of your voice. I knew that I would know you at once, anywhere, if ever we met.

"And then I became Rhiama, Joleckan-word. I forgot my childhood dream. I had become an Acolyte to a Maker. My life was no longer my own, nor did it include the possibility of love. So my dream disappeared, and I never thought of it again. In time, I even forgot the memory of it.

"When I first saw you in the Council Palace at Los'ang, I did not recognize you. I felt attracted to you somehow, but I could not explain why. Do you remember the day the Strangers arrived?"

In answer, he tightened his grip on her hand, knowing that she would understand that as an affirmative.

"Do you remember my watching you," she continued, "as you stood with the other Makers on the steps of the Cantorium? I was studying you. Suddenly your face had become familiar, but I could not recall where I had seen it before or why I should remember it. I thought about it...about you...for many days and still did not remember the dream.

"When we met again at World's End, the remembrances welled up even more strongly than before, but I still could not place them. I knew you as one of the Makersraad, nothing else. Only now, here on the Pillars of Beginnings, where all of Omne first had life, have I remembered that dream.

"So you see," she said, laughing lightly, "we have really been one for much longer than either of us have realized. I was the figure in blue of your dreams; you were the face and the form and the voice in mine. It just took us all of these Cycles to re-discover ourselves."

"And the Words of Joining have made us one," La'am said. He tried not to think about how their joining would be greeted by the Makersraad. Two Makers thinking, behaving, loving, being in all things as one would undoubtedly alter the entire functioning of the Council. On the other hand, the words of the Makers echoed within. La'am remembered Iam'Kendron and the Words of Joining, and knew that no matter what the Makersraad might think, their Joining was correct and complete and perfect.

And necessary.

Because after this night, La'am thought, looking up again at the stars, and after the day that is to come, the Makersraad and so much on Omne will be forever altered. This is but the beginning.

The night died without the two Makers being fully aware of it—or of anything except each other. Then suddenly the eastern border of the sky flared long arms of scarlet and pink that swept within the stars and extinguished them as they wheeled inexorably toward the west. La'am and Laral stood side by side to watch, entranced by the newness of the spectacle. The eastern sky gradually brightened, then the first sliver of the returning sun crested the Veil of Heaven. Unlike the darkly red sun that had settled in the west the night before, this eastern sun was new, fresh, vibrant, and glowing with energy and heat.

When it was fully risen, La'am spoke.

"We must hurry now. This revelation is great and wondrous, but it is not the whole. There is more that we must know. Come."

Laral opened her mouth to reply and to re-affirm her commitment to La'am's quest, when a third, unanticipated, and wholly strange voice breathed through the morning air.

"Welcome, my children. Welcome home."

It was not a mentrans pattern resonating through them. No, this was a *voice*. It was real, human, vocal, wavering through the air. Yet it was not all-powerful or all-consuming, as the ritual implicit in the night just passed might have demanded. The voice was gentle, patient; it sounded slightly amused at the Makers' surprise.

"Welcome, my children, to the Place of Beginnings. We have waited long for you. Come."

La'am and Laral turned toward the voice. They saw a form, undefined and vague. It shimmered near an opening in the cliff. They walked toward the light. The light disappeared into a cave. Without hesitation, the Makers entered the darkness, just as the light-figure had done. Their robes, which had been transcendently bright in the full light of morning, continued to glow but now through their own inherent powers. The blue Makerslight guided them along a smooth-walled corridor hollowed out in the Pillars.

The passageway continued for what could have been a mile or more, level most of the way but occasionally dipping downward for a few feet. The two Makers walked easily on the smooth rock. They did not speak, but they held tightly to each other's hand—not out of fright but out of an over-powering sense of unity and mutual understanding. They were, in fact, one being inhabiting two bodies.

They had no idea how long they spent in the passageway—it seemed alternately like moments and hours. But finally the passageway opened to form a immense cavern, brilliantly lit with blue-white fires. The walls sparkled, polished to a resplendent smoothness beyond La'am's vividest imaginings. Clear crystals embedded in the living rock fractured the blue light, as they entered, showering La'am and Laral with prismatic glory in precisely the colors and intensities that now appeared in La'am's robe.

In the center of the cavern stood the form they had followed—the light they had followed, really, since they could see through it. It...the form—whatever it was—pulsed and shimmered as if alive. No, not *as if alive*. It *was* alive. It spoke for the third time.

"Welcome, my children. I am Jamison. Or rather"—here the two humans were strangely aware that the voice had taken on a distinctly humorous tone—"I am what remains of Jamison. His consciousness, if you will. His essence. Perhaps his soul."

"His patterns," La'am added.

"Yes, you would define it thus," the voice answered. La'am felt sure that if the light had been corporeal, the head would have been cocked, the eyes narrowed in slight surprise at La'am's comment. "You have learned well, my children. I welcome you here, to the womb of Omne. I have been waiting for you."

"For us? How...?" La'am began, then cut himself off. The light-being was too far beyond La'am's experience for him even to conceive of relevant questions. He waited for the voice to continue.

"I have been waiting for...what?...a thousand years—Cycles, as you call them now." Almost to itself, the light-figure added, "I must remember to use the new words."

Again, the Makers felt the self-confident laughter embedded in the voice. The tone was an uncannily human expression of buoyant laughter bubbling below the surface yet filtering through the awesome solemnity of the voice, as if the disembodied speaker had just made a joke and was waiting to see—and judge—their reaction to it.

"Of course," the voice continued, "I have not been waiting for you two personally. We did not know precisely how events would turn out, nor how long it might take for you to discover us. But I have been waiting for someone, or should I say some two, who were finally ready.

"A thousand ye...Cycles, waiting for the children to grow up...." Jamison's voice trailed off ruminatively, then resumed. "But this does not answer your questions, nor mine." The voice shifted to more formal, nearly ceremonial registers. "I am Captain Jamison, Master of the *HomeSearch,* discoverer of this planet, and founder of the Council of Makers. Who are you? What are your names?"

La'am stepped forward.

"I am La'am, Master of Makers on Omne, Master Maker of the Pillars of Beginnings, Iam'Kendron-word, Davian Charl'an-born of the Northrill Vale." His voice bounced oddly from the crystalline walls. It was his but subtly not his.

Jamison made a small sound; La'am define it as a verbal equivalent of a nod of acceptance. In turn, La'am bowed toward the light-figure.

Then Laral spoke, with equal confidence and force.

"And I am Laral, Master Maker of World's End, Joleckan-word and Freyma-word, Rhiama Petran-born of the Eastern Ranges—now wife to La'am of the Pillars." At her final words, La'am tingled with an unexpected pleasure.

Wife. Husband. One. So they would be defined.

The light in the center of the cavern dimmed slightly as if to reduce the brilliance reflecting from the walls. La'am and Laral could now see additional spots of light scattered through the chamber. These new lights seemed similar to the Jamison-light—less intense perhaps, but similar. Jamison apparently noticed the Makers' quick glances about them.

"These are my memories, my aids. These are the others who have preceded you to this spot and who have joined me in waiting. Still others await deep within this mountain. Our lights are our substance, our essence, our reflection of the greater....

"But that must wait. For now, you are seeing all that you are capable of receiving and understanding. The greater Light must wait." The voice broke off. For a moment, it seemed as if La'am and Laral were suddenly alone in the vast cavern. They did not move. They did not speak. They could wait upon the Light.

"I..., we have been waiting for so long, that now I am reluctant to begin," the voice said after a timeless pause. "Nevertheless, let us proceed."

The light moved slowly toward them, until it hovered within inches of their faces. La'am thought he could dimly perceive the form of a face within the light, but the image quickly passed. Then another light was next to him, its movement so gentle and unassuming that he scarcely noted it until the radiance was less than a yard away. He turned slowly to peer deeply into the shifting colors of the light.

And saw....

Heart lilting in the joy of recognition, he started forward. The light dispersed, like the merest soap bubble on Seed Time air, leaving renewed emptiness, softened now by closeness.

As La'am turned to speak his joy to Laral, Jamison's voice broke the spell.

"Come into me. We have much to learn of one another."

CHAPTER THIRTY-TWO

Captain Haardt paced nervously along the far wall of the former public room of the High Magister of Omne. It was now the third day since the death of Jorik and the flight of the Master Maker La'am. In the intervening days, Haardt had meticulously consolidated his strangle-hold on Omne. He now controlled the entire Makersraad. The surviving Makers were closely imprisoned in the lowest chambers of the Magistry. The rooms were not really dungeons; he had quickly discovered that here were no prisons worthy of the name anywhere on the planet. But the chambers were windowless enclosures nonetheless, where the movements of the Makers could be monitored. It took only a few hours to rig up electronic surveillance along the corridors. His most trusted men were guarding all the entrances and exits, as well as the individual doors. His orders were explicit—and were being followed to the letter. There would be no communication among the Makers. Their apprentices, with the exception of Jorik's Ky'lan, were locked in their own chambers elsewhere in the Council Palace. Ky'lan lay unconscious in a room in the Magistry.

Even more importantly, Haardt thought, he had effectively destroyed the power of the Masters by the most efficient and most permanent tactic possible—death. The Master Makers had been utterly shattered. Jorik had been killed. Jabeth had been executed. And La'am....

Haardt paused in his nervous pacing, then resumed. That was the real problem, Haardt knew. That was the source of his nervousness.

What of the third Master Maker? Where was the instigator of all the trouble he had faced in the past three or four days?

No one had seen him since the episode on the beach, when he had attempted to kill one of Haardt's men. Haardt's most competent trackers had failed to locate any signs of the man. Finally, all Haardt could do was to dispatch landers and scouters to each of the outlying Sanctuaries, first to pick up and bring all of the Makers back to Los'ang, then to destroy the repositories themselves. Without records, documents, artifacts—Haardt hoped—the Omnans would be more tractable. Without the constant physical presence of those leftovers from a legendary and distant past, these troublesome rumors about mythical messiahs might be more easily silenced.

And, Haardt realized, the show of force involved in destroying the Sanctuaries might be an effective object lesson. Not that there was any danger of an organized resistance. He stifled a snort of contempt for the sheep that surrounded him. The peaceful, almost uneventful surrender of the Makersraad was a case in point. Not one Maker had so much as breathed an objection to being transported back to Los'ang. They had been without exception quiet, tractable, cowed by the superior force and martial knowledge so obviously at Haardt's disposal. He had half expected at least some outbursts of rage or anger, but his men reported no such occurrences.

To all appearances, then, Haardt was the undisputed master of the entire planet. The chief of the Makers was dead. The Makersraad was effectively silenced. The High Magister a pliant boy, easily manipulated. And as a consequence Haardt felt no need to fear any individual or group remaining on Omne. These natives were too firmly entrenched in their beliefs and in their absolute reliance on the Magistry and the Makersraad to even conceive of independent action.

He stopped pacing again. His face darkened and he struck his palm against the stone wall. The stinging cleared his mind and helped him focus.

He was the master of Omne.

Except for La'am.

Haardt shook his head.

"That bastard won't fade away into the wilderness and wait patiently for death," he said to himself, striking his hand a second time against the wall—as the stone were the living flesh of the Master Maker La'am. "He's out there somewhere, plotting something. But where, and what?"

The Maker would act, Haardt knew, and would do so precipitously, without warning, and in ways totally unknowable to the Ex-Serv. Haardt knew firsthand that there was more than legend to the Makerspower. His man was still blinded, although the medics' report sitting on his desk across the room placidly assured Haardt that the loss of vision was temporary. Streiter, however, had undergone a radical personality alteration as a result of his experience; the man would be unfit for any further service once Haardt returned to his home base. And Streiter had been a good man.

Haardt cursed silently.

Then too, Jorik had threatened Haardt with the same blue fire. Haardt shook his head in physical negation. He refused to take parlor tricks seriously as a weapon of force, especially against trained ExServ men. He had been surprised, without preparation. But his own weaponry had carried the day. Jorik was dead and was no longer a threat.

But La'am was also a Master. He wore the blue robe. And he was loose on Omne. Haardt had had each of the imprisoned Makers questioned by Corcoran—an effective man, although tending sometimes to more softness than Haardt could quite countenance. Yesterday, Haardt had personally interviewed the three Corcoran had recommended for further interrogation. Haardt was satisfied that two were ignorant of any knowledge of La'am's whereabouts. Jeriam of Towerwatch was merely truculent, but Corcoran had wisely assumed that hidden knowledge might have been at the bottom of the Maker's abruptness and sullenness. The second one, Kaleb of the Lesser Pillars, had been passed on to Haardt because he had seemed particularly nervous. Haardt approved of Corcoran's meticulousness, but again, the trail died. Kaleb was the newest member of the Council and had apparently undergone a number of traumatic experiences since his former Master died. He was by nature timid. His nervousness was easily attributable to the unsettling circumstances he suddenly found himself in.

Haardt crossed the room again and dropped heavily into the chair behind his desk. He picked up a paper and scanned it, toying with its edges. Abruptly he crumpled the sheet and flung it across the chamber. It struck the wall and fell to the floor.

Jathanan.

Jathanan of Harborwatch. The third Maker Haardt had interrogated. She was another matter entirely. He had immediately recognized her stubbornness and strength. He felt the aura of command about her when she had entered. She had walked into his presence confidently, insolently, in fact—not as captive before her conqueror, but as a queen before a commoner. Her attitude had surprised Haardt. She certainly did not have any of the physical qualities that might have justified such an enormous sense of self. She was old, to be sure, old and wrinkled and care-worn. But Haardt was certain that she had never been more than plain at best. She had never been sought for her feminine charms. Her features were raw, angular, sharp—too strongly defined to fit anyone's definition of softness and compliance. Coupled to that was the fact that she was the Maker of one of the smallest and least prestigious Sanctuaries, if Haardt's understanding of the seniority in the Council was as accurate as he supposed. She had no family, no close friends. Even her Acolyte seemed distant and reserved in speaking of her. She had no obvious source of power among the Makers of Omne, other than the bare fact of her age and her biting tongue.

She had been less than prepossessing, too, in the formless gown Haardt had provided for her from the ship's stores. After the execution of Jabeth and the imprisonment of the others, Haardt had ordered the Makers stripped of their robes. He was not superstitious, not did he believe that the robes themselves carried any occult powers. But he knew that the robes were potent symbols of power on Omne. The male Makers had been issued loose jumpsuits, while the women had been given draped and entirely unflattering short dresses. Before, the Makers had seemed, to be blunt, more than a little awesome; now they were merely ridiculous. Except for Jathanan, they wore their new clothing self-consciously. But she seemed unaware of her clothing, her imprisonment, or her helplessness when she swept into his presence.

"What do you want of me?" she had demanded as soon as her guard thrust her into the chamber. Haardt had been startled; she had taken the initiative from the beginning. "Why do you disgrace me by summoning me to you?" she asked before he had a chance to answer her first question.

Haardt had not responded immediately. He leaned back and studied the old woman. She did not speak again. She returned his stare with her own; her eyes challenged him in ways that had brought better men than this old bitch to their deaths. Her face remained expressionless, except for the sharp glint of hatred in her deep-set eyes. Corcoran had been right, Haardt decided. The harridan knows something, and she is confident because of that knowledge. She dares me, baits me, even knowing that I could destroy her with one word. She knows something.

"Jathanan of Harborwatch," Haardt began, pausing after the title. The woman nodded fractionally in response. He took that as a small sign of victory.

"Where is La'am?"

She gave no answer. She did not move.

"Do you know where he is?"

Again, silence.

"Do you have any idea where he might have fled?"

Again.

Haardt leaned back in the chair and smiled. He was rather enjoying the challenge. He had become angry once before in front of a Maker, and the results had brought about this entire mess. This time he was in control—in several meanings of the word—and he would get the information he wanted.

He reached into a side drawer in the desk. Her eyes flickered to follow the movement of his hand, then snapped back to his face. He pulled out several items, one at a time, and laid them on the polished wood of the desk top. As he spoke, his fingers rested lightly on two or three of the items.

"Old woman, you have no idea what I hold here, do you?"

She still did not move or signal an answer in her expression, her eyes. She remained as coldly silent as the stones of the Magistry. But then, Haardt reminded himself, he had expected nothing else.

"I won't tell you the names of these," he said, almost casually, "since you would not appreciate the subtlety of the horror embedded in the words. Let me instead tell you what they are capable of doing." Watching her reactions closely, he did just that. He explained the functions of neural whips, of cell disrupters, of brain scramblers. His voice moved with dispassionate coldness from pain to mounting horror. The woman remained impassively still, however, with not even a widening or narrowing of her eyes to indicate that she had registered the information. He completed his grisly catalogue.

"I am a master with each of these weapons, as are several of my men. In my hands—or theirs—these instruments kill, maim, and torture, as I command."

His voice took on a harshness he had carefully kept control until now.

"I could rape you—or have you raped, which would be infinitely more pleasurable to me—torture you, kill you so slowly that each second would seem an eternity. These powers are at my disposal. I have used them when necessary in the past. Believe me, old woman, I *have* used them." He pushed them to one side of the desk and leaned forward to face her directly. "I do not want to resort to such primitive means of gaining information, but be assured that I will if need be.

"Where is La'am."

Jathanan waited for a moment, then answered with a long, mocking laugh that was bitter and cracked with age.

"Captain Haardt," she said, infusing scorn into both the name and the title, "do you honestly think you can frighten me with your little stories of pain and murder? Do you think that I can be intimidated into talking—even if I had anything to say—by the sight of a row of strangely fashioned lumps of dead metal?"

She held up her right hand and shook her head slightly, as if in interruption of her own words.

"Not that I do not believe all that you have said. I believe you." She stepped toward the desk and laid a thin finger on the shiny surface of one of the items. "I believe with all my soul that this could reduce me to a whimpering idiot in less time that it takes me to speak this sentence." She touched another one. "Or that this could destroy my mind completely, leaving my body, such as it is, untouched. And I believe that you would treat me as you have threatened if you felt that you would thereby gain what you wish.

"But I also believe..., no, I *know* that you will do none of these things." She turned her back on him and walked over to a low bench beneath the window. She lowered herself into it with the patient care of age. She smoothed the ugly gown across her legs and drew herself up, as if she were presenting herself before royalty. Only then she looked at her interrogator.

"Excuse me if I sit. I am old and tired. But to continue. You will do none of these things, will you?"

Haardt felt clots of rage forming in his throat. He would show her, he would order the guards to..., no, he would take the neural whip himself, in his own hands and right here, right now, in this chamber, he would....

But he did not. He remained seated. She sat across from him, studying him, calm and self-assured.

"Why will I not?" he finally asked when he felt he could trust his voice.

She looked at him, piercing him with her eyes. "For two reasons. The first is simply that you are not the kind of man to inflict pain for the pleasure of doing so." She paused, raising one eyebrow. "That I should say such a thing surprises you? Captain Haardt, you are ruthless and cunning, that is true. You are insensitive and cruel. But so far, every action you have taken has furthered your own aims and purposes, no matter that they have destroyed us or disrupted our lives. You may in fact be evil, according to our morality and our traditions, but I doubt that you are so according to your own. I do not credit you with any nobility of purpose or dedication to any causes other than your own personal well-being. But neither do I accuse you of a perverted pleasure in giving pain. Had you wished to do so, you would have used those things on me, instead of merely telling me about them. Surely you must have realized that a woman of my years would have little fear of death, regardless of its form.

"As for forceful violation of my person...." She shrugged her thin shoulders and half smiled. "Believe me, the act would be as nothing to me. I do not assent. My mind refuses to accept the act. My body would undergo a temporary inconvenience, that is all."

Haardt blinked rapidly. "And the second reason?" he asked.

"Obvious," she said, in a tone that suggested that even a child should know something so rudimentary. "You have no way of knowing when I speak the truth. I could babble for hours about La'am's probable plans, about his hiding places, about his destinations—and you would have to dispatch men to every point I mention, on the slight chance that one was the truth. Oh, I know that you could torture me and ultimately force me to put aside any lies and speak directly and truthfully. And I know that you would use torture if it became necessary.

"But to do so would not be to your best interest. You know by now that the Makers have developed certain..., uh, abilities..., powers, if you like. They stem from our minds. We can withstand much more than you would expect. How could you tell if my anguished revelations were truthful or merely carefully staged acquiescence to your tortures? I am, you know, capable of doing a superb acting job if my world depends upon it—and it does!"

The last words split the air, venomous and irrevocable with threat. Haardt moved as if to speak, but her voice cut him off.

"You are angry at me, and you fear me. Well, think one step further, *Captain* Haardt. You came in one vessel. It is a large one, to be sure, and well complemented with men. But do you have enough men to search every hiding spot on an entire planet, to investigate every tear-filled cry I might utter—and still post guards about your own encampment, about the doors to our cells, and about the Council Palace. Do you have enough men that you could still carry on your insidious operations in the rhiam fields. How thinly can you spread yourself, and yet remain even marginally effective?"

With a smoothness and an abruptness that left Haardt speechless, the old woman rose from her seat in a single fluid motion that gave the lie to her groanings and creakings about age, and swept to the door.

"I will leave you now. Your guards will, I am certain, escort me safely back to my prison."

She turned her back on Haardt, thrust the heavy door open with her stiffened palms, and walked through the open doorway.

"To her cell." Haardt ordered crisply, struggling to regain command of the situation—and still not quite sure when and how he had lost it.

* * * * * * *

Jathanan marched down the ancient corridors, her heart throbbing and her knees so weak that she thought they would give out before she reached the lower chambers. She willed her body not to, and concentrated all of her energy on keeping up the façade of power she hoped she had created.

She barely noticed the corridors they passed through, or the increasing darkness as her captors led her deeper and deeper into the confines of the Magistry. She felt another sudden flood of weakness. She wanted desperately to stop and lean against the damp walls; she needed to shake uncontrollably until her body had rid itself of the overload of tension and fear...and relief. It had been close, but her estimation of the man had been good enough. Her plan had worked. He would now be so concerned with her and with her responses to his demands that he might, just might, delay taking further action. Every hour, every minute, every second that Haardt sat silently and confused, wondering how much a certain old woman knew and how best to drag that information from her, improved the boy's chances of finding the solution. He might even make it to the Pillars of Beginnings safely. Careful not to let any emotion show on her face or in her movements, she smiled to herself.

Oh, the lies she had told in there just now! If Haardt ever found out how thoroughly he had been gulled....

Suddenly she wasn't as weak or as tired as she had thought. She led her guards briskly to the room they had chosen as her cell.

And her tomb.

* * * * * * *

But Haardt was not thinking of reprisal. As soon as Jathanan left the room, he felt an inconspicuous snap in his head, as if a thin cord connecting him to someone...something...else had severed. He stared at the closed door, reconstructing the abortive investigation. He had found out nothing, while she....

What had her real game been, he wondered? She was right, of course. He would not carry out his initial threats, because now he was certain that she *did* know something, and that she was capable of resisting him to her last breath. She could tie up men he could not afford to expend in following false trails and digging out nonexistent messiahs. She had him, he thought morosely, and she knew it.

That last perception was the most dangerous thing about the entire interchange. The woman must be watched closely. Haardt touched a small button on his belt.

"Corcoran."

"Sir?"

"Transfer the Maker of Harborwatch from her present cell to one on the far side of the building, as far away from the other Makers as possible. Treat her firmly but properly. See to it that she speaks to no one, not even the guards as she is transported. I want at least three locked and monitored doors between her and any of our men. No one is to see her, enter her cell, or in any way contact her alone. At least three must be present at all times."

"Yes, sir." Corcoran's voice betrayed no surprise at the unusual orders.

An hour later, a written report of the transfer had been delivered to Haardt's desk.

* * * * * * *

That had been yesterday. The intervening night's sleep had been restless and disturbed by unremembered but distressing dreams. Now, a day later, Haardt remembered the encounter as almost a dream itself. He could not believe that the old woman had so completely dominated him. What could he have been thinking of in letting her live.

He stood up abruptly and strode toward the door. She was fully as dangerous as this La'am. Perhaps more so, since she was older and more experienced, even if her robe was yellow instead of blue. He was in the act of reaching for the door when a sharp rap sounded from the other side. Startled, he stepped back a pace. Then he stopped, returned to his desk, and forced himself to answer calmly.

"Enter."

Corcoran slid through a narrow opening. His face was flushed. He clutched a scrap of paper in his hand.

"A message from Southern Patrol, sir."

Haardt looked at the man. Corcoran was excited and had obviously read the message.

"Give it to me."

Haardt scanned the scrap. The message was terse: a blue-robed Maker had been seen near the mining operations in the southern plains. The scouts reported that three of the ExServ men were following the Maker into the nearby forest. His capture was imminent. The message stopped there.

Haardt pursed his lips thoughtfully.

"Anything further?"

"No, sir."

"The Maker has not yet been captured, then?"

"I don't know, sir. I brought this to you as soon as I received it. Perhaps an additional message has arrived by now."

"Check it out."

Corcoran activated his communicator and spoke briefly with the ship. "Nothing, sir. We will contact the southern patrol for more information."

"Good," Haardt said. "Do it." Corcoran disappeared through the door. Haardt turned his attention to his desk. He shuffled through a number of papers there. Reports on the mining operations—satisfactory for a beginning, but they must be expanded as much as possible in the next few weeks, in order to allow sufficient results and still have time to mask the evidence. There were reports on the status of the two largest settlements, Los'ang and Heartland—some vague suggestions of unrest, but nothing one armed man could not handle. Reports on the histories of the Makers and of the High Magister, as nearly as the information could be gathered—they contained nothing beyond what Haardt had anticipated. A formal request by Panraak for an interview with Captain Haardt. Haardt slapped the paper down onto the desk—the officious little man was beginning to prey on Haardt's nerves. He wondered vaguely what the problem was this time. Panraak could be counted on to bring up a triviality.

Corcoran returned, entered the room silently, and approached the desk.

Haardt looked up.

"What is it?"

"The ship cannot raise the southern patrol, sir?"

"What!"

"They can get nothing but static, sir, as if a scrambler were operating near the lander."

"That's impossible!"

"Yes, sir. But that is what the ship reports."

Haardt would have spoken further, but just then a crisp buzz sounded. Corcoran bent over his communicator once again. When he faced Haardt a few seconds later, his face had drained of all color.

"Sir, the computer-miners have been destroyed."

Haardt opened his mouth but could not speak. Corcoran continued.

"Their memory banks have been short-circuited, as was the main memory bank on the lander. The patrol leader managed to make emergency repairs, enough to send a request for rescue and aid. But he says that the Maker escaped and that operations in their sector are completely stopped until repairs can be made to the computers."

"La'am," Haardt said, "that bastard." But underneath the anger, he felt almost relieved. The blow had fallen. The man had revealed his hiding place. Soon now, Haardt would have him.

"Get me the Maker of the Eastern Ranges, what's her name…."

"Joleckan, I believe, sir."

Haardt nodded. "She's closest to the south. We'll see what she has to say about this."

Corcoran stepped outside, relaying the order to the guard. He started back inside, only to stop when the communicator buzzed again. When he straightened, he rushed into the room.

"Sir, additional messages are coming in. All of the computer-miners, everywhere, are malfunctioning. None of the landers seem damaged, but the mining operations have come to a standstill. Everywhere. At first, the patrol leaders thought that localized malfunctions had occurred, but then they discovered that all of their machines were out. *All* of them. One called the ship, then another, and another. The memory banks of the miners are out entirely."

"What about the Maker?"

Corcoran whispered something into his communicator.

"Escaped, sir. Our men followed him through the forest for a while, lost him, picked up the trail again, then lost it. He appears to have fled to the shore. There was a heavy fog there, and our men could see nothing, sir."

"He has wrought better than he knew."

The unexpected voice echoed through the chamber. Haardt jerked his head up to see Joleckan of the Eastern Ranges standing in the doorway. Just as Jathanan had been the preceding day, Joleckan was garbed in an unflattering gown. She carried herself with none of

Jathanan's regality, however. She looked as bluff and plain as any peasant woman. Her skin was coarse, her hair thick and gray and tangled. Her hands, clasped tightly in front of her, were broad and worn. Even from across the room, the blunt fingers and thick knuckles were obvious. Had Haardt seen her under any other circumstances, he would probably have written her off as little more than a farmer's wife, a country drudge. But here, now, confronting him within the stone walls of the Palace, she seemed to radiate danger.

"What do you mean?" he blurted out, without thinking that since he had summoned her, he should have spoken first. Then he swore to himself. Damn, now she has me on the defensive also. How do they do it?

"La'am," she answered. Her voice was sweet with pleasure at his anger and frustration. "He seems to have severely disrupted your operations."

"No such th...."

She interrupted him, her voice now harsh and flinty. "He has destroyed your machines, not only in my Eastern Ranges, but throughout Omne. That much I overheard. I do not know how he did it. Perhaps he does not know himself. But the important thing is that the Makers have stopped you, no matter how temporarily, no matter how trivially." She nodded her head. Her gray hair moved in disheveled swirls on her neck and shoulders. "And," she continued, "this is of course but the first of many such disruptions."

Haardt started to respond to the challenging tone, but abruptly altered his strategy. It was time for him to take the offensive.

"Where is La'am?"

"I do not know," she said simply.

Haardt was almost surprised by the forthrightness of her reply. The timbre of her voice persuaded him that she spoke the truth. Why could not that witch of yesterday been as honest?

"What do you know of him, then? Of his whereabouts?" Haardt asked.

"Little. He was near the Eastern Ranges—or at least on the plains to the South. Since the lapsing of the Makerseat there, the plains have belonged in name to the Eastern Ranges. They are part of my responsibility. I have felt him there. Do not ask how I know," she said, cutting of a question forming in Haardt's throat. "I know. The Eastern Ranges are *mine.* Little happens there without my being aware of it. And certainly something as portentous as the presence of the Master of all Makers would claim my attention."

"How...," Haardt began, then something the old woman said sunk home. "The Master of all Makers?" he repeated. "What are you talking about? There is no such thing."

Joleckan seemed to enjoy herself. She gave the impression that she was nothing more than a harmless gossip, full of juicy tidbits to be shared, settling back in a comfortable chair, although she remained standing stiffly before the Stranger. Her hands, still clasped, did not move.

"You didn't know, then, did you," she answered. "I thought not. I don't even know if the others know yet. Jathanan might. But if she does, you will never find out from her. You have tried, I trust."

She seemed to enjoy the momentary expression of frustration that escaped Haardt's control and flitted across his face.

"But I will tell you anyway," she said. "Like all members of the Makersraad, I can sense the presence of the other Makers, particularly when they enter my own territory. I don't expect you to believe that. To you, our claims must sound like merely so much superstition. You are, of course, free to deny anything I say. But I can sense a Maker. Nothing can deny that. I felt it when La'am landed on the southern coast yesterday. And I knew that he had been altered. I do not yet know what he is, but he is already far beyond my powers, probably beyond the powers of any in the Council.

"I warn you, Captain Haardt, for your safety and your life, to beware of him."

She ceased speaking. Again Haardt had the distinct impression that she would have enjoyed her triumph more had she been seated before a roaring fireplace, surrounded by half a dozen toothless crones.

"Where is he now?"

"I don't know."

"But you said...."

"I said that I could sense him in the Eastern Ranges. He is no longer there. He left shortly after he arrived, within a day. By sea, I think. I cannot think how else he could have escaped along that the coast."

"Where would he head?"

"I don't know."

"Why would he have landed there in the first place?"

"I don't know that either, unless he wanted to visit the ruins of the Makerseat of the Two Isles, which he did in fact visit. Other than that I can help you very little. He was there; he is there no longer."

Haardt glanced at Corcoran. The officer had been listening intently. He might have some ideas later from the woman's comments. Haardt walked slowly back around to the opposite side of the desk. He hesitated for a few seconds before sitting down, then looked up.

"Why do you give this information so freely. None of the other Makers would speak to me of it. Jathanan threatened me, in her own acerbic way, when I demanded from her what you have just given me. Why?"

Joleckan looked content, serene and quiet. A thin smile played over her lips, but she sighed deeply before speaking.

"I told you these things because.., because I am of the old and will find no place within the new."

"Explain yourself."

"Jathanan is older than I, yet in some ways she is much younger. She is strong and durable. She knows well how to adapt. One living in the isolation of Harborwatch must do so, or the tedium will lead to insanity." Her voice took on a distant, echoing hollowness that startled Haardt. "Likewise Jeriam of the Tower will survive, I think. His mind is solemn, always dwelling on portents and signs. In what is to come, he will see the culmination of his visions. He will live to see his darkness transformed into light. So it is with the others, most of them. Old Jabeth would not have survived. You yourself fulfilled that prophecy.

"Nor will I. My Sanctuary is destroyed. My Acolyte wanders lost in the wilderness and I can no longer feel her life. I have lived all of my Cycles in the Eastern Ranges. I did not want to be a Maker, but the call is irresistible. One has little choice. I have served as well as I could and, I think, have done good for many. But I will not survive. When the new comes, I will not see it."

"What are you talking about woman," Haardt asked, frustrated to find himself again, unaccountably on the defensive. "No one is going to harm you. What is this nonsense about?"

"Still talking of nonsense, are you? You will learn. You see, I am no longer necessary to Omne. Somehow, my powers are being—or will be—assumed and surpassed by another. I do not who, or when, or how. But I know that I am no longer needed.

"As for what I have told you...none of it was new to you. Your spies had already ferreted out much of it, and as for the rest, well, you will learn it yourself far sooner than you would have wished." She sighed again. Her eyes seemed glazed, almost unfocused—or rather, focused on a spot above, behind, and beyond Haardt. He knew that if he turned to look in the direction of her steady gaze, he would see nothing. He shuddered.

"I am tired, tired and unhappy," she said. "To continue like this would be torture beyond anything you could inflict. Therefore, I will not survive. I so choose."

As she spoke, her shoulders drooped. For the first time since she had entered, her hands dropped to her side. She breathed a small sigh that was less speech than merely the emptying of old and tired lungs. Without a further sound, she slumped to the stone floor of the chamber and lay still, her face drawn and gray. Haardt leaned over the polished desk.

"Help her up. Get her out of here," he snapped at Corcoran. "I have had enough of this."

Corcoran darted forward and knelt down. He slipped his arms under Joleckan's bulk and lifted. The Maker was a dead weight in his arms. Suddenly frightened of what he already knew to be true, he pressed his ear to her breast and listened. He laid her head carefully on the stone floor and stood.

"She is dead, sir."

"What?"

"Dead, sir. She is dead."

"She did not want to live," Haardt said softly, stunned. "So she willed herself *not* to live."

He stood and walked slowly to the window facing over the water toward Los'ang.

One more dead. And he was no closer to understanding this peculiar people than he had been five minutes before. A strange people, he thought, and getting stranger with each passing day.

* * * * * * *

Half a world away, on a blackened finger of lava thrusting into the golden sands of World's End, a robed figure paused in her lonely journey toward the sea. She drew a sharp breath and cried out. There had been a single sharp, passing stab of pain just beneath her ribs.

It was there, then it was gone and almost forgotten. When she spoke with La'am later that night, Rhiama did not remember it even as sufficiently important to mention it to him.

CHAPTER THIRTY-THREE

Haardt's nights were getting more and more wearisome. He consistently slept poorly, then woke early—often the only thing he would see through his window was the hideous black blankness of the Veil of Heaven. He hated darkness, had hated it since he was a child. He no longer saw the creatures and shapeless terrors that had once haunted him during dark nights, but he hated them nonetheless. Especially here, on this hell-hole. On the *Wanderer*, there was always light...always.

If it were not for his reputation—and, of course, for the fortune he would glean for himself and his crew—he could have abandoned this planet to the ravages of some other privateer. Nothing except reputation and fortune could be sufficiently important to force him to remain.

On the morning following Joleckan's death, Haardt startled awake even earlier than usual. For the first few seconds of wakefulness, he lay unmoving, as if paralyzed. His face felt damp and cold with sweat. His heart raced so fast he could hear its violent thump echoing from the walls and ceiling. His eyes flew open, and he stared wildly at the stone walls. They were inching closer, he thought, closer and closer and suffocatingly closer. *And he couldn't move!* He tried to call for his adjutant but could not force the words out.

Then moment of panic passed as quickly as it had come. He flailed out with one arm, knocking something metallic from the small stand near the head of his bed. More slowly and carefully, he raised his other arm. His limbs would move again. He sat up. His body felt stiff, as if it had not been used in a long time. He touched the stud on his lamp and looked toward the window. Heavy hangings had been drawn across the abysmal nothingness beyond. He heaved himself out of bed, still weary and unrested. Soon, soon the mining would be complete....

Then he remembered.

Damn that man, he thought. Damn that blue-robed bastard!

The delays caused by the malfunctioning memory banks would take days to repair. The deadline for his report was drawing nearer, and for the first time in his career, Haardt felt himself losing control.

He breakfasted early, dissatisfied with the all-pervasive aftertaste of some native spice in the food. He thought of ordering a meal from the ship's stores then decided against it. There was nothing wrong with the accursed stuff as food, he reminded himself. His medics had examined it and claimed that the stuff—rhiam—was instead unusually healthful. He ate it, but he did not feel required to like it.

By the time the meal was over, he had worked himself into a mood of mild pleasure. The morning was beautiful where the Veil of Heaven lit up the sky with a play of unknown colors. And he had pinpointed a recent location for the remaining fugitive Maker. Today, he would....

His plans were interrupted by a timid knock on the door of the outer chamber that adjoined his sleeping room. Haardt strode into the outer chamber, crossing the large room with three strides. The adjutant had just opened the doors to admit Alisandr den Panraak.

Haardt stopped in the center of the room, half wishing that he could disappear back into the sleeping chamber. Of all the people on this planet, Panraak was probably the last one Haardt would have chosen to see. But he had no ready excuse to dismiss the man and he was feeling unusually generous, so he waved the man in, somewhat cavalierly to be certain, but he was sure that the little man would not even notice.

As a matter of fact, however, Panraak did notice, and his clear awareness of the Captain's ill-concealed contempt did not make his self-imposed task any easier. He shuffled from foot to foot as if building up the impetus to speak.

"Well, what is it?" Haardt demanded, his good humor vaporizing as quickly as had the earlier moment of panic. "I am busy today. Don't waste my time."

"Captain Haardt," Panraak said. His voice was pitched high, almost a squeak. He stopped, flushed, cleared his throat and began again. "Captain Haardt, it has come to my attention that you are engaging in..., well, shall we say, rather unorthodox methods of exploring and assessing this planet. Rumors...."

"What rumors," Haardt asked, more sweetly than Panraak might have expected—but then, the archivist did not know the ExServ officer well enough, even after the long flight to Omne, to recognize the danger signals.

"Well, sir," Panraak continued, apparently heartened by the mild reception he was receiving, "the men mention forays into the rhiam fields and burning crops. Sir, this sort of thing will surely enrage the native populace, since they depend so completely upon the crop for...."

Haardt lost his patience.

"Sir!" he bellowed, "I strongly urge you to stick to your own studies and leave me to tame this planet. I will do things my way, in my time, without any interference from you. Is that clear?"

"Yes, sir, but...."

"No buts. You are here on an official capacity for the Comity. Fulfill that commission and leave all else to me. What I do, I do of necessities far beyond any you might imagine. And what I do will make it far easier for the Comity to assimilate the material wealth of this world."

"I realize that, sir," Panraak squeaked again, "but that is precisely my concern. My job is to study this people, this culture." He ignored Haardt's snort of contempt. "This culture, I repeat. And frankly, I do not see how it *can* be assimilated. The differences are too great. We worship technology and deify metals. We apotheosize computers and conquests. We spread from world to world, remaking everything and everyone we find into our own image—and I am not sure that I very much like that image any more.

"But these people...they are innocents. They have no technology, no machines, no war. In fact, the words for those concepts simply do not exist in their tongue. I cannot sanction any actions which so endanger a native population as your do. Indeed, the deaths which have occurred in the past days have...."

"That is sufficient, Lon Drehmel." Haardt's tone cut through Panraak's words like laser through ice. The voice spoke of determination and stubbornness blended with anger and pride. "You may leave." Haardt turned his back on the archivist and disappeared through the door into the inner chamber.

"I...." Panraak started to remonstrate. Then, realizing that any further words were futile, he sighed and left. Once in the corridor and well beyond the guard stationed outside Haardt's door, he stopped and leaned heavily against the wall. He had tried to be reasonable. He had tried to warn Haardt. But Haardt had chosen not to listen.

That was Haardt's problem.

But in spite of what had just happened, Haardt could not be allowed to continue. Panraak had done what he could officially, as a member of the discovery team *and* as an official emissary of the Collegium. He had remonstrated, and his remonstrance had been met with the contempt and deafness he had anticipated. He had only one recourse, although to take it would be dangerous to him personally. But he could not stand by and watch a madman destroy a human culture that had evolved so perfectly and so completely over so many centuries. More was at stake here than a few grams of minerals. This was Jamison's treasure planet indeed, but not for the reasons that Panraak had first suspected. He had studied the ancient documents closely. If only half of what he had read was true—if only a quarter of what he suspected—then these people....

But now was not the time to speculate on what might ultimately and disastrously turn out to be more myth than reality. Panraak straightened, took a deep cleansing breath, and hurried along the corridors, scarcely pausing until he stood panting outside a thick black door. One ExServ man stood along side the doorway. He was not at strict attention, Panraak noted with some pleasure, but he was armed. Panraak took a moment to catch his breath, then addressed the man.

"I must see the High Magister. I have found some documents...." Panraak allowed his voice to trail off uncertainly. If Haardt's orders had not been changed since yesterday, that should be sufficient.

The guard looked down at Panraak, grunted, and moved aside. Panraak knocked softly on the door, amazed as always at the resonating boom his small fist made. A remarkable wood, this ranya, he thought.

The door opened to reveal an Omnan, although not the High Magister. Panraak did not know the man. His face seemed flushed, but whether from exertion or from anger, Panraak could not tell. The man did not speak. Panraak bowed.

"I am the Archivist Alisandr den Panraak. I wish to speak to the High Magister."

The Omnan started to say something, but before he could, Zeta'Om's strong tenor called out.

"Let him in, Brandt." The Magister's voices sounded strained, as if he were struggling to keep some strong emotion from spilling over.

The door opened wider to allow Panraak to enter the new quarters of the High Magister of Omne. The rooms were obviously not as spacious as the old ones now housing Haardt. The outer, public chamber was perhaps a third as large, and even to Panraak's untrained eye, the grain in the stonework was coarser, the finishing polish less lustrous and resonant. There was no stone latticework at the open window. And no woven hangings on the walls. But there was good lighting and the floors and walls were clean and smooth. He glanced at the young man standing in the doorway to the private chamber. Oddly, Zeta'Om seemed more at home here than he had in the more pretentious chambers several passages away, but his body spoke of tension. Panraak felt the sudden conviction that he had walked in on the middle of an argument.

Panraak bowed again.

"My lord, may I speak with you concerning...." Again his voice trailed off. The Magister made a small movement with his hand. Brandt swung the doors closed. The guard outside would not be able to hear now.

"Forgive me, sir, for intruding this early," Panraak said. "But I must talk to you of a matter of the utmost urgency." His face was tight with tension.

For his part, the High Magister found himself trying to stifle a smile. He liked Panraak, better in fact that he liked any of the Strangers. He was in awe of Haardt and recently had grown to fear him. But with Panraak, he somehow felt a common bond. And he enjoyed the archivists' obvious pleasure at unraveling the myths and lore of Omne, becoming more and more excited by what he had discovered each day from the ancient documents and artifacts. What would the little man want to talk about this time?

But Panraak's message was not humorous. It did not concern matters of interpretation of forgotten languages or arcane passages in books written by men long-dead. No, this time Zeta'Om found himself sitting straighter in his chair, his muscles tensing as the man related the details of his interview with Haardt.

Then the full consequence of what Panraak was doing sank in.

Alisandr den Panraak, of all people! The little man, the—what was the word Haardt used whenever the archivist was not around? Yes. The little *mouse* was apparently turning against its Master.

Zeta'Om wanted to interrupt, but Panraak's words were too fascinating, too enthralling. He was indicting Haardt as a cheat and a liar, a murderer, and an exploiter! All the doubts and questions Zeta'Om had felt before and tried to suppress now returned full force. He had tried to convince himself of the truthfulness of Haardt's claims from the first. But the deaths of Mord'am, Jorik, and Jabeth had confused him. He needed Haardt; he wanted desperately for the Stranger to be in truth the Wordsmith. Haardt had treated him fairly, as if he were truly an adult. They had spoken often of the power Zeta'Om would soon hold over all of Omne—and to a young, ambitious, perpetually frustrated young man, such promises had sounded sweet.

But beneath the promises, the doubts had remained. Now they were gaining in strength as Panraak continued. He spoke of things that brought fear to the Magister's heart.

Wholesale burning of rhiam fields in the southern plains and along the Highland Marshes? But had not Haardt already mentioned some small, localized explorations of the composition of the soil in the rhiam fields. To hear Panraak speak of it, one would think that Haardt intended on denuding every field in Omne.

And wild stories of Haardt destroying the Sanctuaries? Impossible! True, the Makers were presently staying in the Magistry, but only on the invitation of the High Magister. Haardt had explained that the Makers should be nearby in case the Strangers needed counsel concerning the ancient scripts. But the Sanctuaries themselves were inviolate; yet Panraak spoke of fires, of explosions, and of death.

"And now that Joleckan is dead…," Panraak said.

Zeta'Om's head jerked up, his own reveries destroyed.

"Joleckan?" he asked. "The Maker Joleckan is dead? How?" Suddenly he was on his feet and moving toward Panraak.

"I don't know. She was with Haardt and...and then she died. No one will say more." Panraak raised his hands in a gesture of helplessness, as if to say that he wished he knew more.

Zeta'Om turned away and walked toward the window. He placed his hands on the casement and lowered his head. He did not move for a long time. Panraak glanced quickly at Brandt, who motioned for him to wait, to be patient.

Zeta'Om had not left his own chambers since that frightful evening when Jorik attempted to assassinate Captain Haardt with the Makerslight. Jorik was dead—that Zeta'Om knew. And Jabeth and Mord'am. But Joleckan? And who else?

"Where are the rest of the Makers?" he asked without turning.

"Imprisoned in the lowest chambers of the Council Palace," Panraak said softly.

"Imprisoned," the young man repeated, lingering on the word as if he had never heard it before.

"And...," Panraak began. He fell silent.

Zeta'Om turned to face him.

"And what?"

"And, sir, Haardt has stripped them of their robes."

"Stripped...!"

"He has locked the robed away in another chamber and will not allow the Makers or the Acolytes to see each other, to speak to each other, to communicate in any way."

Zeta'Om's fist slammed against the stone wall behind him. Panraak's words rang true. Judging between truth and falsehood and recognizing truth had always been among the Magister's chief functions—and now, for the first time since the Strangers arrived, the High Magister forced himself to confront all of the things he had seen and heard. His mind made instantaneous connections that he had chosen not to make before. And he knew.

Panraak spoke truth. Which meant that Haardt did not.

Suddenly Zeta'Om stripped away all of the layers of self-deception and pride and fear that he had wrapped himself in for so many days. How could he have been so blind! He had believed everything Haardt said, he had remained immured within these walls like a child, swallowing the lies Haardt caused to be filtered down to him. He returned to his desk and sat down. His hands knotted where they gripped the wooden arm of his chair.

And still Panraak talked on—of increasing death, of devastation of Omne. And now Brandt's voice joined the Stranger's.

"It is as I have warned." Zeta'Om turned to face Brandt. He stared at the Cantorium singer as if he had never seen the man before. The cold, flat expression in Zeta'Om's eyes frightened Brandt, but he kept speaking. "I know little about such things. We in Los'ang hear only vague rumors from the outlying areas. No travelers have arrived for days, just third- and fourth-hand tales of tales. But even rumors have a kernel of truth; and the smallest kernels of what I have heard would still be impossible. Rolf," he said, dropping into the intimate diminutive that only emphasized more the naked pleading in the voice. "Rolf, listen to him.., to me.

"Why do you think I came here this morning? Don't you know that once I entered the Magistry, I became as much a prisoner as you are."

Zeta'Om started to say something, half-rising from his chair. Then he dropped back. Brandt continued: "I have heard too much—and this morning I have told you what I know, even though then you refused to believe it. We are all prisoners here. Believe me, Rolf.

What this man says is the truth—the bitter, unbelievable, impossible, but absolute truth. We must act."

"But how, Brandt, what can we do?" Zeta'Om refused to look at Brandt, and Panraak understood at once what the two had been arguing about before he arrived.

"We could escape into the city, warn the Singers, spread the word among...."

"But what good would that do. People would die—*Omnans* would die. The Strangers are armed and will kill. They have already killed. I shudder to remember Jorik...and to think that I could have accepted his death as just." There was a long moment of painful silence. "I do not know what we can do."

"But perhaps," Panraak's voice edged in quietly, "perhaps if you were free, you could contact La'am."

"What good could that do? He is only one, just as I am only one."

Brandt opened his mouth as if to speak, when the door burst open and the guard stepped in, accompanied by two more armed men.

"Singer Brandt."

"Yes," Brandt said.

"You are to come with me."

Zeta'Om was on his feet and heading toward the door before the guard could move. "By whose orders. And by what right? I and I alone command in the Magistry and on Omne."

"By order of Captain Haardt." The guard nodded to the man behind him, who seized Brandt by the arm and propelled him from the room.

"Brandt!" the Magister called.

"Remember!" Brandt had time to yell, then he disappeared into the darkness of the corridors.

The guard turned to face Zeta'Om. One hand rested lightly on the holster at his side. "You are to remain in your chambers."

Zeta'Om turned white with fury.

"I demand to speak with the Captain. I will not be spoken to like this in my own...."

"You will be silent and stand back, or I will force you to do so."

Panraak laid his hand on the High Magister's arm to restrain him. "It is best to do as he says, sir. Haardt will do as he threatens."

Zeta'Om cast a long look at the darkness where Brandt had disappeared, then nodded. His shoulders slumped for a moment, then he straightened. "But the matter does not end here," he said. He stared at the guard who, ignoring him, left the room. "It only begins."

The doors swung shut.

Panraak looked up at the High Magister. "I will do what I can for your friend, although that is a promise that carries little hope and great fear. But I will try. Please remain here. You are safer if you do."

Without waiting for an answer, Panraak opened the door and stepped through. The guard glanced at him and nodded, waving him on with a curt gesture of his hand. In the other hand, Panraak noted, the man carried a drawn weapon. The time for laxness had passed. Whatever Haardt had decided to do was now irrevocably set into motion. The crisis was coming—and with or without his planning it, Panraak suddenly knew that he would find himself in its focus. He had begun the movement toward this moment. Now he must try to bring it to as positive an ending as he could.

Without looking back, the little man hurried down the corridors toward his own apartments.

CHAPTER THIRTY-FOUR

The next day was unusually quiet in the Magistry. Anyone used to the normal functioning of the place would have immediately felt uncomfortable at the cold, watchful silence that seemed to radiate from the walls themselves.

But then, everyone who knew what the Magistry was like before the coming of the Strangers was safely locked away. The corridors were empty, except for Haardt's men, standing silent guard before secured doors or stationed at equally silent monitoring devices. The thick stonework swallowed the occasional sound of a crisply spoken order or of a single man striding along deserted corridors.

To all intents and purposes, the Magistry seemed dead.

Haardt remained in the rooms that had once housed the Magister. Speaking into a number of commlinks, he was busy coordinating the newly expanded mining operations. By working through the night, his men were able to repair the damage done by the rogue Maker, although they still did not quite understand what he had done or how he had done it. Even the best computer hackers on the crew were stymied by the multiplicity of changes the Maker had made to the deep-memory cores. In more than one instance, they had to dump the entire sequence of memories and off-load replacements from the few undamaged machines in the belly of the *Wanderer* that had not yet been deployed for mining. But however the technicians had managed it, the computers were again functional, and Haardt ordered even more men out in the landers and scouters, stripping the guards and patrols in Los'ang to the bone. Time was pressing hard on him. He had to hurry if he was going to harvest his fortune and still remove all evidence that it had ever existed.

But on the credit side, he now had the entire governing bodies of the planet safely under lock and key—or, in the case of La'am, neutralized in the wilderness somewhere south and east of the capital. From there, he would be able to do little to circumvent Haardt's plans.

The rest of the Makers, those still living, remained imprisoned. Their guards reported that several had somehow received word of Joleckan's death. None had spoken of it directly to their captors, but one or two of the guards had overheard quiet references to the dead Maker, and at least two of the remaining Makers were refusing food or drink—apparently grieving for the dead. Jathanan had neither moved nor spoken for over a full day; she simply sat cross-legged on the floor of her cell staring at the wall. She had been so since shortly after the death of her fellow-Maker, but the man posted outside her door had sworn up and down that no one had entered, that no message could possibly have been sent to her. He had been summarily replaced.

The breach in security bothered Haardt, since his orders had been explicit: all of the Makers and their Acolytes were to have been kept strictly incommunicado.

Still, it was a minor breach, nothing to worry about.

Inside the various cells, the imprisoned Makers and Acolytes kept their own council. They caused no problems. In fact, they were so silent that the lack of sound only added to the overall eerie sense of the place.

The Singer Brandt sat just as quietly in his cell, a windowless cubicle somewhere near the waterline of the Magistry. He had been led down several flights of steps, and the corridors they passed through were increasingly damp and musty. His guard had thrust him into the room and slammed the door shut. He had heard the metal grating on metal, and assumed that he had been locked in. He did not try the door to see if it was secure.

On a narrow ledge built into the outside wall, he found a small length of candle and a match. He lit the candle. It gave out enough light for him to see the moisture glistening on the walls, and in one or two places the mortar had disintegrated almost completely. He studied the room for a few minutes, until he had it captured in his mind, then he blew out the candle. In the darkness, he crossed to a low cot—the only piece of movable furniture in the room—and lowered himself onto it. The cover was damp and smelled of mildew but he paid no attention to that.

Since then, he had neither seen nor spoken to anyone. Twice he had been fed a reasonably decent meal of rhiam cakes and thin wine, and several times in between, earthen bowls of water had been slid through a rough slit cut in the hardwood door. Once, when the panel sealing the slit was removed, he caught a glimmer of light on metal and decided that the bowl had been pushed through the small opening by someone using one of the Stranger's weapons.

Apparently, he was not going to be starved or tortured. Yet.

For the rest of the time, he sat in darkness. He concentrated all of his training and his memory on trying to gauge the passage of time, and on working out ways to out-think and out-maneuver Haardt—the latter more an exercise in futility than anything since he had no illusions about his ability to escape or in any way combat Haardt directly.

So after a few frustrating hours, he shifted unconsciously from planning strategies to doing what he knew best and did best. He began reciting the chants and lays that he had spend his adult Cycles learning. Once he forgot himself sufficiently that his voice carried through the thick wooden door and he was interrupted by a sharp banging and a muffled voice that said, "None of that. Quiet in there." After that, he sang almost inaudibly, pitching his voice so that it died out before it reached the middle of the small room. There were no echoes, not even to his sensitive ears. Hour after hour, he sang and remembered and, somewhere deep inside, he concentrated on strengthening his resolution to escape...somehow.

The High Magister Zeta'Om remained cloistered within his chambers. The guard outside his door heard nothing and saw nothing. As far as the man could tell, the room was empty. He did not know when the High Magister rose from the chair behind his desk where he had been sitting for hours, and walked into the private room. The guard had no idea when the High Magister stripped himself of the nondescript day-robe he was wearing and, naked, fell to his knees on the stone. When the guards changed at nightfall, neither knew that the Magister was still on his knees, lost in an agony of weeping that lasted for the entire night. Only when First Light filtered into the sleeping chamber did the young man move. He stood, stiff and hurting. His knees were bleeding from being pressed into the stone for hour upon hour. His legs threatened to buckle under him, and once he almost fell as he crossed the small room and carefully washed, using the bit of water left in his basin from the day before. He toweled himself off with the day-robe, then dry-eye and resolute he opened his wardrobe and reverently removed the flawless scarlet robe of the High Magister of Omne. Haardt might have taken the Maker's robes and locked them away, but he had not removed Zeta'Om's. Yet. He cinched the robe closed with a length of undyed rhiam cord.

Had the guard standing outside his door looked into the High Magister's eyes at that moment, he might have kept his watch more cautiously.

* * * * * * *

The second day of the internal siege of the Magistry was virtually a mirror-image of the first. Word had arrived just after First Light (about the time Zeta'Om was robing himself) of the success of the renewed mining operations. Haardt began to unwind slightly. He allowed himself to release some of the tension that had been building in him for days. He was firmly back in charge. The rogue Maker had made no attempt to destroy the restored machinery. Nothing was interfering with the mining operations. All of the computer-miners were working perfectly. The prisoners were quiet and clearly under his control. His word was law, entirely and utterly, throughout the planet, even though, he admitted to himself, public notices were still issued in the name of the Makersraad or the Magister.

And true, the rogue Maker still had not been sighted. But what was one man against the might of an ExServ ship, fully weaponed and poised for battle?

Haardt did not worry about the only other fugitive from the Makersraad—the young woman who had once been the Acolyte of Joleckan of the Eastern Ranges and who disappeared on the day the Sanctuary there was destroyed. Nor did he suspect that as he sat comfortably in the former chambers of the High Magister, that the Maker and the Acolyte had arrived safely at their destination, the Pillars of Beginnings, and were studying intently the unclimbable cliffs.

When night finally fell, La'am and Laral were still isolated on the narrow strand of white sand; Captain Haardt, on the other hand, had settled down for sleep. This time, he hoped, without the interruption of dreams. The heavy drapes hid him from the blankness of night. Within the chamber, a single power torch glowed dimly.

Zeta'Om was not sleeping, nor would he *this* night. It had taken him most of the day to remove the masonry. He had worked quietly and slowly, always alert for any sounds from the guard beyond the door of the outer, public chamber. He chipped away at the masonry carefully, using a thin ranya strip that he had worked loose from the decorative edge along the side of his desk. The wood was old and time-hardened. It was as strong as metal now, and quieter when he probed the thin layer of masonry on the back wall of the sleeping room. He cracked the masonry away bit by bit, letting it drop into the basin. When it was full, he carried it to the window and dumped it, grateful that this wall overlooked the water and that the currents today were swift. The bits and pieces of white cement disappeared almost immediately. When the basin was empty, he returned to the wall and began chipping again.

There was a streak of white dust on his red robe, but he simply brushed it away. Normally he would not perform such labor while wearing the ceremonial robes of the High Magister, but this time, he told himself again and again, what he did was not merely labor. For the first time since his Installation, he was acting as the Magister of Omne. He was working to save his people and his world. And he would do so as befit a High Magister.

The old passageway had been plastered over long Cycles before Zeta'Om's birth, but he knew of its existence from old documents and floor plans that he had been forced to study as Ranulf Mathomson, just as he knew of every passageway, chamber, and hidden niche in the labyrinth of stone that was the Magistry. After all, the building was his heritage. After the first few flirtations with youthful rebellion, he had studied intently and with great pride.

Initially, he had been hampered by the lack of any tools appropriate to the task. His nails broke against the stone-hardened lime, leaving thin streaks of blood that quickly dried from red to brown. Nor were his wooden eating utensils appreciably better. They shattered and splintered almost immediately. He had tried one thing after another, searching the sleeping chamber and even thinking about dismantling the bed itself before he remembered the loose strip of ranyawood on the desk.

He had pried it loose. Part of it broke off with a sharp crack that echoed through the room. He froze, his heart in his throat, and waited for the guard to throw the door open and come in to investigate the noise. Nothing happened. After a full minute, Zeta'Om allowed himself to relax enough to slip silently into the sleeping chamber and begin probing at a thin crack in the masonry, high up, near the lintel of the blocked off doorway.

The High Magister worked quietly but quickly and effectively. Slowly, the outline of a squat door appeared on the smooth wall. And even more slowly, the long-hidden wood of the door was scraped clean. Twice he was interrupted when Strangers brought in meals. Each time, he was able to brush himself clean and emerge from the sleeping chamber before the men came into the inner room to find him. Neither time did the guards speak to him, or even look at him except to make sure he did not try to wedge his way past them and escape. He took care not to come too close or to give them any reason to be suspicious of him. As soon as they were gone, he ate a handful of cakes and returned to his work.

The opening was cleared before daylight died, but even so it was several hours after nightfall before Zeta'Om dared to try the door. He could tell from examining them that the leather hinges were dried and cracked. They were caked with lime dust, but they had held through the Cycles. Finally, when he hoped that the Magistry would have settled down to rest, he slid back the wooden bolt and pressed his palms against the heavy wood. He pushed.

Nothing happened.

He pushed again, putting more of his weight into the movement.

Still the door did not move.

He stepped back and studied the panel. The wood fit closely into the stonework. With his naked eye, aided only by a dim light from a lamp, he could barely see the crack that separated wood from stone. Perhaps the mortar had infiltrated the cracks as well, in effect welding the door closed. He slid the bolt back and forth several times, making sure that it was disengaged fully, then pressed his shoulder against the panel and pushed.

It gave. Just an inch or so, but it moved. The leather hinges creaked, and for a moment Zeta'Om was afraid that one would split. But it held. He leaned harder against the panel.

With a long drawn-out, creaking sigh, the door swung inward, revealing a vacant blackness—the passageway the High Magister had sought. He stepped inside and pushed the door closed. It would not close completely, which was perhaps just as well. There was no bolt on this side, and Zeta'Om did not want to risk being trapped in the narrow corridor. From here, he knew, he could in time reach any point in the Magistry. With luck, without being seen.

He had brought no light. He needed none. He was the High Magister and this was his place. He touched the closest wall with his fingers. Patterns formed inside his mind. He closed his eyes, closing out everything external that might distract him, and focused on the patterns.

There. That one. Still with his eyes closed, he began moving along the passageway.

His first stop was obvious. He wanted—needed—to find Brandt, but he did not know where Brandt had been taken. Panraak might, however. And Zeta'Om knew precisely where the archivist was quartered.

* * * * * * *

It was disconcerting to awaken to such total darkness, Panraak thought as he lay in his silent chamber, even after these weeks on the planet. Back home on Auricus, there was always *some* light. The stars, the moon—ah, the lovely golden moon of Auricus. Or city lights reflecting mutely on an occasional passing cloud. Everywhere, there was always at least a flicker of light. He considered the memories longingly, pleasurably, lingeringly. Auricus was not like this world, he decided for the thousandth time.

Panraak lay still on his bed, his eyes closed. He was caught midway between wakefulness and half-asleep and was absently wondering what had awakened him. He was unaccountably certain that he had not just drifted up out of sleep, although he could remember nothing specific. Certainly now it was quiet enough. But there must have been something to rouse him from the sleep: a sound, perhaps, or a smell, a distant echo. Something. He waited patiently.

He was almost asleep again when it came again. It wasn't much. Just the faintest scrape of stone on stone, coming from somewhere near the head of his narrow cot. He twisted his head until he was facing the source of the sound, but he still could see nothing.

He waited.

The sound repeated itself, this time continuing for a few seconds longer. The sound of stone against stone, moving slowly.

Assassin! was his first thought. Then he realized that there was no one on this world who would need to resort to surreptitious murder. Haardt would simply have him arrested...and as far as he knew, he had nothing to fear from the natives. He seemed to get along well enough with them.

"Who's there?" he finally asked, keeping his voice low.

"Zeta'Om." The answer was so soft that he could barely hear, softer even than the noise that had alerted him.

"Wha... what do you want?"

"Help me. Quickly."

Touching the switch on his torch as he moved, Panraak rolled his legs off his cot and stood. He saw nothing except what he had seen when he went to sleep earlier that night: a small room with a cot, a wooden wardrobe, a desk and chair in one corner, both covered with documents and records and notes and files. And a worn tapestry on one wall. That was where the sound was coming from. He slipped toward it, his naked feet cold against the stone floor.

With a shaking hand, he thrust aside the ancient, threadbare hanging. In the darkness behind it, he saw a thick black line marking the place where one portion of the wall had separated from the rest, opening into blackness. Midway up the line was something lighter, pale and moving. The High Magister's hand was clenched around the thick bulk of a stone doorway. A secret passage, Panraak breathed to himself excitedly. Then he forced himself to calm down and assess the situation coolly. Of course. Given the configuration of this building, with its thick stonewalls and meandering passageways, there *had* to be secret passages.

Panraak leaned toward the door and pressed his own fingers through the narrow crack and pulled. Regardless of who had constructed the passageway, or when it had last been used, the truth was that the panel refused to move more than a few inches. Panraak braced one foot against the solid wall and inserted both hands into the cleft, pulling until he felt as if his shoulders would separate from his body. On the other side, he heard small sounds as the High Magister apparently bent all of his strength to moving the heavy panel as well.

A wisp of air curled around the door. It smelled old and musty, damper and cooler than the air in his room. It carried the dankness of centuries-undisturbed moistness and mildewed earth.

Then abruptly, there was a small *snap* somewhere and the door gave way with a grating crunch. Once it began moving, it moved smoothly, as if the massive construct of stone and mortar weighted no more than a feather. Panraak leaped out of the way as the stone slab swung inward. He looked quickly to see what kind of hinging apparatus had been used, but in the dim light of the glow-torch, he could see nothing.

He started to speak, but the High Magister swept rapidly past him, a dusky red blur in the dim light. Panraak whirled on his heels, but already the High Magister was at the corridor door. He paused only long enough to call over his shoulder, "Where is Brandt?"

Panraak gave the directions to Brandt's cell as quickly as he could, speaking in a hoarse whisper. When he finished, the young man nodded.

"I know the place," he muttered. "Are you guarded?"

"No," Panraak said quickly, then added, "At least I do not think so."

"Good."

The High Magister opened the door cautiously, listening and watching. There were no guards. As the two men stepped out into the corridor, Panraak brought the door quietly to, lest anyone chance to pass by and notice that his sleeping chamber was empty.

Zeta'Om knew the passages of the Magistry by memory. Without hesitation, he took Panraak along a series of twisting, convoluted, narrow and obviously little used passages. They saw no one, passed no one. More than once, when the entered areas of absolute blackness, Panraak followed the sounds of the Magister's bare feet slapping softly against stone. But neither of them stumbled. It was only a matter of ten or fifteen minutes before they stood in a shallow doorway a dozen yards further down the corridor from Brandt's prison. One ExServ man stood guard over the barricaded ranyawood door. He was armed, Panraak noted, but not particularly alert. He was slumped against the wall, on his feet and awake but not expecting any danger.

The two men watched for a moment. They had to get rid of that man somehow, but quietly and quickly. Unarmed as they were, they both knew that they could not afford an alarm.

"I'll try to get him," the High Magister whispered. "Wait here." Even as he began to move, however, hoping to surprise the guard and overpower him before he could communicate with any other of the Strangers, the High Magister felt Panraak shoulder past and burst into a run. Zeta'Om grabbed to stop the archivist, then withdrew into the shadows. Let him try, he thought.

It took a few seconds before the guard became aware of something moving down the dusky hall. Then he snapped upright, his hand scrabbling for the weapon at his side. He started to twist to face the unknown danger, and raised his weapon.

"Help! Help!" Panraak squeaked breathlessly. He seemed to recognize the guard, because he added, "Help, Monsara. Quickly, quickly! They've attacked the Captain! He needs help!"

The guard opened his mouth to question the intruder, but Panraak gestured wildly up the hall.

"No time! Run! Save him!"

The guard hesitated an instant more, glancing back at the solidly barricaded door twice before starting down the hall at a half-run. After a few steps, he broke into a full run, his feet pounding against the floor. He passed Zeta'Om without noticing the darker shadow within the shadow. In a few seconds, he was out of sight, and after a few more seconds, even the echoing tread of his boots disappeared.

Panraak motioned Zeta'Om forward.

"Hurry! I don't know how long he will be gone."

The High Magister reached the door in seconds, but Panraak had already discovered the heavy lock hanging from a gleaming metal hasp that could only have been installed within the past few days.

Panraak stared at the lock, then looked up at the High Magister. The archivist's face was pale, his eyes dark shadows.

"It's locked."

"Can you open it?"

"I have no keys."

The High Magister glanced up and down the passageway, as if he were pinpointing his location and reconstructing the route that had taken them there.

"Keep watch," he whispered.

He backed away from the door until he was pressed against the opposite wall. He spread his arms and legs, as if he were trying to cover as much of the stonework as he could. His robe flared behind him. He leaned his head against the wall and closed his eyes. For a moment, he stood motionless. Then his eyes began to flutter beneath his eyelids and his lips moved soundless.

Panraak's eyes darted up and down the corridor. He saw no one. He tried to concentrate on any sounds that would indicate that the guard was returning, but his attention was drawn inexorably to the High Magister. By now the man's face had drained of almost all color. His fingers were dead white in the pale light, and his naked feet looked as if they had been carved of snow-white marble. Except for the fluttering of his eyes and the moving of his lips, he could have been a red-draped statue.

Then Panraak heard words. Or rather, he heard sounds that should have been words but were not. It was as if his brain had short-circuited. The phonemes were Standard, the sounds of vowels and consonants were familiar, syllables fell where they should have, and the rhythms of what the man was saying were so familiar that Panraak felt as if he should understand every word. But he understood none of it.

The words grew louder.

"Shhh," he hissed, then stopped himself. The man knew what he was doing. Let him continue. And anyway, they had no choice. Without a key, there was no way Panraak could get into the room.

The voice grew louder and stronger, until it echoed up and down the passageway. Panraak's eyes widened and his breath quickened. He tried to watch both ends of the long passageway, knowing that now a brigade of hundreds could march metal-shod toward them and he would not be able to hear them.

The voice reached a climax. Zeta'Om abruptly tore himself from the wall, breaking contact with the stone, and thrust both hands directly in front of him.

The lock held solidly, hanging from its steel-alloy hasp.

But the door behind it disintegrated. The lock hung in the air for an instant, then clattered to the ground. It struck with a hollow clank that startled Panraak. He heard the sound as it echoed off the walls...and realized that until that moment, the passageway had been absolutely silent.

There had been no voice, except in his own mind.

"How...?"

"No time," the High Magister said abruptly.

Brandt stood waiting for them in the center of his room. He was fully dressed.

"I felt you," he said simply when the high Magister stepped through the doorway.

"Come," Zeta'Om said.

He led the two men hurriedly to a small alcove opening off the main corridor.

"Brandt, follow this corridor to the third branching and turn to the left. Go to the fourth room. In the far corner of the room is a small door. Open it and go down the steps. You will come to a small sea-chamber. My boat is there—you remember, the one we used to use out on the harbor on calm days. It is still in good condition. I have seen to that. Take it, and get to Los'ang as soon as possible. Alert the Singers and have them spread the word throughout Omne. We may not be able to withstand the Strangers, but we must try. We cannot sit idly by and watch them destroy our land."

Brandt hesitated.

"Hurry," the High Magister said. "We have no time to waste. Not even Haardt will be able to ignore what I did to the door."

"But you, Rolf. Are you not coming, too?"

"No. I am the High Magister. My ignorance and pride led to much of this disaster. There may yet be a way for me to avert more bloodshed. I will remain here and deal with Haardt as best I can."

"But Rolf...."

"Rolf would go with you," Zeta'Om said softly. "He would go with you and repay the love of a birth-friend with a lifetime of love. But the High Magister must stay."

Brandt started down the corridor. Panraak hung back, unsure of what he should do next. Zeta'Om placed a hand on the archivist's shoulder.

"And you, Lon Drehmel, you must go with Brandt."

"But I...."

"Haardt will blame you for Brandt's escape. The guard will report your presence here. Haardt may suspect me, but he knows that you have shown sympathy for us and for our cause. He might not kill you, but for now you would be safer outside the Magistry than within it. Go!"

The last words were spoken in a tone of command that neither Brandt nor Panraak could deny. Brandt retraced his steps and gripped the unhappy Panraak by the forearm, propelling the Aurican into the darkness.

Zeta'Om remained where he was for a few moments more, until all sounds of the retreating pair died away. They would escape, he was sure, although he did not know what good they could do. Still, it was worth the effort, even if only to remove Brandt from the danger that Zeta'Om's own stubbornness had placed the singer in.

He turned and proceeded cautiously back toward his own chamber, avoiding the main corridors and slipping from shadow to shadow. Far too soon, however, he began hearing shouts of alarm, cries of anger and excitement. He would have to hurry.

He returned to the hidden passageway through the side wall of a long-unused store-room where he and his brothers had long ago hidden from their tutors and played children's games. In the total darkness of the passageway, he followed the rough wall with one hand, counting branches and openings until he arrived at the proper one. He ascended a narrow stairway, its steps dusty and dry, then followed another passageway until he saw a glimmer of light. The door to his sleeping chamber was still slightly ajar, letting in just enough light to be noticeable. Zeta'Om's sensitive fingers trailed along the wall. When he reached the doorway, he searched the smooth face of the door for the hand grip, found it, and pulled.

A brilliant light flared in his sleeping chamber. He threw his hands in front of his eyes, blinded by the brightness. From behind the spiraling explosion of light and color, he heard Haardt's mocking voice.

"Welcome back, my lord High Magister."

Then the same voice, in a cold and infinitely threatening tone, said, "Take him to the cell."

CHAPTER THIRTY-FIVE

With the coming of daylight, Haardt allowed himself to relax a bit. In the preceding hour or two, the situation on Omne had altered, largely to his benefit. It was true that he had lost Brandt and Panraak, but the latter had been little more than an intrusive fool, certainly no threat to the ExServ or to Haardt's private mission. The man knew less than nothing about what was really going on and would be equally ineffectual as part of a fighting force—either Haardt's or the Omnans'. No, taken as a whole, Panraak was a cipher that could be ignored.

The other escapee, the Singer Brandt, was a greater unknown. He seemed to be a nonentity, a minor functionary from the city who was important primarily for his friendship with Zeta'Om. Haardt had alerted his men to watch for the fugitive but had taken no other measures.

The High Magister was now a prisoner in name as well as in fact. Even though Panraak had distracted the guard outside Brandt's cell, the Magister had obviously engineered the escape, although Haardt was not quite certain what the purpose of the attempt might have been or how the Magister had destroyed the door so completely without damaging the ExServ lock. No one had heard any sounds, either of explosions or of tools sufficiently powerful to have removed the door in the short time it was left unguarded. And there were no remnants of the door to be found immediately outside. Nor were there any marks of flame or heat or disrupters on the bare stone walls. It was as if the wood had simply disappeared. And that, of course, was impossible.

But there was nothing Haardt could do about unraveling that mystery right now. The Magister would not talk about how he had done it...of that much Haardt was certain. Since being taken into custody, the young man had not spoken a word. Haardt shrugged and turned to more immediate tasks at hand of securing his position and coordinating the mining operations.

Less than ten minutes later, he was interrupted. Corcoran knocked lightly on the door.

"Come."

The officer entered, carrying more updates on operations in the far north. Haardt and his lieutenant reviewed the reports and spoke unhurriedly for several minutes more.

The communications buzzer broke their muted conversation. Haardt depressed a switch, listened to a static-distorted voice, and surged to his feet.

"The courtyard," he said tersely as he strapped on his weapon and headed for the door. "Something is happening."

Corcoran fell in immediately behind the Captain. They passed through silent halls until they arrived at a huge chamber, perhaps originally an audience room of some sort, but one that Haardt had never seen used. The room was empty except for a handful of tapestries and thirteen thick wooden sconces set at irregular intervals along the interior wall. He crossed the room, his boots ringing hollowly on the stone floor. A single door opened from the room onto a long narrow balcony that extended along the Magistry, flanking the courtyard on two sides. From the balcony's height, one could not only overlook the Magistry courtyard but see beyond the low wall that surrounded the building and across the river to the city of Los'ang.

As soon as he strode onto the balcony, Haardt knew that the guards had been correct in alerting him. Something was dangerously wrong. Even the air felt thick with unnamed tensions; there was a restlessness about the place wholly at variance with what Haardt had become used to.

Half a dozen of his men were standing along the parapet, their weapons drawn, their eyes alert.

Haardt glanced across the river toward the town. He could see nothing unusual. Turning to the closest, Haardt asked harshly, "What's the matter?"

"We're not sure yet, sir. No one seems to know for certain. We have reports of mobs forming in the center of the city." The man gestured across the courtyard to where the Cantorium thrust above the rest of the buildings. Haardt squinted. He could make out a few figures on the Cantorium steps, but from this distance nothing more.

"The patrols have been in contact with us here," the guard continued. "There has been talk about the Wordsmith but...."

"So...," Haardt said, more to himself than to his man. He nodded as if in confirmation of something he had thought might happen. So that had been the High Magister's ulterior purpose. Brandt was a Singer of the Cantorium at Los'ang. How better to stir up the Omnans than to remind them of the prophecies of the Golden Age to come under the Wordsmith. Zeta'Om couldn't escape and do that himself, but he had released the one who could. Perhaps the boy was deeper than Haardt had given him credit for.

"The Wordsmith again," Haardt said after another moment or two. He had hoped that La'am's disappearance and the imprisonment of the remaining Makers would squelch the irritating superstitions. Instead, the opposite seemed to have occurred. And now the Omnans were moving, for the first time.

Looking across the water, Haardt could now see files of men and women streaming from the narrow streets and along the harbor toward the bridge leading to the Magistry. Hundreds of people snaked out of the city. Even this far away, he could hear the low murmur of their voices—angry voices, disappointed voices, frustrated voices.

"Shall we stop them at the bridge, sir," a voice behind him asked. There was only one way for the people to get to the Magistry, unless some few might be paddling across in primitive boats. Bar the bridge across the river, or the bridge from the Council Palace to the Magistry, and the natives would be unable to get any closer.

"No, not this time." Haardt made his decision quickly and intuitively. "I have an idea. Since we can't bottle this Wordsmith thing up, let's see if we can turn it to our advantage. Come with me."

Turning on his heels, he left the balcony.

* * * * * * *

The mob had thinned out by the time it reached the stone buttresses of the river bridge. Most of the men and women and all of the children had remained near the boundaries of the city. Only the chosen deputation from the Cantorium, joined by perhaps three hundred of the angrier city folk, forged ahead. They did so in spite of loud vocal protests by Brandt and Panraak.

"Don't you see, this is suicide?" Panraak called shrilly, striving to achieve by voice what had proven impossible through reason.

He and Brandt had arrived in Los'ang while it was still dark—an eerie experience for him, although the streets had been dimly illuminated by flickering torches. They had passed through the city unobserved by anyone, as far as Panraak could tell—certainly unobserved by the patrols Haardt undoubtedly had located there. Brandt had led them along a circuitous route that seemed to wander without purpose through the outskirts of Los'ang but that had finally brought them to the Cantorium steps.

Panraak had hidden in a deep doorway while Brandt disappeared into a nearby building nearby. While the Singer was gone, a small patrol of Haardt's men had passed within half a dozen feet of Panraak. He had shrunk back against the door, his heart thudding with fear. One of the men had glanced directly at him, and for an instant Panraak felt his body freeze—blood, breath, everything stopped until the man turned away and the rest of the patrol continued past without so much as pausing. Panraak shut his eyes, forcing himself to begin breathing again. A hand dropped onto his shoulder. Before he could yelp in surprise, another clamped over his mouth.

"Shhh," the Singer hissed in his ear. "Come with me. Quickly."

They scuttled across the narrow street. In the distance Panraak could see the last of the patrol turning a corner. No one looked back. He followed Brandt into another doorway and from there into a small, stark chamber. The walls and floor were of stone. There was one chair in the room. And one person.

"This is Hom'ar, the eldest of the Singers," Brandt said, gesturing to the old man seated on the chair. Since there was no other place to sit, Brandt and Panraak remained standing while Brandt related their experiences in the Magistry. As the young man spoke, Hom'ar had become visibly agitated, angered, and finally livid.

He rose from the chair and paced back and forth across the far end of the small room.

He had lived too long with the visions of the prophetic lays to see them perverted and abused, he said angrily. He would confront the Strangers at First Light. He would demand proof of their identities should they continue to arrogate the honors and rights of the Wordsmith to themselves. And should they fail to fulfill the prophecies in the least element, he would demand their immediate withdrawal from Omne.

"But don't you see," Brandt had pleaded, "that is precisely what the Master Maker Jorik attempted...and he is dead. They killed him while he stood before them and uttered words of power against them. You cannot try to force them. You do not even have the power of a Maker. And they have weapons we do not understand and cannot hope to stand up against. They will slaughter anyone sent against them. Please, Hom'ar. We must find another way."

Hom'ar turned sorrowfully to face Brandt. He could read the truth and the concern in the younger man's face.

"I understand what you say. But what I have vowed is *precisely* what we must do. Did you not listen to the words which you yourself brought to me from the High Magister. He remains in the Magistry to work against the Strangers as he must. I am a Singer; I must work according to my office. I am commissioned to preserve the Lore of the Wordsmith. If that Lore is being distorted and altered and destroyed, I must rectify it."

Brandt tried to speak but the old man held out his hand to forestall any argument.

"I know that I might die, Brandt," he said, his voice gentler now, the anger leached away, leaving only sorrow and compassion. "But I am old. I will die soon anyway. But for now I must act according to the traditions of my office and the expectations of Omne. To do otherwise would be to become one with the enemy we confront."

"If I deny my duty, how can I expect others to fulfill theirs."

He sat down heavily in the chair. Panraak started to speak but the old man stopped him.

"Please leave me for a time," Hom'ar said. "Take him to the preparation room, Brandt, and wait there until First Light. Then return here."

Brandt nodded and, taking Panraak by the elbow, left the room. They would wait elsewhere for the coming of light. In the meantime, the Singer of the Cantorium of Los'ang would study and meditate.

When they returned to the Singer's chamber a few hours later, Hom'ar was not alone. He was accompanied by most of the senior Singers. They stood in a single row around the perimeter of the room. Hom'ar was giving orders to the others, explaining what must be done, organizing them, urging them. He looked up as Brandt and Panraak entered.

"Punctual, as always, Brandt. I am glad that you are here. We have chosen those to accompany me." The old man gestured with his right hand toward the half-dozen men behind him. "We will speak with the Strangers. We will demand to meet with the High Magister, as is our right. And then we will take action as required by our knowledge.

"You, Brandt, and you, Stranger, may accompany us as far as the bridge. Then you will return to the Cantorium."

"But...," Brandt said.

"Then you will return to the Cantorium," Hom'ar repeated. His tone left no room for discussion. "Brandt, you are charged with the safety of this Stranger. And with the continuity of the Singers of the Cantorium of Los'ang, should we not return—which, I fear, seems likely. However, your duty remains the same in any case. The old Omne is passing; we all feel that and perhaps, even after all these Cycles of awaiting it, we regret it. But we cannot change it. Regardless what occurs today at the Magistry, our world is dead. We bequeath its remains to your care."

The note of finality—fatality?—in the old man's voice inhibited Brandt from speaking. He knew Hom'ar well enough to know that arguments would be futile. The Singer had spoken. Brandt would obey.

Panraak was less amenable as to what was about to happen.

"Wait," he called as the line of singers began to move. "Wait. You can't do this. I know Haardt. He is ruthless and cunning. He will not hesitate to kill you, if he feels it will advance his cause."

Panraak spoke for a few moments more, volubly, sincerely, convincingly—and entirely without success. He was, in fact, bluntly ignored. Without another word to him or among themselves, the Singers filed from the chamber. Brandt and Panraak followed close behind. As soon as they entered the street, they realized that more had been happening that morning than just a clandestine council of Singers. The streets were packed full of people but they were behaving strangely, at least as far as Panraak was concerned. They were obviously concerned. Their expressions, the way they held themselves erect and tense, their few muttered words—all suggested worry and fear. But there was no shouting. No overt anger. No mob scene that might break into violence at any moment.

Instead, as soon as the line of Singers passed, the people fell in behind them, streaming along the narrow streets. When they passed the first intersection, Panraak glanced both left and right and saw more people filling the streets that paralleled the one he was on. But still there was no shouting. He shivered.

After a block or two, the main group passed one of Haardt's patrols. The three ExServ men were standing close to each other on a corner, silently watching the people passing. None of the three moved to raise a weapon, and the Omnans in turn completely ignored the three Strangers.

"They will report to Haardt," Panraak whispered to Brandt as soon as they had passed the three. Brandt nodded. He seemed unconcerned. Whatever objections he had voiced to old Hom'ar's plans had long since vanished. Brandt was of Omne; he would play his part exactly.

Before Panraak was fully prepared for it, the procession had left the city and approached the bridge leading to the island of the Magistry. Before his foot could touch the bridge's stonework, however, a hand grasped his upper arm and held him back. As Hom'ar had decided, he was to be barred as well from stepping onto the bridge leading to the island. He did not struggle. That, he knew, would be useless. But as he stood silently next to Brandt, he did hug himself in frustration as he watched nearly three hundred men and women walk past him...to meet their doom.

* * * * * * *

When the Singers and those accompanying them passed through the great wooden gates that separated the Magistry from the bridge across the Harbor, they were not surprised to see a line of Strangers standing before the main entrance to the Magistry. The men were armored in metal, and armed as well, each carrying a small, deadly-looking tube that glinted harshly in the light. The guards seemed to be masked, with thin metal sheets covering their faces and most of their bodies. They stood as unmoving as the stones behind them, a jarring note of alienness in an otherwise totally Omnan scene.

One of the Strangers stepped forward. The Omnans shuffled to a halt, halfway across the courtyard.

"What do you want," the Stranger asked. His metal sheathing made his voice sound odd. It seemed higher pitched than the Omnans were used to, and it echoed shrilly against the stonework. The words carried no inflections that Hom'ar or the others could detect. To their ears, it was as coldly inhuman as the crashing of two rocks or the clash of waves against the shore.

"We wish to see the High Magister," Hom'ar answered. His voice was deep and resonant and challenging despite his age and blindness. A chorus of voices took up the call, until the courtyard resounded with the name of Zeta'Om.

From his hidden position in the massive central chamber, Haardt smiled tightly. This was precisely the response that he had counted on. Let the natives come running to their traditional leader, even though the young man was now entirely within the ExServ's power and a prisoner to boot. Even had the people below him known the full facts of the High Magister's imprisonment, Haardt thought sardonically, they would still have come bleating like sheep to the one they looked upon as their Master.

Haardt, Corcoran, and Zeta'Om waited for a few moments longer inside the open doors of the chamber above the courtyard. From there, they had seen the mob crossing the bridge, had heard the shouted demand and its echoing murmurs of concurrence.

Haardt measured the moments, listening to the rising cadence of demand. When the swell reached its peak, he spoke a single word.

"Now." As simple as it was, Haardt's word was a command. The High Magister faltered a moment before recovering his sense of calm. Then, his face as impassive as if it had been carved of stone, he moved toward the balcony. His scarlet robe of office swirled at his heels. At the doorway, the young man stopped for a moment more.

"Remember," Haardt whispered in a voice that he knew the young man would hear, "you life depends on what you say. And the lives of everyone here and at the Council Palace."

The young man did not move.

"Believe me."

The High Magister nodded fractionally, then straightened his shoulders and crossed the narrow balcony until he stood next to the parapet.

Haardt's smile broadened. That one understands the use of force, he thought. He will speak carefully.

The smile might have faltered, however, if he had known all that the young man was thinking.

Zeta'Om held his face expressionless as he faced his fellow Omnans clustered near the far end of the courtyard. He raised his hands, and the turmoil below fell away immediately. A deep silence settled over the Magistry.

I know what he wants me to do, Zeta'Om thought as he studied the intent faces of those below. I know what he want me to do, and I know what he will do if I fail. This Stranger thinks that he controls all of Omne, but he is about to learn differently. I know what is expected—demanded—by the Strangers...and for the first time in my life, I truly know what I must do."

Through the gracefully cut stone of the balustrade, he was easily in view of everyone crowded into the courtyard, as well as those massed beyond the stone bridge, although to the latter he would have been little more than a faint splash of scarlet against the gray of the Magistry walls.

He started to speak, but his first words were drowned out by an abrupt surge of voices calling his name. He raised his hands again, motioning for quiet, and waited patiently until the roar of voices again had nearly subsided. He could hear only a few individual voices crying out for answers.

"Why do they burn our fields?"

"Why do they rob and kill?"

"Who are they?"

"Who are they?"

Zeta'Om signaled again for silence. He realized at that instant that he was young; that he was inexperienced; that he was horribly frightened—of the men in the room behind him, of the people clustered below, of the voices that rang through his own memory and reminded him of his weakness and his failures.

But he was High Magister still.

He threw his arms open, as if trying to embrace all of his world. His red robe swelled with the movement, until it seemed two arching wings about to lift him from the solid stonework of the balcony toward the Veil of Heaven.

I might be the last of the High Magisters of Omne, he thought grimly and triumphantly. His Name insidiously suggested that such was indeed true—but he *was* the High Magister nonetheless, and in this place, he *was* Omne. Let the Makers muddle through in their Council Palace—or in their dungeons below me, he amended to himself—*I am the Master here.*

"Omnans!"

He felt his voice straining to make itself heard as far back as possible. The undercurrent of murmuring settled to almost nothing. No one moved. Not even the armed Strangers lined up threateningly, directly below him.

"Omnans, I know why you have come. I, too, have been concerned about our land, about the changes that have taken place since the arrival of the Strangers. I feel with you the confusion that such times bring, when the old must give way to the new. When the life we had is not yet dead, but the life we are to enjoy is not yet ready to be born. I know, I feel, I grieve—and yet I hope, indeed, I rejoice."

Still withdrawn into the shadows of the adjoining room, Haardt allowed his inward smile to touch his lips. The boy knew how to speak, he had to give him that much credit. So far things were going perfectly.

On the balcony, Zeta'Om continued.

"I have heard your voices crying for answers. I have felt your hearts aching for assurance. I have heard and I have felt. And I have looked into myself to search out the answers.

"And I have found them!"

The crowd surged forward a dozen steps. Haardt edged toward the doorway leading to the balcony, carefully remaining shadowed from the mass of people below but wanting to study their faces and gauge their reactions.

This was the crucial point, Haardt knew. The boy was in control now. But how long could he keep that control?

"You have heard of the Prophecies, of the Portents and Omens," Zeta'Om said, investing each of the key words with implicit emphasis. He had not raised his voice but suddenly it seemed to echo from every corner. "You have heard of earthquakes, you have heard of fires and of frosts. You have seen the blue fires of the Makers blazing from the Council Palace. And you have seen the silver ship descending through the Veil of Heaven to land almost on the steps of the Cantorium itself—and that on the Feast of Passing, the holiest day, the observance of the passing of the Wordsmith from this land.

"You, Hom'ar of the Cantorium"—the High Magister's pointing finger shot out as if to pinion the old man—"you attest to the truth of these things, do you not." The old Singer, standing with his head bowed in the front of the crowd, nodded mutely then raised his sightless eyes to meet his Master's.

"Yes, Magister," Hom'ar said distinctly. "I do." The words sounded like an admission of defeat. To accept what the Magister said as truth was to tacitly admit that the Stranger was the Wordsmith—and that the destruction of Omne was inevitable. One could not fight against the wishes of the gods.

Zeta'Om studied the old man for a long moment, then dropped his hand to his side.

"You have heard the rumors that the Wordsmith has come," he said. "You have heard the whisperings that all is now to become a paradise."

He paused long enough to let his words sink into the minds and hearts of everyone present. Several along the farthest edge shuffled nervously.

"What you have heard is true," Zeta'Om said softly. "He *has* come."

Silence cloaked the courtyard. It was a silence so deep and absolute that Haardt would have sworn he could hear hearts beating, breath inhaled and expelled from three hundred sets of lungs. The sequence of ideas Zeta'Om presented was not quite what Haardt had expected but it was more than satisfactory. Haardt straightened slightly, awaiting the cue that he knew would come soon. This boy was good! And more to the point, Haardt's plan was working.

"The Wordsmith is come," Zeta'Om said, shifting into a consciously archaic diction and structure. He felt himself growing taller, his robe fuller and moving voluminously with the breeze from across the Harbor. He did not raise his voice, but it was as if he could see his words flying beyond the walls and encircling all of Omne with their truth. "I have seen him. I have spoken with him. I have seen his powers, and I am afraid.

"I am afraid for what his coming will mean to each of us.

"I am afraid for the good things that must pass, for the happiness that will no longer flow unhampered through out lives.

"He comes, and he brings with him an End and a Beginning. We must work to make that Beginning a reality. We must work to turn to our advantage the inevitable pangs of birth. There will be pain. There will be danger. And there will be death."

The people in the courtyard waited breathlessly. Zeta'Om was no longer looking down at them. His eyes were bright and piercing, as if seeing beyond the limits of human vision. The High Magister was speaking Truth. And they waited for him to continue.

On Zeta'Om's part, he was as stunned as his listeners. He had intended to walk onto the balcony and condemn Haardt and the other Strangers as imposters. He would have died immediately; he knew that for a fact. But he had been willing to embrace death. Perhaps thereby he could make restitution for his ignorance and weakness.

But to his shock, he heard himself speak words he had not anticipated. And now he was seeing sights he had never imagined. Instead of hundreds of hopeful faces staring up at him, waiting for his final words, he saw a limitless vista of indigo surrounding a sphere of saffron flame...and before the flame, two silhouettes spreading their hands and, like the images of the Wordsmith worked in fading threads on ancient tapestries hanging in the Council Palace, opening their fingers to release the powers of life throughout Omne.

His final words came unplanned and unpremeditated but more true for all of that.

"There will be pain and death, my friends. *And yet there will also be great joy, joy beyond all imagining!"*

Haardt was surprised by the speech, but he was content. It would serve his purposes as well as what he had initially demanded the boy say. Taking the final phrase as his cue he strode stiffly onto the balcony until he was standing next to the young man. He sensed the tenseness in Zeta'Om, the quavering of breath in the boy's throat. The boy was highly wrought and, as far as Haardt could see, on the point of nervous exhaustion. The boy's hands were trembling uncontrollably and his eyes seemed fixed and glazed, staring straight over the wall of the Magistry. He obviously would not be able to control the crowd for much longer. It was time for Haardt himself to take charge.

"Hear him!" Haardt bellowed—needlessly, since there was not a person present who was not hanging on the words of the High Magister. "He speaks truth." Haardt's voice outstripped the High Magister's, billowing harshly over the heads of the crowd like the ominous storms of Dark Time roared over the Lesser Pillars to ravage Heartland.

"I am Haardt, whom you call The Stranger. That is but one of my Names. On other worlds, I have other Names; here I resume an Ancient One, long unused, but mine nonetheless. I am the W...."

"No!" The syllable tore itself from Zeta'Om's mouth. His body shook with the intensity of the denial. He scarcely registered the shock that flooded over the faces in the crowd, over the guards, over Haardt himself. The scar on the Magister's forehead burned hot and red and angry, and his right hand flashed in an abrupt cutting gesture that seemed to separate the Stranger from the Omnans he was trying to destroy.

"No," the young man repeated, pitching his voice to reach the Pillars of Beginnings, if such a thing were possible for a human voice. "He lies! This man is a murderer, a thief, not the Wordsmith. Wordsmith lives, comes, *is*. But this is not He. Wordsmith is...."

The blade was quick, silent, and effective, even though Haardt disliked such primitive weaponry, preferring instead the cleaner death offered by laser guns. The knife penetrated between two ribs, puncturing the lung before reaching the tissue of the High Magister's heart and carefully piercing it. The boy swayed drunkenly and started to topple forward. Haardt twisted the blade to lock it in place, then pulled backward. The High Magister staggered back until Haardt was carrying his full weight against him. The thrust would be fatal; Haardt was a master with a blade. There was still life, but only for a matter of moments. The boy would not be able to speak, but Haardt could use the silence to his own advantage.

"I am the Wordsmith." The claim echoed hollowly through the courtyard, roiling like filthy water through the air. Each word was spit out like a threat. Haardt stood on the balcony, the High Magister next to him, shoulder to shoulder with him. Zeta'Om's head drooped, as if to signify the truth of the Stranger's words and the acquiescence of Omne to the Wordsmith.

From the courtyard, however, a single voice returned the claim and coupled it with a challenge. Hom'ar of the Cantorium, blind master of Lore and faithful servant of truth, fulfilled his office as Singer.

"You lie."

The rest of the people took up the chant. They surged forward, bare-handed, angry, and frustrated. Someone reached down and dug a stone from the courtyard pavement and sped it unerringly at the balcony. It struck Haardt a glancing blow on the temple, stunning him. He stumbled backward. He lost his grip on the knife still embedded in the High Magister's back, and Zeta'Om slumped to the floor.

As if that movement were an unspoken command, more rocks hurtled toward the balcony. The guards lined up at the Magistry doors backed up, waiting for Haardt to give the signal to open fire on the mob. Dazed by the unexpected blow, Haardt struggled to drag the High Magister back into the chamber with him. He worked his way to his feet, pulling the High Magister up with him, as if he intended the dead-weight flesh of the Magister to serve as his shield. He took a step back toward the chamber, staggered under the weight of the scarlet-robed figure, and slipped on a stone made slippery by the Magister's blood. A knife-sharp shard of rock aimed at his head missed by a fraction, but instead buried itself in the forehead of the unconscious High Master.

Under the force of the blow Zeta'Om's head snapped back and his body toppled heavily, dragging Haardt with him to the cold stones of the balcony. Finally, someone from the hidden chamber—Corcoran, Haardt thought dimly—shouted a terse command, and the cold hissing of lasers filled the courtyard. Red lines of fire cut down the unarmed Omnans, slicing flesh, severing bone and tendon, fusing muscle to bared bone. Again and again the lasers sang out. Stones dropped from lifeless hands, adding their clashing clatter to the sudden cries of pain that rose from the courtyard.

Again and again the lasers spat death. One of the Stranger guards fell, struck in the mouth by a fist-sized rock. He fell backwards, his finger still depressing the firing stud. his beam traced a smooth arc upward, cutting a thin black-edged furrow in the granite of the balcony above him. For a moment he choked against the blood pouring down his throat and cutting off his air, then he convulsed once, twice. His weapon dropped to the stone. He died.

But he was the only one of the Strangers who died. Of the hundreds of Omnans in the courtyard, however, only a handful survived.

Above, on the balcony, Corcoran somehow reached Haardt before any of the flying shards of granite had injured the Captain too seriously. Gripping Haardt under the arms, Corcoran pulled him back into the shadowed room. Zeta'Om remained lying on the stones, pale beside the bright crimson of his own blood. He did not move. Haardt, on the other hand, revived quickly. In a moment, he sat up, throwing off the confusion of the stunning blow. He shook his head from side to side, then stopped when the pain threatened to make him pass out. He raised one finger and gingerly touched his temple where he had either been grazed by a second stone or had struck the balcony when he fell. A thin trickle of blood framed the left side of his face in scarlet.

He sat for a few moments longer, recovering. He seemed oblivious to the turmoil outside.

Gradually he rallied, though, and stood and walked shakily over to the doorway. Corcoran followed less than an arm's distance behind, as if he feared the Captain would fall again. From the inner edge of the doorway onto the balcony, Haardt could see most of the blood-stained courtyard below. Already the Omnans were, for the most part, dead or dying. A few had vaulted the high stone wall along the side of the courtyard in a desperate attempt to throw themselves into the waters of the Harbor. Perhaps they would survive by swimming to shore, although his men were already on the walls, firing sporadically at the fugitives. Still, the chances were good that at least one of the swimmers would survive, and then the news of this massacre would spread throughout the city. He raised his head and tried to focus on the distant press of bodies on the other side of the bridge. Observers on the shore might not have seen the actual fighting, but once the laser fire began and the cries of the dead and dying rose into the air, they could not be expected to take long to come to the obvious conclusion. Already the crowd seemed to seethe and boil, as if it were trying to come to some sort of decision—cross the bridge and confront the Strangers themselves, or take refuge in the City and plan their further strategy. In spite of the pain in his temple, Haardt could think clearly enough to understand that he would have to take immediate and decisive action to forestall any further violence or rebellion. From here on, he must be in complete control. He must rule with an iron fist or the entire mission to this god-forsaken planet would be delayed, if not destroyed. He would secure the place, even if he had to exterminate every native to do so.

But if there were an easier way, it might prove ultimately more effective, efficient, and, hence, profitable. And he would take it.

He turned, motioning Corcoran to his side. He was about to speak when the inner doors to the chamber swung open. Eyes wide with shock, his lips tinged with gray, his laser still drawn and his thumb not quite touching the firing stud but held ready, one of the guards Haardt had set to watch the entrances to the Magistry entered.

CHAPTER THIRTY-SIX

"What is it?" Haardt roared angrily at the man. He was still dazed slightly and in considerable pain. "And holster that weapon!"

Corcoran glanced quickly at the guard—a man named Milner, serving on his first mission with Haardt. Corcoran stared pointedly at the weapon and nodded. Haardt's blustering had threatened to send Milner deeper into shock. The man's arm had raised instinctively at the sound of Haardt's voice, and for a second it looked as if he intended to fire at the Captain. His thumb trembled next to the firing stud. Something in Corcoran's eyes, however, caught his attention. His gaze cleared and—suddenly struck by the insanity of what he was doing, Milner dropped his arm. His thumb slid slowly away from the stud.

"Out!" Haardt yelled, as if he had not noticed the man's actions. Perhaps he hadn't. Or perhaps in his own shock, the implied threat to himself simply hadn't registered.

"Sir," Milner said uncertainly. To Corcoran's eyes, he looked as if he had just awakened from a long and exhausting nightmare. There was a smear of blood along one sleeve of Milner's uniform. But as he spoke, the man stood a fraction straighter, Corcoran noted, and his hand, while still holding the laser, did not shake. "One of the patrols...," Milner started to say.

"What about it?" He seemed to be recovering as well. He put one hand to his temple, as if feeling for the pain, then pulled himself erect and faced the guard.

"One of the patrols from the town, sir. It has brought important information."

"And?"

"One of the Makers, the last one, La'am...."

"What about him?" Haardt's eyes glinted coldly in the darkness of the room. Corcoran could almost red the Captain's thoughts:

La'am—the one who had caused this entire cataclysm. The one who must be captured, interrogated, and, if necessary, executed.

The guard hesitated and for the first time dropped his gaze away from Haardt.

"Well, out with it," Haardt ordered.

"He has been...found."

"Where?"

The guard hesitated again. Corcoran could read lines of worry as they traced an intricate pattern across the Captain's face. Obviously the guard was in no hurry to report. He would have been if there had been a successful completion to a difficult assignment. Therefore....

"Where is he? Out with it!" Haardt thundered. His voice echoed through the large, empty room.

"In the Cantorium, sir."

Haardt didn't speak immediately. Instead, he turned to Corcoran. "Wasn't that place searched thoroughly?"

"Yes, sir. In fact, it was the first place we looked," Corcoran answered briskly.

"There must have been a secret entrance or chamber," Milner added nervously. "Because when the patrol took command of the Cantorium at the beginning of the troubles this morning, as you ordered, there was no one inside. No one. The patrol made certain of that. There's just that one big room at the top you know, and nothing inside except rows of benches and things. And...."

"Get on with it!" Haardt growled.

Milner swallowed convulsively and straightened. "Yes sir. Guards were stationed along the stairway near the street and at each of the corners. No one went up or down the steps, but...."

"Enough!" Haardt said, cutting off the embarrassed guard's explanation. "I don't want to hear excuses. Is La'am in custody?"

"Not quite, sir!"

Haardt's snort was an even mixture of pain, rage, and frustration. Corcoran tried to catch Milner's attention long enough to gesture that he should get to the point. But Milner saw no one except Haardt.

Would the fool never come right out and tell them what he had to say? Haardt clenched his teeth. Obviously forcing himself to appear calm, he continued: "If not *exactly,* then how?"

"He is in the Cantorium, sir. Of that there is no doubt. There are many witnesses...."

"I don't care about witnesses! Get on with it."

Finally, even Milner appeared to realize that he was straining what little remained of Haardt's patience.

"He is there, sir. La'am. The patrol reports that they can see him clearly. He is standing on the outer platform, in plain sight of any-one in the city. Suddenly, he was just standing there. The patrol can't explain it. The other one...."

"What other one?" Haardt focused part of the question at Cor-coran, who was the officer in charge of the prisoners.

"That's impossible, sir," Corcoran interjected. "All of the Mak-ers are under our control." He touched his breast pocket. "I have the keys to their cells and have checked with the guards not fifteen min-utes ago. None have escaped. None have left the Council Palace since the mob arrived here."

Haardt held up a hand. "Tell me, uh...."

"Milner, sir," Corcoran whispered.

"Tell me, Milner, how was this new 'Maker' dressed?"

"Like the other one, in one of those long robes. It was blue."

"No," Haardt said flatly. "La'am might have been seen on the Cantorium. But both of the other Masters are dead." He could have added "I know because I killed them myself," but he did not.

"Yes, sir. But there *is* another Maker. This one is a woman and she is robed in blue. The two of them stand just within hands-length of each other, staring toward this island. A crowd has already massed at the foot of the Cantorium. We need your orders."

"No orders," Haardt said. "I will take care of it personally. I will come myself. I will finish off this business today. Come on, Corcoran," he added, with a grin that, for the first time since the riot began outside, seemed to Corcoran to reveal the true Admant Haardt. "Let's go destroy a god."

Haardt brushed past Milner as if the other man did not exist. Corcoran paused long enough to whisper a word of encouragement to the man, then followed the Captain out of the chamber. Together, they passed through the corridors like twin shadows of death—one of them a particularly dark, silent, angry shadow. Haardt paused only long enough at the entry to bark an order to increase the guard on the passageways leading to the chambers where the remaining Makers were imprisoned and to post an additional guard on each of the bridges. With his remaining men—nearly fifty, well-armed, sea-soned to warfare on a dozen planets, and best of all unquestioningly obedient to his commands—Haardt rushed toward the river, the bridge, and the waiting city of Los'ang.

The crowd at the bridge pulled back as Haardt's men approached.

"Don't fire unless they attack," Haardt called, but the order was unnecessary. The moment Haardt set foot on the bridge, the mob melted away, opening a passageway for him to the city.

No, more than that. The mob disappeared. One moment they were there, rows of human garbage ten and twenty deep on every side. The next moment they were gone. Haardt barely noticed, however. His attention was locked on the Cantorium. From this distance, it towered above the low stone dwellings of the city. Haardt could already see two small brushes of blue alone the upper edge.

La'am and the other Maker.

Two *Master Makers.*

Haardt and his men swept unhindered past the bridge and turned toward the city. To all appearances, it was deserted. Well beyond the first rows of structures, into the streets that led to the heart of the place, however, he and his men encountered the first fringes of the crowd. He suddenly became aware of dense clusters of people at intersections, of people clotting the streets on each side of him. And with equal abruptness, he realized for the first time the sheer numbers of people involved, far more than the city should be able to accommodate. How this many people could crowd unnoticed into the rude buildings of the town amazed Haardt; there were thousands of them, lining every street, silent, waiting.

None offered any resistance, however, perhaps because of the weapons evident among the Strangers. Wherever they turned, Haardt and his men found open passageways that closed immediately behind them. There were no hints of any weapons or of any threats from the Omnans. But—and this startled Haardt more than he cared to admit, even to himself—there was also no suggestions of fear.

We just slaughtered hundreds of them, Haardt thought. We cut them down without mercy. Their king is dead. Their planet is ours. They cannot hope to fight against us. *And yet they show no fear.*

For the first time, his steps faltered. He slowed his mindless careening through the streets and began watching.

"Stay alert," he ordered. But the order was not needed, since everyone in the party had by then noticed the same things. The Ex-Serv men held their weapons to the ready and swiveled their heard from side to side, watching for any subtle hints of exploding violence.

An undercurrent of closely-reined hatred simmered through the crowd, but no hand moved overtly against the intruders.

Street through body-choked street Haardt and the ExServ advanced, until it abruptly struck Haardt that perhaps he was not advancing so much as being led. The way the crowds opened before him and closed behind him. Even if they had no weapons except sticks and rocks, there were enough people here to....

But the Captain and his men marched uninterrupted and unimpeded toward the towering stone pyramid of the Cantorium. The figures at the top were now plainly in sight. There were indeed two, standing statue-still. One, the woman, was robed in indigo, as Milner had reported.

Who in hell is that? Haardt thought, replaying for the dozenth time the list of Makers and—as always, accounting for every one, dead and alive. La'am was the male, and the others were dead or under confinement. The woman in blue could not exist.

But she did.

The other Maker—La'am—wore what now seemed not so much a robe as a flowing play of light. The material of both robes fluttered slightly in the faint breezes from the east.

Haardt stopped at the base of the building. The two Makers were staring over his head, staring over the rooftops of Los'ang. They seemed to be watching the Council Palace and the Magistry. Neither paid any notice to Haardt or his men, although their passage through the city had to have been obvious to anyone standing above them on the Cantorium's heights.

Around them, the Omnans pressed closer together. They left a space of half a dozen meters between themselves and the knot of ExServ men at the base of the Cantorium.

Haardt said something to Corcoran, who made a gesture. Immediately the armed men formed a half circle around Haardt and Corcoran. They turned outward, facing the crowd. They raised their weapons to the ready and took aim at the closest Omnan.

No one moved.

No one spoke.

A silence deeper than anything Haardt had ever imagined settled over the entire city. It was as if the place was inhabited by pale stone statues, not living, breathing beings. There was not so much as the sound of a leather sandal scuffing against a loose stone.

The silence was unnerving. Haardt glanced at his men and saw that they were sweating and nervous—not at all like trained mercenaries facing unarmed sheep.

Haardt swore beneath his breath, then moved on. Leaving his men behind to control the approaches to the single staircase, accompanied only by Corcoran, Admant Haardt began mounting the steps of the Cantorium.

PART FOUR

CHAPTER THIRTY-SEVEN

At first La'am knew nothing but confusion. Pressured interfaces massed themselves against the familiar patterns within him and fragmented. For an instant, La'am felt as if his mind were being shattered by forces that surged through him, battering his mind like hammer blows against soft stone. Then, in another instant, the forces spun wildly and resolved into new patterns. They were comfortably similar to the mentrans patterns he had learned to read and feel and live with over the past Cycles, but at the same time these new swirls and whorls of color-sound were subtly but importantly different. They felt intangibly alien, foreign. Yet through them, he could sense the overriding pattern of the being that had identified himself as Jamison—the same Jamison who had commanded a desperate colony-ship fleeing from the Mother Planet so many generations previously.

La'am tried to enter the Jamison-patterns. He tried to meld with them and allow them to flow over and through him, but the attempt proved more difficult than La'am would have imagined. The patterns were there, they were clear and unambiguous, but at the same time, they were not as accessible as had been the previous mentrans patterns La'am had encountered. There was a strange...*taste*...to the Jamison-patterns that was missing from Iam'Kendron's, Mord'am's, Jorik's—from every pattern La'am had ever touched. The sensation was mildly irritating. He was reminded of metal, and there was a jangling feeling at the back of his teeth. The color/sounds were cold, distanced but inviting. La'am probed deeper, suddenly startled by a perception that blossomed from memories he did not know he had, from memories stored in small bits of patterns that were part of larger patterns perpetuated through generations of Makers' lore.

The Jamison-patterns were not organic—at least not in any way La'am could identify. Words for which he had as yet discovered only hazy referents whirled formlessly: *copper, brass, steel, plati-*

num, gold, silver. These were all parts of the Jamison-being; yet he was not wholly inorganic, either. He was not like the metal ships of the Strangers, with their intricate metal-work brains, or like the mindless servant mechanisms La'am had short-circuited in the Southern Plains. Still, when he probed even deeper, he discovered a certain crispness, elegance, and clarity about the Jamison-patterns that strongly suggested the machines of the Strangers. In addition, however, the patterns were less fully articulated than were those of La'am's fellow Makers. They were simpler, less developed, almost primitively formed. But the content, paradoxically, was largely beyond La'am's comprehension. He struggled to isolate certain fragments that he could focus on and try to fully identify; but always other more strident patterns interrupted, tearing his attention to themselves and forcing him to abandon the half-interpreted one. Again and again La'am tried, until finally the Voice dampened the other patterns, gently recalling La'am back to awareness of the caverns. Laral was beside him. Her eyes glistened, and she seemed as puzzled as La'am felt.

"What did you see?" he asked her gently, touching her hand.

"I'm not certain. Most of it was terribly mixed up. Confusing. Then just when I felt that the patterns were coming clear, they would fade. I just don't know. I feel that they were important, but I couldn't control them. Not by myself, at any rate." She looked pleadingly into La'am's eyes.

The Voice spoke. It seemed to come from everywhere and nowhere as it echoed through the chamber. "Neither of you alone is sufficient. You must truly join, become one."

"But...," Laral said, starting to repeat the sternest admonition of the Makers' Lore that warned against precisely the intimate blending and sharing of personalities that the Voice seemed to be urging. Part of the reason for the prohibition, of course, was that the full Makerspower could—until now, at least—only be administered by the Master Maker in conjunction with the full council. Until the death of Iam'Kendron, in fact, there was no recorded indication that any Maker had ever used mentrans to speak directly to another individual. And beyond that, there was always the abiding fear that in such a joining, the dominant personality might overcome the lesser. Instead of two beings sharing equally, one might master the other.

La'am started to respond as well, then cut the words off before they could pass his lips.

This is Jamison, he reminded himself, first Master of Omne and the initiator of both the Makersraad and the Magistry.

Instead of speaking, he bowed his head in acceptance. He barely noticed Laral doing the same.

"You are already one in many ways," the Voice intoned. La'am felt an undercurrent of humor in the tones, bubbles of joy floating close to the surface. "You two are more fully one than any other Makers in the history of the land. We consciously denied the Makers the rights and privileges of marriage and procreation, lest anyone be tempted to found personal dynasties and pervert our intentions for Omne. I am still not certain that the prohibition was justified but our fears for our children demanded it.

"And now two Makers have chosen to disregard that tradition. Two Makers have spoken the Words of Joining. You have wed and bear within yourselves the germination of new life. You hadn't realized that, yet did you, my child?" The voice gave the impression that the entity behind it had turned toward Laral and was addressing paternally. La'am imagined a solemn face, drawn with years but now illuminated by a gentle smile. Then the meaning of the words penetrated and he glanced sideways at Laral, almost afraid to gaze on her directly.

"I know, and have known from the Beginning," Laral replied. She smiled in turn and looked into La'am's startled face.

"Yes," the Voice said, "...you would. I must remember that you have changed since the time of the first Makers—as all Omnans have altered since the Beginning, which is as we had hoped. It remains to be seen whether the alteration is sufficient."

"Sufficient for what," La'am asked.

"That I will show you now. But first, you two must become one. Not merely physically and emotionally, but essentially, spiritually." The Voice paused dramatically. Even so, La'am could not shake the continuing conviction that, as serious as the matter seemed to be, Jamison was pleased and was in fact enjoying himself immensely.

But when the voice resumed, no one, least of all a Maker trained in all of the nuances of voice and word could miss the intense solemnity compressed into in every syllable. Jamison was speaking Words of greater power than any La'am had ever experienced. The sounds were familiar, but the words—the patterns that flowed into him and formed the words—made no sense. He felt again as if his brain had short-circuited. The sounds broke upon him and swirled into new forms. Time stopped. Light and dark disappeared. Nothing existed except the Words.

Then he came to himself again. His muscles were trembling with fatigue, so much so that he was half afraid that his legs would give way and he would pitch forward onto his face. He felt a deep, cutting pain in his chest and realized with amazement that he had neglected to draw a breath since the Words began. He slowly let the stale air seep out, carefully, as if afraid that the movement of his expelled breath might somehow disrupt the intensity of the Words.

"These are the Words of Eternity," the voice intoned, "by which two may become as one. You will be unified in purpose and flesh, in mind and spirit. Behold."

New words formed in La'am's mind. The patterns were so intense that they frightened him, even as accustomed as he had become to mentrans. His mind melted. The inherent boundaries of what had been himself—first as Davian Charl'an-born, then as Iam'Kendron-word, finally as La'am—softened. They grew malleable, insubstantial, and moved like ocean currents through time and space until they encountered other boundaries, equally flexible and permeable and...inviting. The new boundaries defined Laral. La'am recognized the surface patterns that the two had shared in the Cantorium in World's End. Then, just as he began to apprehend deeper patterns, he felt her entering within his boundaries, becoming first Davian, then Iam'Kendron-word, then La'am. The edges merged, coincided, solidified. La'am was Laral; Laral was La'am. Each represented the entirety of the other; each, before unknowingly incomplete, now stood complete.

There was a moment of dizziness. La'am felt a black cloud obscuring the patterns, as if the Veil of Heaven itself had descended over them and cut of all sensation. Then a flood of new patterns burst over them. This time, however, working in tandem, La'am and Laral sorted and arranged them. As one, with one mind, they followed the visions Jamison was opening to them....

* * * * * * *

Earth spun silently, fertile and beautiful. She hung in space, an exquisite diadem of emerald, turquoise, amber, suffused with feathered strands of opal. Centuries, millennia, eons passed uneventfully for her. She remained pendant, unchanging as the stars themselves. She was a brilliant jewel surrounded by the unmarked black velvet of a celestial jeweler's cloth.

The lights came gradually. A few at first, then spreading with unbelievable speed, they diamond-dusted their way across. They engemmed the planet.

With the lights came other changes. The emerald dimmed. The amber receded. The turquoise muddied. The opal shrouds deepened and darkened to white, then gray. Gradually, then more rapidly, she changed. She became less fertile, less beautiful...more tired and careworn.

And finally, a few of us could see that she was perhaps mortally tired, exhausted and fatigued beyond endurance. Her emerald was blighted, replaced by stone and concrete and steel. Her amber deserts and mountains were encroached upon until they, too, were supplanted by monoliths of steel.

She might have survived, even then, had enough cared. But too few did. Even we who understood did not care enough. The temptation to ignore the old, to explore and exploit the new was too great—and we succumbed, as did millions of others. With one difference: we chose to deny the heritage of technology that had laced the Mother World with ropes of light...and that had turned vampire and drained her of vitality, energy, and life.

We chose to reject that.

We found a place: we Named it Omne. *She reminded us of the Mother World before cold brilliance displaced earth-toned warmth. She was fertile and beautiful. She was isolated. She was receptive to us.*

And we to her. The first time, we scouted her carefully. We tallied her resources: wildlife, plants.

And we found it.

The botanists were the first. They were classifying life according to the structures and standards that had grown on another world, another earth. The process was tedious, slow. But they were making progress. Many of the plants resembled superficially those of the Mother World. Others were alien and unknown.

Among the latter was the rhiam.

It blossomed throughout the land. It seeded itself each generation. It required little care. At first the botanists were interested. Its potential as food was demonstrated. It would provide fiber for clothing and thick mats for shelter. It seemed perfect.

Too perfect, in fact. Gradually the botanists discovered its other properties. They correlated its growth to the presence of the nodules in the soil. They defined the symbiosis between the two. And then came the greatest discovery of all—that the rhiam could alter human brain tissue.

The physiologists and psychologists stepped in. They substantiated the early findings...then expanded them. The rhiam and the nodules made kinetic those potentials that had lain hidden within the human mind since the beginning. Under their influence, words became instruments of power. Thoughts created external reality. Anyone living on Omne became different. Potent.

This terrified us. We had seen the power potential in technology. We had seen that power abused and turned against us, against our world. We had seen war, destruction, filth pouring into skies, waters, land. We had seen all—and we had aided it. We were scientists, the leading minds of our time. And we were sick at heart at what we had created.

Here was our chance, we realized, to expiate our part of that treason. We collected ourselves and others sympathetic with us. We organized a colonizing expedition and built a ship...the Home-Search. *We traversed the immense distances; not even the mathematicians could conceive of those dimensions in concrete images. We broke from the Mother Planet, diverting our scheduled course, halting communications, losing ourselves in the vastness of space. We hid our trail so that no one could follow. So that we could remain alone, in peace.*

We arrived here, at the Place of Beginnings. The remnants of our ship still lie hidden here, deep within the caverns of the Pillars, where it formed the core of our community. We had arrived.

Now we had to learn how to live in harmony with our world.

The rhiam took effect. We ate it. We wore it. We lived surrounded by it. And we could see the changes in us.

We banded together to create the Makersraad. Our first purpose was to hide our knowledge. We would bury the sciences that had forced us into exile from another world. We collected the knowledge and recorded it so that it might not disappear entirely, then secured it deep within the Pillars of Beginnings. We expunged the words that would call it forth. We obscured them and made them into legends and lore and lays to be propagated among our children and their children.

We created the Veil of Heaven as a shield between this world and the world we had known. We enveloped Omne in clouds, so that our children would not be tempted to look out—and so that the children we left behind would not be able to look in. We obscured our-

selves from the False Knowledge of the First World and hid in our immaturity.

We created the vision of the Wordsmith, the one who would return and tie together Word and Knowledge. When our children had matured sufficiently, when they had mastered the power of the rhiam and controlled it rather than being controlled by it, when they could successfully integrate the technology of the lost world with the morality of Omne—then and only then would we allow our world to confront the ghost of its past.

For generations, our children have spread over the land. They have populated the places we built. They have preserved the traditions as they were taught. They have, in the persons of the Makers, brought to fulfillment the promise of the rhiam.

The time arrived.

But still we were not certain. Our world was moral—highly moral, without violence or crime, warfare or destruction, without even the words to describe such perversions. Yet we were not certain. One who went before—as ancient to us as we are to you—long ago defined our fears:

> I cannot praise a fugitive and cloistered virtue, unexercised and unbreathed, that never sallies out and sees her adversary, but slinks out of the race where that immortal garland is to be run for, not without dust and heat....

The final test alone remained. And now that test has come.

* * * * * * *

The visions ceased. La'am and Laral had not perceived the message in words as such, but rather in fleeting images, in mentrans color-sounds that increased in depth and complexity as they registered in the Makers' minds. The patterns built on each other, suggesting details which, when investigated, revealed hidden treasures of knowledge.

La'am and Laral remained standing for some time—perhaps for hours—absorbing and relating the knowledge they had been given: knowledge of another time and another culture; of another people, who used and misused machines but who had no Makers, no Singers, no hope for the Wordsmith; and finally knowledge that the Wordsmith was not an individual, exactly, although La'am and

Laral shared many of the powers ascribed to him; but rather...well, rather a reflection of someone, some power beyond their imaginations, beyond even Omne herself although implicit in her as He/It had been implicit in First World and rejected. No, the Wordsmith was a complex: this god-like Essence, conjoined with the people of Omne, the individuals who carried within themselves potentialities which, if properly developed, could bestow upon them the tremendous powers that Jamison and his group had carefully husbanded and developed for their children, in the name of the Wordsmith...when their children had proven themselves adults.

Gradually the Voice intruded again into their thoughts, bringing the two Makers abruptly to an awareness of their situation. They looked about them. The chamber had changed substantially from their last conscious memory of it. The plays of light had faded to soft glows, more subdued, more intelligible, more recognizable as individual entities. The Jamison-being had resolved into a figure and stood before them, not a dozen paces distant, a form molded of living light that had endured for Cycles within the darkness of the mountain's bowels. La'am did not fully understand what had happened, but he absorbed Jamison's unspoken words almost without noticing them, his mind concentrating on the knowledge that his encounter with the Ancients had forced onto him.

The Jamison figure stepped toward them, seeming to float on a cushion of light.

"My mission is ended," he said quietly. "I have watched and cared and kept alive the original dream of the *HomeSearch.* I have seen the reality behind the image of the Wordsmith. Now, there is nothing more for me to do. You have my knowledge. You know what lies beneath the Pillars of Beginnings. You know what infuses this world, what powers are entrusted to you and to the minds of the Omnans. You know how that power must be applied, if the dreams of the *HomeSearch* and the meanings of the Wordsmith are to be realized.

"The Strangers have arrived. We knew that they would eventually. We did not know how or when—indeed, I am somewhat surprised that it has taken them so many Cycles to track our path to this place. But we knew that they would surely arrive. When they did, you would have to deal with them for yourselves.

"You have come searching for the Wordsmith. You sought for the image of salvation after which generations of Omnans have sighed. I tell you that you have found Him. He is in you. His image is formed by the power flowing within your minds. Use it well. Fully...potently...wisely.

"Now, fare well...forever."

That light that was Jamison drew into a glowing point of light that should have blinded them but did not. La'am closed his eyes and shaded them with his hand, but the light still penetrated. It was painfully bright, but at the same time, the pain was strong and pure and cleansing. There was a crisp crackle, as of Dark Time lightning, and then the glow faded. It closed in upon itself until it resembled merely another of the dozens of ephemeral glows now visibly scattered about the chamber. Before, they had been too dim to be seen above the light that the Jamison-figure had emitted. But now they twinkled, rose, and died. And as La'am and Laral watched, one by one they faded and winked out. The final point of light remained for a lingering moment. It was little more than a scarlet speck, like a single eye in the darkness, but La'am recognized the essence it symbolized.

"Farewell," he whispered to all of them, but to that one point of light in particular, "but not forever."

Without turning to face each other, the Master Makers thoughtspoke:

"We must hurry. The crisis has come."

"To the Magistry, then. Perhaps we can save him."

"No, it is too late for that. He is of the old, though young. He has accepted his passing as essential to the conception and birth of the new. He is right. We must not depreciate the meaning of his sacrifice. He shall live, as long as Omne survives."

"To the Cantorium, then?"

After a moment: "*Yes, that is right. We must go now."*

Hand touched hand. There was a burst of blue flame. When the blue light faded, the chamber was empty, silent, and dark.

CHAPTER THIRTY-EIGHT

Darkness...as thick and palpable and complete as a closely woven blanket cocooning head and chest and arms and legs. It stifles breath. Heart hovers between two beats...and stops. Blood grows sluggish in veins and arteries...grows sluggish, slows...and stops. Lungs expand to pull air in, hold the expansion in spite of tissues crying for replenishment...and stop. Life signs dwindle to less than a minute flicker hidden at the core of a darkness that lasts only a fraction of a second outside the self but that inside seems like an eternity. Then an instantaneous explosion of cold fire that spears the flicker and enflames it, releases its burst of light throughout the darkness. Blue at first, then vivid purples that shade imperceptibly into reds, oranges, and yellows...then all color leeches out leaving only pure, stark white. The essence of light, brilliant and engulfing. And then the light fades from white to gray. The unendurable flame withdraws into a secret place surrounded by layer upon layer of intricate patterns. Withdraws but never dies.

* * * * * * *

The muffled gray of daylight first filtered down through the Veil of Heaven and then reflected in glancing shafts from the hand-polished white stone platform, and from there angled sharply through the half-open doors on the south side of the Cantorium. Inside the chamber, La'am and Laral appeared side by side on the Singer's dais. A moment before, they had touched hands in the caverns of the Pillars of Beginnings and thought to be in Los'ang. And then they were there.

Intellectually, they felt no particular surprise at having crossed half the length of Omne in the fleeting space of time counted between two rapid breaths, two *thrumms* of their hearts. The Voice, the Jamison-consciousness had spoken in mentrans patterns to them for a long time about the transference of matter through space—and through time as well, although that power was not necessary here. Emotionally, however, it was difficult to adjust to the sudden alteration in their surroundings. One moment they had been standing in a seemingly endless cavern so deep within the Pillars of Beginnings that they could almost have been at the heart of the planet itself...and in the next, they were standing silently in what they had once considered a huge chamber that suddenly seemed small and crowded and cramped. Around them circled half a dozen rows of rude stone benches, each bench covered with fabrics and cushions primitively dyed in earth-tone browns and russets and golds and greens and reds. After the stark simplicity of the caverns, the place seemed overwrought, overdone, a confusion of angles and shadows that had no meaning and bore no beauty.

For an instant, their minds refused to accept the change, then as quickly as if something inside had snapped open—some synapse they had never understood before or even known existed—they blinked once and knew where they were. The primitive angles and curves and colors resolved themselves into the quiet elegance of the great Cantorium. They recognized the dais on which they stood, from having sat themselves on the stone benches to hear Hom'ar sing the Lore. They stared at the chamber, seeing it as if for the first time. The resemblances between the Cantorium at Los'ang and the dead structure at World's End struck La'am and Laral with the force of a blow: they saw the same stylized arrangements of stone seats; the same circular dais, its edges carved with intricate arabesques and curvilinear designs. La'am cocked his head as if listening. After a moment, Laral did so also. Yes, in spite of the newness of the structure, they felt the same eerie suggestion of living essences encased in the cold stone that they had felt at World's End. But these essences spoke of other horrors than of volcanic lava. They spoke of death in a nearby courtyard, of Omnans twisting beneath the Strangers' weapons and bleeding their blood between the cracks, where it sank without a sound into the soil of Omne. They spoke of death and of destruction and of change beyond the imaginings of either Maker.

Fingertips still touching, the two stood for a long moment, struggling to adjust physically and emotionally. They did not move. Their robes hung perfectly still, as if the two Makers had been standing as motionless as living statues on the Speaker's dais for hours or days or Cycles.

There was a rustle at the doorway. One of the huge panels swung silently inward, allowing a bit more light to penetrate the gloom. Then there was a glimmer of something metallic. One of the Strangers was at the door. He held a long, thin tube, its open end pointing into the heart of the Cantorium.

"Who's there," the man asked. His voice was strong and confident. Neither Maker spoke.

* * * * * * *

Eugenio Solario—just plain "Gene" or "Solario" to anyone not eager for a quick two rounds, a busted jaw and a couple of splintered ribs, none of this "*Eu*-gene" crap for him—glared over the flat roofs that spread in every direction. He shifted his position on the platform, cursing again the bad luck that had gotten him into that scuffle last night and from there onto the Captain's shit-list. He shaded his eyes with his open palm and stared at the clump of buildings on the distant island. It looked calm enough now, but not ten minutes before he had seen the flash of laser fire and knew that the ExServ was finally giving the natives a taste of real power. His finger had twitched sympathetically against the firing stud of his own laser. He muttered to himself and focused his attention back on the streets laid out in grids below his position. People were moving back this way, he noted. There were still small mobs of them by the bridge and along the outer fringe streets, but even in the few seconds he watched, he could see a current beginning. Whorls of movement lengthened and became streams, twining along the streets and toward his position.

His eyes darted along the base of the pyramid, making certain that the others were alert. Mac, the patrol commander, had taken point position at the base of the stairway. His weapon was drawn and pointing steadily at the nearest edge of the mob.

Solario hefted his own laser, grateful for its reassuring weight. He shifted his footing again, and suddenly realized that he was nervous. There was no reason to be, he thought. This was a shit job, he knew that much. This place had been cleared out days before. There was nobody up here, and nobody could climb up here without the patrols seeing it. And anyway, the action was out there. He looked at the island. Still nothing. No movement.

But there was still something, a sense that something was not right. He studied the scene below: the rows of silent houses, the knotted streets, the crowds of people so far away that they seemed small dots rather than humans. Moving slowly but silently toward him.

That was it. He straightened. His finger crept nearer to the stud, hovering over it so closely that he could feel its warm metallic smoothness against his skin.

That was it.

The silence.

Except for the faint sounds of the wind against his ears, it was as if he had suddenly gone deaf. He had seen mobs before—hell, he had been *in* mobs before, and understood the wild cries, the shouts for blood, the mindless keening that rasped throats raw and made the ears ring to meet the fevered throbbing of blood.

He knew all of that. He enjoyed it. Sometimes it seemed as if he craved it.

But down there, there was none of that.

The people clustering below were silent...dead silent. He strained his ears. He could hear nothing, not even the scrape of feet against stone as the mob tightened.

He swallowed hard, recalling the stories that had been circulating in the barracks for the past couple of days. Thank god that all of those Makers were locked up.

He checked out the island again. Still no movement. But it had to come soon. He knew laser fire too well not to know that something heavy had gone down out there. Haardt would have to move now, would have to teach these....

His ears screamed.

It was only an instant, over so fast that if his ears were not ringing like they had been near an explosion of a steel foundry he wouldn't have believed it had happened.

He whirled on his heels, laser up and ready, finger brushing the stud and steady.

Nothing behind him.

The doors to the single room at the top of the pyramid were half open. Inside, as far as he could see nothing moved. He moved closer to the wall, getting himself out of sight of anything that might be inside that room.

Solario licked his suddenly parched lips. His ears were still ringing, a high-pitched buzzing that made him even more nervous than he should have been.

What the hell was that? he asked himself. It had been a sound—a thunderclap so loud that it could have split a world, and so lightning-fast that the sound had died almost before it began. He shook his head to clear his ears. It helped a little.

He sidled back to the edge of the platform, keeping his eyes glued to the half-open doors and the darkness inside them. He crouched down.

He touched his commlink. "Mac?" he said softly. He was shocked at how thin his voice sounded. "Come in, Mac."

Down below, the figure at the base of the stairway moved slightly.

"Solario?"

"Did you hear that?"

"Hear what?" Mac's voice said. Below, the figure turned its head and stared up the length of the stairway. Solario could feel Mac's eyes boring into him, even from this distance.

"That sound?"

"What sound? It's quiet down here."

Too quiet, added Solario with bitter humor.

"There was a, like a thunderclap or something. Loud, real loud. But quick."

Mac's voice changed. "Anything up there?"

"I...I don't know."

"Did you check that room?"

"Not yet. I wanted to see if you had heard...," Solario said.

"Check it out."

Solario heard the buzz that told him Mac had deactivated the link. The last words had been an order. There was no further discussion.

He rose slowly until he was standing but hunched over. No use taking any chances. He slipped against the wall again and followed it to the doorway. There he stopped for a moment, then slowly edged around the stone jamb. He was pretty sure that nothing showed inside except maybe just the outline of his shoulder and arm.

"Who's there?" he shouted.

No one answered. He listened intently. The thunder had finally stopped echoing in his brain, but the high-pitched ringing was still there. It sounded like an electrical current passing nearby. His skin tingled. There was an odd odor in the air that came from the room. Again, it was almost electrical, hot wires and insufficient insulation, maybe.

Except that there was no electrical power anywhere on this planet except in the ships. No wires and no insulation.

The smell faded. He cocked his head and listened again.

"Who's in there?" he repeated. "I'm armed. Come out. Now!"

His arm—banded near the shoulder with strips of silver that caught the outside light and reflected it onto one of the benches just inside—withdrew until only the tip of the tube-weapon remained visible. It stopped just inside the doorway.

No one answered.

Bracing the laser steady against the doorjamb, Solario punched the commlink again.

"Mac," he said, "I don't hear anything inside."

"Have you checked it out?" Mac sounded tense now, tense and more than a little pissed off at Solario. Solario could almost hear the Patrol commander's internal voice screaming at him: *Whadda ya mean, "I don't hear anything!" Get you ass in there and check it out. That's what you're getting paid for. So do your job.*

"I...there's...," Solario's voice stuttered to a halt. He flashed back to a dozen laser fights he'd survived, to half a hundred brawls and battles—most of which he'd started himself, sometimes just because he was bored. He'd faced up to the toughest thugs backwash planets could throw against him. He thrived on danger. He lived for excitement.

And he did not want to go into that dark room.

His ears buzzed—no, he realized, not his ears. The buzzing was real enough, but it was not in his ears. It was inside his head.

"Mac...," he started to say.

"Get in there or I'll have your balls for breakfast."

Solario did not answer. There was no answer. Instead, he thumbed the link off and slid the end of the tube-weapon further into the chamber. Then he moved his arm and the side of his body around the corner, still hugging the doorjamb for as much protection as possible from whatever might be hiding inside. He paused. The ringing in his head surged louder. His eyes blurred, then cleared when his shook his head. And then he entered the Cantorium chamber.

Hunched over to make the smallest target possible, he took two or three long strides inside. He was moving rapidly toward the back row of benches, almost half way there, before he glanced out of the corner of his eye and saw the Makers. He stopped abruptly. He blinked, as much from trying to adjust to the sudden darkness as from shock.

There were two of them. Light was streaming down on them from somewhere, maybe from an opening in the ceiling. It circled them completely where they stood on the raised stone circle in the center of the room. One was a woman, wearing a blue robe. The other was a man. He wore a robe also, but the color was harder to define.

Solario cursed softly again—then realized that this was the man the Captain was hunting for. Solario had him—had *both* of them—in his laser sights. He straightened and aimed the laser at the Makers. "Stand still," he said, "don't move...."

Too late. The woman's hand was a blue-cloaked blur as it whipped up and thrust toward Solario. The buzzing spiraled to a whistle, then skyrocketed into a scream that seemed to pierce his brain from ear to ear. His eyes opened wide and his nostrils flared. His finger clenched convulsively against the firing stud and time slowed enough for him to see the thin beam of clear white fire flash out to incinerate the two figures.

Shit, Solario thought in the next instant. Haardt wanted the blue-robes taken alive. If I killed them, Haardt's gonna....

The light stopped. That's all. It stopped. Solario's jaw dropped in shock. The tingling along his skin increased until it became painful but he did not even notice it. He stared at the darkness in front of him, at the darkness that an instant before had been split by a beam of coherent light powerful enough to drill a hole through the solid stone wall on the other side of the room. Halfway between Solario and the Makers the light had died. There was no sound, no crackle of flames, no sizzle of human flesh where the laser slashed through solid matter and destroyed cells and tissues and flesh and bone. There was simply no light.

There was nothing.

"Wh...?" Solario began.

The second Maker raised his arm, more slowly, and pointed at Solario.

"No!" he screamed. His finger stabbed the firing stud.

This time there was no response from the weapon at all.

Solario started to scream again, but something touched him at the center of his mind. The high-pitched buzzing stopped so suddenly that the abrupt, absolute silence now seemed unutterably painful. Darkness touched him, and coldness. He concentrated on his firing finger, willed it to move just enough to activate the laser one more time, just one more time and fry those....

His shoulders slumped. His firing arm dropped to his side. His laser clattered hollowly against the stone as it fell. Only half conscious, Solario felt himself collapsing. His body caught the edge of the last bench, knocking the air from his lungs and digging painfully into his stomach. He sprawled across the bench, his head coming to rest against one of the brightly dyed cushions.

The darkness and the coldness became complete.

* * * * * * *

La'am and Laral stepped down from the Singer's dais and made their way across the chamber. As they passed the prone form, Laral paused long enough to pass her hand across his temple. She nodded gravely. The Makers took no further notice of the Stranger guard where he lay asleep, but with no internal or external injuries. He would be safely out of the way at least long enough for them to complete their mission.

Still without speaking, the Makers passed through the great open maw of the doorway, then out onto the smooth, polished platform at the top of the pyramid. From their position on the southern face, they could look out over Los'ang toward the Harbor. Further out, beyond the grid of streets, they could see the Council Palace and the Island of the Magistry. As her eyes rested on the Magistry, Laral caught her breath in a sharp hiss. La'am did not respond overtly but his eyes darkened, then closed in pain. Although now there was no movement at the Magistry, the Makers could almost see the roiling cloud of fear and death, of violence and pain and suffering that hung over the cold stones like the smoke from a dying fire. They heard the waning moans of the wounded and sensed the lingering cries of the dead. The men and women slaughtered in the courtyard had forever stained the stones with their patterns, many of them unconscious patterns readable only to the Makers. La'am and Laral felt tears rising and burning as their eyes rested on the building and their minds opened themselves to the hundreds of deaths crowding down upon them.

I can't bear this, one thought.

We must, the other countered so quickly that both thoughts seemed like one. After that instant of hesitation, the moment expanded infinitely to give the Makers time to grieve and to sing a silent symphony woven from the hundreds of individual patterns. One by one, they searched for the residue of each dying soul and gathered it into themselves. One by one, each more painful than the last—and more painfully glorious—they added power upon power, unknown talent to unknown talent, until they *were* three hundred Omnans... and themselves...and something much more than merely the sum of the accumulation.

Finally, only one pattern remained. It was the first one they had sought and the only one that, by unspoken, common consent, neither Maker had touched as they sorted through the miasma of death and pain and terror that the Strangers had created. Then there was only one pattern. They paused, drew a figurative breath through lips as still and cold as stone, and with a single motion burst through its barriers, accepted its story, and were whirled away by the breadth and power and majesty of the exultant, triumphant death-pattern of Zeta'Om, Ranulf-born, Mathom-son, last High Magister of Omne, as he bade farewell to the old and, through the shedding of his blood, helped to usher in the New.

He died well, as if he knew. Laral's thoughts were tinged with overtones of pity and regret. She had never formally met the High Magister and only now, after his death, could she—or perhaps anyone, for that matter—understand the depth of his love for Omne.

He knew, I think, at the end, La'am answered. *His office entailed preparing for the Wordsmith in all things. When he spoke his final truths, he knew. He died well, as a child-father should.*

A sound rose from the base of the Cantorium. It touched their ears and penetrates to the surface of their minds and drew them from their unseen depths back to the present task. They broke away from the compelling attraction of the Magistry and focused on the streets below. Already, the crowds that had assembled in Los'ang at First Light were surging like Seed Time floods, as if they intended to break upon the lower bulwarks of the Cantorium. Immediately below, surrounding the base of the building, was a curious mixture of Omnans and Strangers. The former hung back nearly to the protective shelter of the closest streets. A handful of the latter had formed a thin line along bottom of the stairway. Three watched the crowds. Two had turned their back on the crowd and drawn their weapons and aimed them at the two figures high above them. The Strangers' bodies were poised for battle but La'am and Laral could smell the uncertainty and the fear that rose from them like a tainted fog. They could almost read the Strangers' thoughts: No one was supposed to be in the Cantorium. No one had been seen entering. And the guard stationed at the great doors...where was he? For the moment, the Strangers held their positions but none of them started up the stairway.

Neither Maker acknowledged either Omnans or Strangers. Neither spoke. And, after they had initially crossed the narrow platform and stopped with their feet at the edge of the upper step, neither moved. They stood, waiting patiently for what must come, for the final test. They strengthened themselves for the ordeal of discipline and control. How easy it would be simply to reach out, La'am thought, to send thrusts of Makerspower blazing through the air, igniting the scouters, the landers, the ship itself, its stores, its men—all of the Strangers. That would be the easy way, the sure way.

And the one way that they could not allow to happen.

The crowd swelled further. Many waiting along the streets near the Harbor had heard the cries of pain and terror and seen the lasers flashing in the courtyard to announce the death of Hom'ar and those with him. They had milled around where they were, stunned and indecisive. But now they turned their backs on the Magistry and, as if drawn by invisible cords, felt themselves pulled toward the Cantorium. Already the outer streets of the city—at least those visible from the platform—were almost empty of Omnans. Below, the crowd still stayed well away from the line of Strangers with their gleaming weapons, but hundreds of bodies were pressing forward from behind. The leading edge of the crowd became a ragged line. Over it all rested an eerie silence. The crowds surged forward, but no one spoke. No one raised a voice in anger or in fear.

Across the bridge, something moved in the courtyard of the Magistry. There was a brief glint of metal glimmering beneath the Veil of Heaven, then a darkness that emerged from the gates.

Only then did La'am speak to Laral. He spoke softly, without turning to look at her. His voice sounded strange to his ears, unused and rusty.

"The time has come. Haardt has left the Magistry and comes to us. We must work quickly."

They sank deeper into themselves, pinpointing particular patterns among the hundreds they contained. They chose half a dozen and amplified them.

"—Hear us Jathanan—"

"—Hear us Jeriam—"

"—Hear us—"

"—Hear us—"

They called to the living and to the dead, communicating with the Makers beneath the Magistry and with the patterns of the Makers destroyed by the Strangers. Then the Master of Makers and the Master Maker of World's End poured into their surviving fellows all of the knowledge distilled from the Jamison-consciousness, preparing Omne in all things.

Soon, they were ready.

CHAPTER THIRTY-NINE

Haardt motioned for most of his men to barricade the base of the pyramid. Accompanied by Corcoran and, well behind them, four others, he began to climb the stone stairway to the platform on which the two fugitive Makers waited. He climbed steadily, conscious of the power he wielded and of his superiority over these blue-robed savages, regardless of what that whey-faced traitor Panraak had said, regardless of the parlor magic Jorik and the others had tried to frighten him with. He was Captain Admant Haardt of the ExServ. He had had enough of this planet and of these sheep that passed for humans. Here, on this pyramid where all could see, he would destroy all resistance to himself and to the ExServ. Within the hour, he would control everything, as far as his eye could see.

He approached the silent and motionless figures standing just outside the shadow of the doorway leading into the Cantorium. His men remained several paces behind him. They kept their weapons trained on the robed figures. Their instructions—shoot to kill at the slightest movement—echoed stridently in their minds. Haardt stopped two meters from the man he immediately recognized as La'am. Facing the Maker, he stood stolidly, legs spread apart, hands on his hips, obviating any hints of tension or fear. He wore no battle armor but he would need none to finish this job.

"La'am, isn't it?" He began, sure of himself. He carefully refrained from attributing to the man any of the titles or powers the Omnans credited him with.

The Maker blinked, as if suddenly waking from a deep dream. His eyes rested on Haardt for a second—cold gray eyes as impenetrable as the fog bank overhead. Haardt started to speak, but the Maker parted his lips and responded to Haardt in the ritual tones the Captain had heard before in the Makersraad: "I am La'am, Master of Makers of Omne, Master Maker of the Pillars of Beginnings, Interpreter of Light."

That was a new one, Haardt thought, surprised at the claim. What in the hell was that supposed to signify? Panraak might know, but the traitor had escaped and....

The Maker was still speaking. Haardt jerked himself out of his thoughts and concentrated on the words.

"—Spokesman for the Wordsmith, and Word of Omne. This is Laral, Master Maker of World's End, Interpreter of Light, Spokesman of the Wordsmith and Voice of Omne. We are one."

"All right, then, Master Maker," Haardt sneered, his voice richly laced with sarcasm and cynicism, "consider yourself my prisoner." He turned to include the woman in his piercing gaze. "Consider yourselves both my prisoners."

He brought his weapon smoothly up until it bore directly on La'am's abdomen. The guards behind him shifted as they came to attention, but the aim of their weapons did not waver either. He spoke over his shoulder to one of the men.

"Mac, get Solario."

The man—formerly commander of the Los'ang patrol—nodded and pushed past Haardt. He circled warily around the Makers, never dropping his gaze from them until he was beyond them and disappeared into the darkness of the room. The Makers did not look at him.

The group remained motionless, a vignette carved of living stone, for the moment or two it took Mac to reappear. He supported Solario across his shoulder. Solario's head hung slackly, and his feet scraped loudly against the pavement. Haardt snorted contemptuously. The man looked drunk. Last night he starts a brawl that left two men with broken ribs, and now he can't even stand guard without....

Solario finally saw Haardt and snapped to attention. His eyes wavered slightly, but there was no other sign of drunkenness about him.

"Is he all right?" Haardt asked Mac.

Mac nodded. "I think so. He was just coming out of it when I went in. They"—he pointed his laser at the Makers—"they did something to him. Knocked him out."

Solario nodded and tried to speak, but no words emerged. His gaze fell on the backs of the two Makers and he blanched. He raised his hands to his ears and shook his head, as if he were trying to silence some inner scream.

"Get him back to the ship," Haardt barked, motioning with his laser.

"Yes, sir," Mac said.

He steered the other man around the motionless Makers. Solario went even paler, if that were possible, but did not falter in his steps. As he passed them, the woman glanced quickly at him, but the man—La'am—kept his eyes on Haardt.

"You will come with me now," Haardt continued, directing his words to La'am. "You will be charged with attacking and blinding one of my men, with fomenting unrest and rebellion against me, with destroying Exploration Service property, with defying the Exploration Service, and with hampering its legitimate mission to evaluate the economic impact of this planet upon the Twelve Worlds. Your friend there will be similarly charged, except for the first count."

He paused, expecting a defense, or at the least a denial of his authority to make such charges on Omne. He had played this part often enough before. He waited for the natives to say their lines.

But the Makers remained silent, whether out of fear or defiance he could not tell. The man's gray eyes did not waver. Haardt shifted his weight. He felt a sheen of sweat break out on the palm of his hand, making his laser fell hot and slippery. He tightened his grip on the weapon. If only the bastards would speak, or move, or stop staring at him so intently that he almost felt them boring through him.

"Sir?" Corcoran said softly from his position a few steps behind and below Haardt. Only the voice wasn't soft. It only seemed so to Haardt. He blinked, realizing that he had dropped the barrel of his weapon until it pointed at a spot only a meter or so from his feet. He had stepped backward until his heel grazed the edge of the uppermost step. His ears rang, and he felt dizzy.

"Wha—?"

"Sir!" Corcoran repeated. This time Haardt heard the sound for what it was, a shout that echoed from the stone wall in front of him.

"It's all right, Mr. Corcoran...."

They had almost gotten to him!

"...Everything is all right."

Behind him, Corcoran shifted his position just enough that his boots grated on the steps. Haardt shook his head and slowly, carefully re-directed the laser at the heart of the man in front of him.

"No more tricks," he ordered. He jerked his free hand over his shoulder, motioning toward the ship again, more peremptorily this time. "Come."

"No."

The crowds below had been unable to hear what Haardt had said, but the import of his words had communicated itself clearly enough through his actions. The Stranger brought down from the Cantorium by another of his fellows had been vocal in his threats against the Makers, against the Omnans, against the world itself. He had cursed and muttered as he stumbled down the final steps. When the Captain began speaking again, a thousand pair of ears strained for the faintest sounds, but none came.

Yet when the Master Maker La'am voiced that single monosyllable—*No!*—it had seemed to echo like an explosion through their minds. Omnans near and distant, those at the foot of the Cantorium and those still on the stones of the bridge, those now packed on the short-cropped lawns of the Council Palace, or those stroking tiredly through heavy swells of the Harbor—all clearly heard the Master Maker's denial.

The word seemed a negation of all that the Strangers had attempted. It rang through mind after mind, joyously and compelling.

No!

No!

No!

No to all that the Strangers represented, to all that they had inflicted upon Omne in the name of the Wordsmith, in the name of the Magister, in the name of the Exploration Service and the Twelve Worlds. The words that followed likewise passed unseen from mind to mind, although not as discreet words. Instead the assembled masses heard...felt something else...something indefinable but undeniably the Words of the Master.

"No," La'am said simply. "I will not go with you."

"You...," Haardt began, but La'am raised his hand in a quiet gesture. None of the armed Strangers behind Haardt fired their weapons.

"I will not go with you," La'am repeated. "Nor will any Omnan again obey your words."

Haardt stared at the Maker. There was power in that voice, and an iron discipline, and suffering, and a contempt that startled Haardt with its vehement coldness. Not even Jorik had communicated such pure emotion to Haardt—but then Jorik had been the first one killed. He had not yet experienced the lengths to which Haardt would go to get what he wanted. La'am knew and he hated Haardt. Haardt licked his lips and dropped his eyes to his laser, wondering if he could get off a shot before...then realized that there was yet something more in the man's voice. Underlying everything else...understanding and forgiveness.

Haardt felt himself flush. For the first time, he accepted the hard fact that he might have underestimated these people. Perhaps Panraak had been right.

He started to signal his men to open fire, only to find that he could not move. He was wrapped in suddenly thickening air, in an eddying swaddle of elements that pinioned and immobilized his arms and legs. He struggled to break free. He lunged toward the Master Maker. The air tightened painfully against his chest until his breath rasped out in ragged pants. His heart thumped wildly, sending blood coursing at breakneck speed through his veins. He felt as if his brain would explode. In another instant, he would be crushed.

Then the tightening ceased. He tried to raise his laser. He still could not move but he could breathe easily. Behind him, he heard a stifled moan and knew that his men were caught in the same trap as he.

And that if he could not figure out a way to escape, they were all dead men.

* * * * * * *

La'am watched the fear flicker through the Strangers' eyes. He could tell from their frantic expressions that they had no idea what was happening to them—and he knew what they were thinking. The perception brought him no happiness. Hurting them brought no pleasure, no diminishing of the loss he felt or of the grief they had inflicted upon his world.

What he did was not for himself alone, but for all.

He spoke again. This time he transmitted his thought not only vocally to Haardt and the other Strangers but through mentrans to the Omnans assembled below.

"I accuse you, Haardt of the ExServ, of grosser crimes than you have counted against me. I accuse you of complicity in the deaths of Zeta'Om, High Magister of Omne; of Jorik, Master Maker of Omne; of Jabeth and Joleckan, Makers in the Makersraad; of Mord'am La'am-word, my soul and my self."

In spite of his resolve, La'am's voice trembled. He moved rapidly in another direction, one less painful.

"I accuse you of burning and destroying Omne. Of ravaging our Sanctuaries. Of destroying our archives and our histories and our heritage. Of burning our fields. Of imprisoning us without cause and without authority. Of raping and killing Omne.

"I accuse you of inhumanity.

"I accuse you of all of these crimes, by my authority as the presiding Maker in this land. I demand that you leave this land at once, never to return."

Suddenly, the air around Haardt became again nothing but air. He could move. His hands and legs were free. Glancing over his shoulder he assured himself that his men were also free. Further down, the men still guarding the base of the stairway were moving again, jerkily, as if not quite willing to believe that whatever had bound them had as abruptly dissipated. Satisfied, Haardt brushed his fingers gently against a section of the broad metallic belt he wore, initiating an emergency alert in the ship.

The Maker might be an adept at mass hypnosis, making Haardt and his men believe that they could not move—Haardt ostentatiously flexed the muscles in his arm. But La'am could not stand up against the might of an armed ExServ vessel. The emergency alert would warn the officers on duty in the ship to prepare all necessary measures against the natives. If necessary, Haardt could destroy this planet.

And he would do so, gladly, before allowing these sheep to dare to give him orders.

A second breath-light brush against the belt sent an order screaming to his lieutenant in the Magistry. Within minutes, Haardt thought grimly but with an enormous sense of satisfaction, the Magistry would be empty of ExServ troops...and thus vulnerable to destruction.

And all of these orders were transmitted so swiftly, so silently that the Makers standing before him had no idea that they had just been defeated. Haardt's fingers hovered over yet another stud on his command belt.

La'am laughed. Loudly. Clearly. His laughter spread through the crowd. Then it stopped, abruptly.

Haardt looked startled at the sound. His brow furrowed and darkened with rage.

"You still do not understand, do you?"

Haardt's face tightened even more at this repetition of Jorik's words. For an instant, it seemed as if the dead Maker was speaking, not the living one.

"You still believe that you can command here," La'am said. He gestured toward Haardt's belt. "You were going to send yet another message. To your ship. Send it. Tell them to destroy the Magistry, as a show of your *power.*"

Haardt winced at the cutting contempt embedded in the last word. He hesitated. He had sent two messages through the emergency link. And he had been about to give the order to demolish the Magistry. How had the Maker known. Could he...great gods!...it was impossible for anyone to read *minds*! Wasn't it? Haardt stirred nervously. He glanced at the men behind him, and the men below, and at the swirling mob now closing slowly in toward the base of the Cantorium.

"Tell them!" The laughter had faded entirely from the Maker's voice, leaving only the iciness of dispassionate command. As if controlled by another mind, another body, Haardt's fingers brushed against the belt.

Across the river, on the flatlands where the ship had settled, a sudden scurrying of men—visible as tiny dark splotches against the green and brown of the fields—signaled that the message had been received. The nose of the ship shifted slightly, swiveled until it pointed directly at the Magistry. A thick clot of Strangers abruptly raced through the gates of the Magistry, as explosively as if the ancient stonework had voided itself of noxious elements. La'am and Laral could see the clot of figures as they stumbled toward the Magistry bridge, some pulling others down and climbing over the prone and supine bodies in their anxiousness. Soon, however, all of the Strangers had crossed the bridge. None remained on the Island.

As soon as the last of the Strangers had passed over the bridge, however, the crowds there surged in the opposite direction, rolling across the bridge to enter the Magistry. La'am felt the sudden shifting of their patterns as they entered the courtyard and saw what he knew was waiting for them...what they had feared to see yet also knew was there. The sounds of their grief and their fury did not carry from the Island to the Cantorium, but La'am felt the sweep of their emotions nonetheless.

Peace, he whispered in words inaudible to all except those on the Island.

Peace, Laral whispered to them as well.

Gradually the turmoil ceased.

In the meantime, the ExServ men aboard the ship had apparently completed their preparations. A low buzz sounded from Haardt's belt.

"Give the order," La'am said coldly.

Haardt jabbed at the belt again. Everyone in Los'ang could see the thin stabbing of red light that arced over the Harbor toward the central structure on the Island. A low, communal moan rose from the mob below and there was a convulsive movement toward the Harbor, as if all present wanted to place themselves between the beam and the ancient stones. As if all of Omne would sacrifice itself to preserve the Magistry. Even though none except Haardt and his men had seen the stabbing light before, all knew instinctively and desperately that when it touched something—anything—that object would burst into flames, explode, cease to exist.

The moan rose to a thin keening.

Haardt felt the muscles of his chest contract with crippling force when the thin red beam impacted against the dome of hazy blue light that suddenly formed above the Magistry, deflecting the ship's fire harmlessly upward. He stared uncomprehendingly as the Veil of Heaven absorbed the energy that should have shattered the building, the island itself, and transformed the harbor into a seething cauldron of vapor and boiling mud. At the least, the beam should have caused *some* change in the cloud layer as it ripped through. Instead, the flat opacity of the Veil opened to receive the scarlet thread, then closed and healed itself and was exactly as before. The blue dome deepened for a moment, then brightened from indigo to sapphire, and gradually faded, leaving only a vaguely discernible cluster of figures standing on the buttresses of the Magistry.

Haardt whirled to face the two Makers. His face contorted with rage. "How…," he began, but his fury was so great that words would not come.

"It is not over yet," La'am said calmly, pointing back toward the harbor.

Haardt shifted his attention to the distant cluster of buildings—the Magistry and the Council Palace. A handful of figures were moving slowly from each set of buildings, moving toward the central bridge. Even Haardt could tell that they all wore the saffron of Makers.

"That's impossible," he shouted, his voice echoing like crackling thunder over the roofs of Los'ang. "They are prisoners. The robes have been removed and locked away—"

"Not any more," said Laral. She pointed this time.

Dizzy with the constant whirling back and forth, Haardt stared at the bridge and the road leading from it to Los'ang. He shaded his eyes, even though the light from the Veil of Heaven was, as always, mild and diffuse. His eyes grew wide as he struggled to accept what he saw. He pulled a monocular from his belt and stared through it.

"No!"

Neither of the Makers behind him responded.

"—Eight, nine…ten!" Haardt's voice throbbed with anger as he saw the robes swirling along the walkway. "Ten! Impossible!"

"Ten," Laral echoed. "The Makerseats have been restored. All of them."

Haardt started to speak again but choked into silence as, through the lens of the monocular, two of the saffron robes flickered from yellow to blue to indicate that the wearers were now Master Makers. He tried to focus closely enough on their faces to identify which they were but the distance was still too great.

"Jathanan and Jeriam," La'am said, as if to answer Haardt's unspoken question. "The Council again has three Master Makers."

"And a Master of Makers," Laral added.

Unseen by Haardt, the two Makers touched hands briefly. As they did so, a scene flashed across their minds: *Deep within the Magistry, in the Loral Chamber, the sconces on the wall burst into flame. Twelve flames flickered, then poured their illumination onto the twelve stone seats, smooth and polished and without dust. The High Magister's seat, however, remained shadowed and shattered and blackened.*

La'am laughed again and Laral joined him. Haardt turned to face them. This time his hand did not hover over the commlinks on his belt. Instead, it held his laser, aimed directly at the Master of Makers.

The laughter died.

"You still do not see," La'am said sadly, as if he were being forced to discipline a particularly obnoxious and recalcitrant child who had willfully chosen not to be loved. "You are helpless. For all of your metal and your weaponry and your power, you can do nothing against us." La'am paused for a long time, studying the contours of the Stranger's face. The knots of anger were still there; veins throbbed and Haardt's face was mottled with deep red. The Master of Makers sighed, as if to signal that he was finally turning responsibility for mischoice over to the still-loved child.

"You will leave," he said simply. "Now."

He thrust out his hand and moved it back and forth. His fingertips wove wreaths of blue flame through the air. Next to him, Laral spoke. Her voice was gentle but imperious as she spoke, not to the

Stranger before her but to her people where they clustered anxiously at the foot of the Cantorium.

"Return to your homes, please. Go quickly and silently. Night is coming. Go, please. Now."

Her final word was as much a command as it had been when La'am had spoken it moments before; but as it registered in the minds of the Omnans who received it, either as physical sound or as an unconscious awareness that they would soon recognize as mentrans, it was suffused with love, with a compassion and warmth that had been missing from La'am's voice when he had spoken to the Stranger. As her words floated down over the crowd, the people heard, understood, and dispersed. As quickly as a warm wind from the west would melt the morning haze off of the fields, the crowd dissipated. It had disappeared almost before Haardt and his men noticed anything around them moving. Even the knots of indigo and saffron moving slowly from the bridge toward the city suddenly sped up, as if they were intent on reaching the shelter of the stone building as quickly as possible before darkness fell. Throughout the city, silent figures slipped into the nearest doors. Windows shut quietly, expectantly. Within seconds of her uttering her final word, Laral, La'am, and the Strangers remained alone outside. Above them, the Veil of Heaven darkened.

La'am broke the heavy silence.

"Captain Haardt, you will leave this world."

As one, La'am and Laral began speaking. Haardt strained to hear the words but although the sounds were familiar he could not understand the words they made. His face communicated his confusion. He tried to step toward the Makers but could not. He urged his finger once again to touch the firing stud, but it refused.

For their part, La'am and Laral barely noticed the Stranger. The time for that had passed. They were safe from anything he might attempt, enrobed in the Makerspower and filled with Words. They spoke Words of Light, but this time they consciously twisted and distorted them. They impelled the unseen powers sleeping beneath the Pillars of Beginnings to awaken, to reach out and strike the Veil of Heaven. They imagined the impermeable, unchangeable Veil thickening, darkening. They imagined not just night, but absolute darkness settling over the face of Omne, hours before the natural dying of the light.

The Veil obeyed. Like a pall of midnight sleep, the Veil of Heaven lowered until it engulfed first the two Makers standing on the Cantorium, then Haardt, then his men clustered below, and finally all of Omne.

The loss of light was so rapid, so unexpected that at first Haardt feared he had been blinded. He remembered all too vividly Streiter's nearly fatal encounter with La'am. His laser dropped with a clatter to the stone platform as he frantically felt the contours of his face, his eyelids, with his hands. In that instant, he did not notice that he was suddenly free to move; his only concern was for the abrupt loss of his vision. Then his ears registered the sudden cries of fear and confusion from the four men on the steps near him, and from those remaining below. If he had been blinded, they all had been blinded. With a shaking hand, he fumbled at the contacts on his belt, opening communication with his ship.

"Haardt here." He forced his voice into a measure of calm. He might not understand exactly what was happening, but he was still and always Haardt of the ExServ. "Report."

"I don't know what's going on, sir. Everything went dark out there. We have lights and power here in the control center. But lights are out all over the rest of the ship and throughout the compound as well."

"Get the generators…."

"They don't work, sir. We've already tried." Neither the disembodied voice crackling through the commlink nor Haardt took note of the extraordinary fact that the man had interrupted his Captain. "We can't…"

Haardt waited for a moment. "Well, can't what?" he demanded.

"Sir, we can't even get a *fire* to light. Incendiaries, lasers, even matches, sir. They burn—God knows they burn! But there's no *light!*" The young man's voice was spiraling into treble ranges. He sounded less and less like a hardened ExServ veteran and more and more like a frightened boy. Haardt caught the rhythms of the man's terror and swallowed hard.

"Who is this?" he asked softly.

"Scott, sir."

The name brought a face instantly to mind: the man was younger than most. This was only his first or second assignment with the ExServ. He was impressionable, willing to work.

"Okay, Scott." For the moment, the darkness and the Makers and the Omnans and this entire misbegotten planet took second place in Haardt's attention. He was Haardt of the ExServ, and his ship was in trouble.

"Yes, sir."

"Tell me what happened over there."

"It looked like all the lights went out at once, sir, except on the command deck. I…, we checked the screens. Nothing registered, sir, inside the ship or outside. Just darkness. Hours before dark was due." The voice began to waver again.

"Steady, soldier," Haardt commanded.

"Yes, sir."

"Are there any problems at the ship?"

"Problems, sir?"

"Casualties." Haardt wasn't certain why he used that word. There was no reason to expect any problems other than momentary disorientation.

"Just a moment, sir. Let me check."

Haardt waited for the crackling voice to return. He felt a prickling along the back of his neck, as if the two Makers standing up there with him were watching him through the darkness. Neither of them spoke or moved. Except for small mutterings and the shuffling of feet on the steps, Haardt could have been alone on the structure… alone in the universe, for that matter.

"Captain Haardt?" Scott's voice sounded. "Yes, sir, there are." Haardt's throat tightened. "Two of the men were working with welding torches outside, repairing one of the landers. When the darkness fell, one of them tried to shut off the torch. He thought the flame was out. He reached across the mouth of the torch and…," Scott stopped.

"And what?"

"And he lost his hand, sir. The other man swears that there wasn't even a glimmer of fire, that the welder *had* to have been out. There wasn't any light, but there was heat enough." Scott paused for a moment. "He'll have to lose the hand, sir."

"It was not our intention to hurt," a man's voice broke in.

Haardt cocked his head, trying to pinpoint the source of the sound. He had no way of telling if he had turned around in the darkness, if he was facing the Makers or looking across toward the ship. Cursing inwardly, he also realized that he had no idea where he was on the platform. For all he knew, he could be a step away from a tumble down half a dozen stories. The fall would surely cripple him, if not kill him outright. He shivered. Suddenly the darkness ceased to be merely the absence of light. He felt more, something almost alive crouching in blackness that shrouded his eyes. Sweat broke out on his forehead, rapidly chilling against the air. He felt suffocated and forced himself to draw a deep breath, as much to calm himself as to reassure himself that it was still possible for his lungs to function.

"It will worsen," the man's voice said quietly.

"I…, I don't…." Haardt's voice wavered. His dread of darkness was rapidly overcoming him. Accustomed to the constant light of the ship in space, he had rarely subjected himself to total darkness until he had arrived on Omne. And even here, he had kept lights burning to shield himself from the blackness of night. He knew intellectually that his fears were groundless, infantile—but they were horribly real nonetheless.

"This is night, Captain Haardt," La'am said. Haardt turned a quarter turn until he was facing the direction of the sound—he thought. He did not dare lift his feet as he moved, instead shuffling his boots noisily over the stonework. The Maker's voice continued: "This is night on Omne. There are no Stars here, no Moon, as there were on Earth. Here there is only darkness. We know this night. We can bear it. You cannot. Already your men shudder with fear. I hear it in their voices, in their breath. Surely you must hear it also. Soon they will panic, and then many will be hurt. Some may die.

"Take command, Captain Haardt. Take command and leave this place."

Haardt's legs began moving, as if of their own volition. Certainly he had no conscious wish to take the first blind step but his legs chose otherwise.

"Help," he cried into the darkness.

"Here," Corcoran said. The voice was comfortingly near. Haardt swung out with one hand and touched something…the crisp fabric of an ExServ uniform sleeve.

"Corcoran?"

"Yes, sir." A hand brushed against his arm, then tightened into it in a solid grip. "I'm at the top stair, sir."

Haardt moved toward the sound. He slid his foot forward until the toe of his boot hung over emptiness, then lowered his foot to the first step. One down. How many hundreds to go?

Another voice spoke nearby, on Haardt's other side. He did not immediately recognize it but it sounded familiar. Another hand grasped his other arm.

"Can you see anything?" he asked.

"No, sir," said the second man.

"Nothing, sir," Corcoran answered a split second later.

They supported each other, three blind men negotiating a steep casement of narrow steps. They moved carefully, probing constantly with their feet. Haardt concentrated so hard on seeing where he was walking that his eyes began to throb even though no light was reaching them. His head throbbed as well.

How many now? Fifty steps? A hundred? How far yet to go?

There were no answers.

A few moments later, he suddenly remembered his belt. He had been using the commlink, but the utility belt also carried a small hand-held emergency torch. He scrabbled at the belt, trying to find the stud that would release the thin cylinder.

"Wait," he panted, frightened at the discovery that he was winded, verging on exhaustion. The other two men halted. Off to the side, he faintly heard the noises of the last two men that had joined him on the platform. They sounded as if they were a few steps further down and to the left.

"My light," he muttered, as if to explain. He held it straight out in front of him and waved it back and forth as he depressed the stud. Nothing. He held it against his open palm. No light, but there was a small tingling of heat.

Heat, but no light. He shivered again.

Cursing, he dropped the torch and grabbed Corcoran's arm again. As he did so, the Maker's voice dropped down on him like rain through a thundercloud. "There can be no light, not for you, Captain Haardt. Ever again. You do not belong here. Your machines do not belong here. We are Omnans. We are Omne. We belong."

"Damn you," Haardt screamed, then bit his tongue to stop the screaming from continuing.

"You are almost at the bottom, Captain," the woman's voice called down to him. "A dozen steps more and you will be at the level."

At that moment there was a harsh scrabbling to his left and the thump of a heavy body striking stone. One of the two men over there cried out in pain, and Haardt thought he heard the *snap* of a bone breaking.

"What is it?"

"Fell, sir," came the answer from slightly below.

"Are you all right?"

"My wrist, sir. Broken, I think."

"Can you make it to the ship?"

"Yeah…uh, yes, sir."

Haardt managed the final few steps carefully, and finally his boot rested on solid stone that extended uninterrupted as far as he could reach with a sweep of his foot.

"Over here," he called. The others joined him, including the ExServ guards that had remained stationed at the base of the stairs.

"Everyone here?"

"Yes, sir," Mac's voice said.

"Anyone hurt?"

"No one down here, sir."

"You are facing your ship, Captain Haardt," the Maker's voice whispered. Haardt jerked. Corcoran was still close on one side, the other man on the other—but it had sounded as if the Maker were speaking directly into Haardt's ear. He twisted his body around, throwing both of his companions off balance. They fell, leaving Haardt momentarily alone in the darkness. "You are facing your ship," the voice repeated. "Return there. Now."

Haardt reached out with both hands but could feel no one.

"Corcoran?" he called, but his voice suddenly sounded dampened, as if he were yelling into a baffle. "Corcoran!"

There was no answer. Ahead, quite a ways to his right, he thought that perhaps he heard someone moving. But before he could place himself more definitely in the darkness, the sounds began.

They were unnamable, unidentifiable, indefinite. Yet they struck to his core, stirring ancient forgotten memories of childhood. They resurrected phantoms from nightmares, from dreams both waking and sleeping. Each was in some way himself. Each sound represented a *thing* hovering on the verge of becoming visible. And even worse, Haardt realized at the same instant that he became conscious of himself running, careening down the smoothly cobbled street, that the sounds were *herding* him! He was lost. He had no way of knowing where he was heading. He did not know where his men were. He did not know what was hounding him through the blackness, murmuring at his ears, flickering along his cheeks, his nose, his fingertips, just out of sight, out of touch, out of hearing.

With a sudden, wrenching cry, Haardt stumbled on something soft. It caught at the toe of his boot and yielded just enough to trip him. As he fell, his mind flashed over possibilities: a stray cloak guided by the marginal breeze into his path, another of his men sprawled in the darkness struggling toward light, a body torn and bloody waiting for his fevered embrace, a *something* beyond his imagining set to trap him and savage him and….

Jarred by the impact with the stones, he lay for a moment, his cheek resting against cold smoothness, listening to the harshness of his own breathing. He blinked rapidly, clearing moisture from his eyes and hoping wildly for the least glimmer of light.

Finally he rose and ran for hours…minutes…days…seconds? Who knew. Time ceased. His mind stretched to the limits of his endurance and then exceeded them again and yet again. He could no longer accommodate his fears. Each time he paused to catch his breath, a new sound emerged, each more primordial than the last, each more primitive and threatening. The air was peopled with phantasms of sounds, with breathings and scrapings and muffled sobs and distant echoes of half-heard screams. Haardt ran. He did not notice when his feet left the smooth cobblestones, when they settled heavily into the invisible grasses of the damp marge-lands, or when they brushed roughly through the rhiam stubble in the fields east of Los'ang. He noticed nothing until his left boot crushed against something hard and cold and unyielding, something that responded with a clarion *clang* that out-shouted all of the phantom sounds.

At first he didn't know what he had struck. He reached down, feeling through the silence—then straightened in absolute terror. As the *clang* echoed and died away, he realized that the sounds were gone—*all* sounds were gone. It was as if he were deaf as well as blind, isolated into himself by the darkness. Then he raised his foot and kicked out again. And again. And again. The metallic ring echoed sweetly in his ears. His hands caressed the cold rungs…*his* rungs, leading into *his* ship. Somehow he had found his way to the encampment, to his vessel.

He clambered shakily aboard, still blind, and felt his way along passageways that should have been light but that were as dark as tombs. He wracked his memory for the correct turnings, bumping his nose more than once against a closed bulkhead, then swearing as he fumbled with the latches and catches than held them closed.

And then there was a glimmer.

He thudded to a halt. He wiped his eyes with the back of his hand and closed his eyes tightly. With them closed, it was pitch black. He opened them. The glimmer was still here, ahead, hazy but persistent. He moved toward it, and it became a definite glow. By the dim light—reflecting from metallic surfaces and suggesting a stronger source of light just ahead—he threaded his way through now-familiar corridors. He ascended to the bulkhead separating the command center from the rest of the ship. The door was outlined with a thin strip of light.

Panting, he pushed the door open.

And was surrounded by an explosion of brilliance.

CHAPTER FORTY

The faces of the men were pinched with anxiety and fear. They apparently hadn't heard him coming; when he burst through the door, they spun as if one and stared at him. None spoke, not even Corcoran, who was already there, standing before the command console, his face whiter than seemed humanly possible. Haardt glanced quickly around. All of the command staff was present.

He opened his mouth to bark out an order, feeling the need to re-establish his control over these men who were staring at him as if he were some piece of filth drug in off the streets of some disreputable spaceport. He opened his mouth...and the intercom crackled. The last voice Haardt had ever expected to hear came through the instrument.

"Captain Haardt. This is Alisandr den Panraak, Lon Drehmel of Auricus."

Haardt stared at the grid. What was the officious fool up to this time? Haardt jabbed at the switch that opened a line to the archivist.

"Panraak, what the hell—!"

"Shut up and listen to me." Distorted and fuzzed by the commlink, the sound was more serpentine hiss than human vocalization. Even so, Haardt's jaw dropped and he stopped speaking.

There was a muffled snapping sound from inside the commlink, and when Panraak continued, the words were more intelligible: "I am Alisandr den Panraak, Lon Drehmel of Auricus, Archivist of the Twelve Worlds, and Consultant to the Makersraad of Omne. I have a message for you from La'am, Presiding Maker of the Council of Masters:

" 'Captain Haardt, you are now safely aboard your vessel. Your men are likewise safe. We are sorry for the pain felt by two of them. The rest are uninjured. None have been lost. A few may have bad dreams for some time, but those will pass.

"'Now you must leave. We have counseled, warned, urged you to depart and leave us in the peace of our traditions and our beliefs. You chose to ignore us.

"'Now we command. If you remain on Omne beyond this hour, you will never see the heavens beyond the Veil of Heaven. You know what we can do.

"'Leave now.'"

Haardt made a convulsive movement with his hand, as if to slam his palm against the commlink, but Panraak's next statement stopped him: "I add one comment, Captain Haardt, for myself. I argued against you coming here, almost from the beginning. I could almost wish that I had never found those documents, that my ambition and pride had not urged me to follow their mystery. Almost. But now that I am here, I choose to remain here. Old Omne is gone; something new is rising in her place and I wish to aid in that birth. As an archivist and a historian, I hunger for that knowledge.

"Now I urge one final thing. Do not return. Do not allow others to follow in your steps. It may be impossible to stop them; I fear that it is. But do your best. What you...what *we* have seen today is but a fragment of the Makerspower. I shudder for us should we disturb it further.

"Remember this—and *do not return*."

The link hummed and died. Silence spread in almost tangible waves through the control center. It was unbreakable, unanswerable. All eyes were on Haardt. He sensed the fear and uncertainty that undermined any illusion or discipline or control.

Suddenly the lights in the ship flared on. Light billowed in from the corridor behind Haardt, and he knew without any doubt that power had returned everywhere on the vessel. At that instant, his crew were blinking blindly, stupidly—everyone not already in the painful white incandescence of the control center.

"Corcoran," he said. The man jerked as if he had brushed against a bare electrical wire.

"Sir!" The response was half a second delayed, then the word came out rushed.

"Call roll of everyone on board."

"Yes, sir." Corcoran turned to a panel and began touching buttons. His voice rose and fell in murmurs as he spoke. There was no other sound in the room. No one else moved. Haardt remained where he was, next to the open door.

After an interminable time that lasted perhaps thirty seconds, Corcoran turned again to face Haardt.

"All present, sir, except Panraak. Two injured. Both will live."

Haardt nodded to indicate that he had heard enough. Corcoran focused his attention back on his panel.

Haardt crossed to the command console. Everyone present and accounted for...except the traitor. Everything ready for takeoff...he froze.

"Corcoran."

"Yes, sir."

"Check the storage compartments."

"Yes, sir."

Haardt winced at the brightness of the lights and counted seconds. Fewer than thirty passed before Corcoran slowly straightened and said, "Empty, sir."

"Empty!" Haardt's voice was a thin screech that echoed painfully across the metal panels and bulkheads. There had been a dozen compartments full of the nodules already prepared and stored for transit. He *knew* that they were there, damn it!

"Yes, sir. Completely empty." Corcoran's face showed his own strain at having to relay this message to Haardt.

The Captain cursed savagely under his breath, then, as if he no longer cared who heard him, he cursed again out loud, volubly and fluently in seven languages and even more dialects. He cursed the planet. He cursed the Makers—the one called La'am in particular. He cursed the ExServ, he cursed Panraak, he cursed Jamison and anyone and everyone who had ever had anything to do with this damnable place.

Then, roughly, he gave the orders.

As scheduled, within the hour the ship rose silently into the Veil of Heaven. Unseen by anyone on the surface, it passed through the cloud cover and finally broke into the clear, star-filled sky.

* * * * * * *

La'am and Laral remained on the platform and followed the dying sounds of Haardt's precipitous flight through the empty city. When they could hear no more, they moved silently to the edge of the platform. Even though it was dark, they felt no fear for their footing. They knew every inch of the Cantorium, with their inner eyes as well as with their outer.

For as long as it took for Haardt to return to his vessel, the two Makers remained immobile. Their ears heard no more, but they followed him with their inner senses. They felt his fury when he fell;

they felt his agonized terror at the sounds that pursued him through the empty streets. They felt his crushing relief when he touched the lifeless metal of his ship.

Then they turned their attention away from the Strangers. At the edge of the Harbor, where cobbled streets decanted into crisp white strand, a light bobbed beside the water. It was the only light visible—and of all those present in the center of Los'ang that day, only two truly saw it. It rose and fell with hypnotic regularity, as the hand that bore it walked solemnly toward the city. At the edge of the city, it stopped, then moved again.

La'am and Laral watched it approach the Cantorium. When the light stopped yet again, this time at the base of the great stairway, the faint aura resolved itself into several figures. Two were dark and draped in darkness. The rest wore vivid swirls of indigo and saffron. Laral called down to the nearest Maker.

"Welcome, Jathanan, Master Maker of Harborwatch."

Robed in nearly flawless indigo, with only the faintest tongues of saffron along the cuffs and hems, the old woman began to climb the steps. La'am and Laral released a flood of Makerslight to illuminate the steps. The two dark figures followed the Master Maker Jathanan. Then the remaining nine Makers of Omne began the ascent as well.

At the same moment that Haardt saw the first glint of light in his vessel, Jathanan reached the platform and moved without direction to a position on the southwest corner. The two dark figures hung back long enough for the Master Maker Jabeth to pass them and take his position on the southeast corner. The remaining eight Makers filed past as well and formed a shallow crescent behind La'am and Laral. The blue glow of the Makerslight increased, until the platform was as light as day.

Panraak stood before La'am and Laral. He huddled near Brandt. He was frightened but controlled. He had long argued with Haardt on behalf of these people. Now he had chosen irrevocably to cast his lot with them. He was divesting himself of much: his lands, his titles, and his prestige on Auricus. He was throwing away his possible—no, his *probable* appointment as Chief Archivist of the Twelve Worlds. He was turning his back on honors and rewards that the discovery of a planet as rich as this would have made his. He was throwing all of that away.

And for what?

Ah, that was the great mystery. Because he truly did not know. Perhaps for nothing, perhaps for everything.

The two Makers smiled at him—down at him, it seemed, as if they were much taller than he, although he knew that was not true. Without speaking they stood for a long time. Panraak had no means nor any desire to know precisely how long they stood there. It sufficed him that they smiled at him and studied him and smiled again. Whatever test they might have been giving him, he seemed to have passed. Only gradually did he notice that they were either intensifying their Makerslight, or the Veil of Heaven was lifting. At any rate, most of the city was dimly visible. He glanced over his shoulder. The field where the ship lay was still shrouded in darkness, a roiling blackness like smoke from an oil-glutted fire. He looked down. Even though there was no sound, the streets had filled again with Omnans, all looking either at the edges of the darkness or upward toward the illuminated heights of the Cantorium.

The woman—Laral—spoke. Panraak did not know if she spoke to him or to La'am but he felt himself tense at her words.

"He has arrived. They are ready."

La'am looked at Panraak and nodded his head.

Panraak fumbled nervously at the communications belt he had been given by the old woman in blue. He forced himself to remain calm, to remember word for word the message that he was to transmit. Coming from him, a member of the expedition, one of Haardt's own kind, and a member of the nobility of Auricus and the political hierarchy of the Twelve Worlds, perhaps someone would listen.

Not that the warning would have much effect, Panraak thought. There would always be more Haardts, men willing to risk all—especially the *all* possessed by innocent others—for adventure, fame, wealth, whatever drove them. Perhaps Haardt himself would return. Perhaps not. But the warning had to be given. Only then could Omne turn away from the suffering of the past and face toward its new present...and its future.

* * * * * * *

When Panraak ceased speaking, he dropped the belt to the stone surface of the Cantorium. It struck with a ringing thud that echoed through the silence. He studied the faces that surrounded him, the faces thronging the streets below—the planes of cheeks and forehead, the clarity and depth of eyes, the strength of jaw lines. How could Haardt ever have thought of them as sheep? They were not innocuous. They were strong, enduring, possessed of strengths and powers few could imagine...even, perhaps, themselves.

And they were awakening, each of them, led by the Makers.

The silence that followed Panraak's transmission endured for some few minutes less than an hour. Then there was a loud roar, and the Veil of Heaven rose from the fields, high enough to graze the tips of the hills surrounding Los'ang.

The plains beyond the city were empty. The ship was gone, carrying with it all of the Strangers except Panraak.

La'am and Laral stepped forward to the edge of the platform.

"Thank you," she said to Panraak.

He nodded, wondering whether he should bow as well. There was that much old-fashioned regality about her. "I am not sure it was enough, though," he said.

"It was. The message is safe and will be delivered." La'am spoke that time.

"But what if Haardt should choose to disregard the warning?"

"He might," La'am said. "But the message itself is part of the machine-minds, the computers on his ship. It cannot be removed or erased. Others will hear and understand. Not all are like Captain Haardt." Here La'am smiled again and laid his hand on Panraak's shoulder.

Then the Makers faced the people below. La'am and Laral raised their arms toward the east, where the darkening edges of the Veil indicated that night—true night, natural night—was beginning to finger the Ranges.

La'am spoke. He did not shout, but Panraak knew that everyone within sight of the Cantorium would hear his words as clearly as if they were standing next to the Maker. He faded back until he stood in the line between two of the saffron robed Makers. This moment belonged to La'am and Laral.

"Omnans, behold!" the Master of Makers said. "The Strangers are gone. They came to rob and to cheat and to despoil. And now they are gone. We have won. We have lost lives. The best of us have died to preserve our world. Yet we have won. We have kept ourselves free from stain. We are now ready.

"I have stood upon the pinnacle of the Pillars of Beginnings. I have stood with one who is myself, and in the presence of the ancient ones, we were unified and become as one."

Laral continued so smoothly that it was as if La'am had not stopped speaking. "We have seen the purposes of the Ancients. We have spoken with the shade of Jamison. We have penetrated the mysteries of the lays and the legends and the lore."

"Of the Wordsmith," La'am said.

With a sweeping gesture that encompassed not only the remaining Makers, the Singer Brandt, and Panraak, but also the masses pressing toward the Cantorium, La'am thundered: "Behold the Wordsmith! He is all of Omne. He is all of us. Through us he shall be revealed!"

Beneath his words, Laral began speaking the Words of Light. La'am joined in. Their voices blended—hers bright, lilting, gentle against a counterpoint deeper, rich, strong. They echoed each other in a startling harmony. Then a third motif was added to the Song. Jathanan of Harborwatch modulated her querulous notes into a triadic resonance. One by one the Makers sang as the Song unfolded. Brandt—who did not yet know it but was now the Singer of the Cantorium of Los'ang—felt the stirrings of the rhythms. He stepped quickly and quietly through the shadowed doorway of the Cantorium and ascended the Singer's Dais. He closed his eyes and raised his eyes and sang, his voice echoing through the hollow chamber and spilling out into the evening air.

Even Panraak was caught up on the visions implicit in the Words. They touched him in deep places that were secret even from himself, and spun him outward. He almost perceived the images the Words formed, images of Sun and Moon and Stars wheeling through virgin skies. The music reached a climax so powerful that Panraak was not certain he would...could...would want to survive it. After this, what more could life offer.

But there was more. Brandt's powerful surge twined through the Maker's songs. The acoustics of the Cantorium, designed so lovingly by Iam'Kendron in unknowing anticipation for this precise instant, brought the two strands together. They merged, melded, transcended song and became color/sound/patterns that flowed down on the people below. First one, then a handful, then all, the hundreds of Omnans assembled below caught the vision of the color-sounds. As one, they engaged their minds fully in the ritual of the chant. The volume did not increase appreciably but the strength of the Words pressed against the ancient stonework, rose to touch the Veil, to spread over the land in a network of mentrans patterns that circled more swiftly than light and touched every point: World's End, Towerwatch, Harborwatch, Heartlands...and the Pillars of Beginnings.

As one, all of Omne changed with the rhythms of the words.

And the Veil of Heaven diminished. It thinned to a tenuous gray, little more than a gauzy haze. Beginning in the east, it withdrew itself from across the face of Omne, ending in the distant west.

At that moment, as the last tattered remnants of the Veil evaporated, the setting sun touched the seas, staining them red and gold and silver. Across the darkening sky, stars appeared.

La'am could sense patterns of wonder, fear, amazement, and turbulent joy as they spread throughout Omne in answer to half-formed questions. He could sense his own powers amplified by the Makersraad. He propelled his patterns again across the land, sharing the revelations of the Pillars of Beginnings with every receptive mind. He almost believed that if he turned at that moment, he would see four more figures standing in the ranks of the Makersraad, pouring their strength into him: the Master Maker Jorik, a gray-robed Acolyte, a young man wearing scarlet, and an old man wearing a dusty, travel-stained robe.

But he did not turn. He did not need to see them to know that they were with him. Instead, he focused his thoughts and spoke to his world:

"Wordsmith is come. We are Wordsmith. We are the children of our parents, children no longer, no longer to be hidden and protected from the universe in which we must live. The Strangers are gone. They have fled to the stars that gave them birth. Perhaps they will not return. More likely they will. But we shall never again be what we were. The Veil of Heaven is gone. We are again one with the sun, the stars, the universe. We are thrust into it to survive.

"We will survive.

"We *will* survive."

As he spoke the final words, the opalescent sun sank into the sea, throwing Omne into night...a night such as at the Beginning, resplendent with light, with stars, with the Eyes of the Wordsmith.

La'am and Laral embraced, holding each other tightly. Their floods of joy created pattern after pattern within them.

EPILOGOS

Panraak had discovered a friend in Brandt, birth-friend of the late High Magister. Since Zeta'Om's death, Brandt had been restless until one afternoon when he accidentally met Panraak in the corridors of the Makers' Palace. The archivist was looking for a particular chamber, one that held the oldest documents still existing on Omne. Brandt had guided him there, then worked with him to locate the document he wanted.

Panraak had suggested that the two of them might begin putting the materials salvaged from Haardt's destructive rampage into some order. It was high time, after all, that Omne had a competent archivist to preserve the vestiges of her past. Oh, the Makers and the Singers had been adequate for centuries, but now that the fragments of knowledge had been joined, now that the immense storehouses beneath the Pillars of Beginnings could be tapped for interpretations and explanations, it was essential that La'am, Laral, Jathanan, and the others know fully what had been preserved from the First Days.

Together they tackled the job, working side by side, mind with mind, until Panraak almost felt sometimes that he could sense the Omnan's patterns. He hoped eventually to be able to share in that intriguing mode of communication now so common on Omne. The time would come.

Now, Panraak and Brandt were finishing up the first room. All of the documents had been sorted, labeled, filed for eventual retrieval.

Panraak looked at the other man.

"Will it work?"

"What?"

"Will they come again?" Panraak's voice was almost a plea for reassurance. Brandt recognized the lingering guilt Panraak radiated in his patterns—guilt for having re-discovered Omne, for having initiated the search that had led to so much change and loss...as well as to inestimable advances.

"Does it matter?"

"Well, yes...doesn't it? I mean, if men like Haardt should try to return, to take over. If they come again, better armed, forewarned about the Makers, about...everything...."

Brandt did not answer immediately.

"I don't know how La'am or the others would answer your question, but I don't think it really does make any difference. We are not the same as those children Haardt found here. We have grown...beyond ourselves. We are something new. If they now know about us, we also know about them. Before, we had only myths and legends. Now we know the realities behind those myths. They will not find it so easy next time to impose themselves on Omne...if there is a next time.

"We have much to learn, of course, but we shall learn it quickly. We will be prepared, but in the way that the Ancients wanted us to be.

"Now, how about we tackle that next room?"

Panraak smiled and nodded. He acknowledged both his companion's answer and his question. Panraak nodded his assent... wordlessly.

ABOUT THE AUTHOR

Michael R. Collings, a retired Professor of English, is the former director of Creative Writing and Poet-in-Residence for Pepperdine University in Malibu, California. He has written books and articles on Stephen King, Orson Scott Card, science fiction, fantasy, and horror, as well as volumes of poetry. He currently lives in Meridian, ID—returning to his state of birth after almost sixty years—where he and his wife, Judi, make jewelry and enjoy watching the seasons change.

www.ingramcontent.com/pod-product-compliance
Lightning Source LLC
Chambersburg PA
CBHW032002240626
47153CB00003B/1078

9781434402813